I0686899

Crashing Into Destiny

Wings of Artemis, Volume 3

Rebecca Royce

Published by Rebecca Royce, 2016.

This is a work of fiction. Similarities to real people, places, or events are entirely coincidental.

CRASHING INTO DESTINY

Chapter One
Diana Mallory, all grown up.

If there was a way to get my twelve-year-old brother to pay attention to what he was doing, I had yet to find it. Asher sung to himself and daydreamed. He couldn't have cared less about doing the job we'd been sent to do. I wasn't even angry with him. Asher was a musician at heart, not an engineer. Unfortunately, in the world we lived in, none of us were going to get to play music for a living.

We had to know how to fix what broke, and right now what needed our attention was the remote alert system keeping zombies from getting through our black hole and killing us all.

Around us, machines buzzed and clicked. I loved the noise. I understood electronics. Digital systems never wanted anything from me except to be fixed and updated. I was the perfect engineer. When I repaired, I wasn't the sometimes glitchy daughter of the president of the Mars station. I was Diana Mallory, goddess of lasers, or Diana Mallory, queen of the engine room.

My twelve-year-old brother, Asher Jackson, danced himself straight into the tool closet and knocked over every water wrench I had in the place. He jumped back, his eyes wide and terrified. He turned slowly toward me. Asher really didn't like when anyone yelled at him. Luckily for him, I wasn't a yeller by nature.

We didn't particularly look alike, except for our brown hair, and even then our different fathers were both brunettes so our genetic similarity didn't rely on our having the same mother. Asher had his father's curls and our mother's expressive blue eyes, which he often used to his advantage. Being cute had always been his most dangerous weapon of manipulation; people simply wanted to give him what he wanted. Including me.

He smiled sheepishly. "Whoops."

I pointed at the mess, and he shrugged before he bent over to start picking up the wrenches.

"Sorry, Diana."

I nodded before I rubbed his hair out of his eyes. His curls got in his face all the time, and there was no taming them except for the time we'd shaved his hair all off. He'd hated the look. Even at six years old he'd been vain about his curls.

"It's okay." I bent over to help him. Asher didn't want to be here. I knew it, and he knew I knew it. He'd gotten into trouble for missing curfew on the Mars' station when he'd gone to hear a band play, and Uncle Cooper, his father and one of my mom's six husbands, punished him by making him come out on Artemis, one of their ships, to help me repair the alert beacons.

The alert systems had been sending out false positives to the station, making us gear up for upcoming battles that never happened. For obvious reasons, we needed that to stop. The expense of sending out a shuttle every time one of the beacons went off was getting out of hand, and our war ship captains didn't know which way was up anymore. Or so the council, led by Mother, said all the time.

Asher's gaze rose to meet mine. "How many more of these do we have to do?"

Was he serious? He couldn't be. I put the last wrench back in the case and closed the closet. Beacon A2TFH was okay. I noted the lack of a problem in the log and moved on to the next one. So far only two showed any errors at all. What was happening here? They weren't even part of the same system.

"Diana," Asher tugged on my arm. "I asked you a question."

I turned to look at him. The day he'd been born, two days after my tenth birthday, I'd fallen hopelessly in love with his baby blue eyes. There were seven children in the family now, including myself, and I adored them all. Hopelessly. I'd do anything for any of them anytime. And they all knew it.

There were two hundred more sensors to look at. "You should go into the gaming room and write your music. I want to hear it."

My statement should settle it. He didn't want to check the systems with me, and I didn't want to be his punishment. He should want to be with me— or go somewhere else.

Asher didn't move. "I'm supposed to help you. Dad says I need to know how to do this stuff or no one will ever let me on their ship. He also said I broke the rules, so now I have to do the punishment. And that it's good for you to have someone to talk to."

I felt the burn of Uncle Cooper's not so subtle criticism as much as I ever did. Not only did he think spending time with me constituted a punishment for Asher, but he'd also sent my twelve-year-old brother to babysit me so I wouldn't get so lost again in my own head that I forgot to talk.

They needed their twenty-two-year-old daughter to be presentable on the station. Not weird. Not off putting. Not too odd to be the daughter of the president.

Asher's face fell. "What did I say to make you upset?"

"Nothing, darling." I ruffled his hair. He still let me do that even though he resisted with everyone else. "Write your music before it makes you nuts. I won't tell."

He threw his arms around me. "You're always the best." He turned and then stopped. I wasn't sure why. Had I not been clear? Did he not understand he didn't have to do this with me? What more was I supposed to say?

Finally, he spoke. "Mom says you're going to have to take a job soon. One that's not with the family. You're coming of age."

Work or marriage by twenty-three—yes, she was correct. No one could ever make me get married—in either the single or plural version of the institution the laws were clear: it was always the woman's choice. Only if I didn't, I had to get a job and be useful. Staying in the arms of my family and working on their ships and equipment would be too easy. I had to go out on my own and help society. Or the third option, which felt like no option at all, I had to join the Sisters of the Universe and never be seen again outside of their protected walls. My family didn't bring up that potential outcome, and I was glad for it. I didn't think I was built for constant self-deprivation, meditation, and never seeing the outside world again.

Asher knew the rules as well as I did. Why did he stand there and wait? After a moment, he ran to me again and hugged me tightly. He'd always been a hugger, particularly when he was sad or upset. When he was two years old and my mother had been pregnant with our half-brother Colin, the Sandler Cartel had attacked the station for the first time.

We'd hidden in an air duct together. He'd held onto me like I was the only thing keeping him alive. He squeezed me like that again. In a family where our parents played politics to keep us all alive, Asher and I understood each other to be the resident oddballs.

Or at least I understood him as much as I did anyone. People weren't like machines. I couldn't always figure them out. I couldn't fix them.

"Thanks." He let go then scurried down the corridor of Artemis to the game room, where I knew he'd hidden his sheet music. Later, he'd enter them into the computer where he could listen to what he composed.

I got back to the matter at hand. These beacons had become the difference between life and death. For years, Mars Station had left the Black Hole open for travel. No one here wanted to return. The other side of the universe, the world humans had travelled so many years ago to escape Earth when it had been nearly destroyed by disease and war, had become hell. I'd been born on the other side.

When I was five, my father and uncles had come back from where we now lived to rescue us. I'd spent a year in the black hole traveling to the Mars Station and then the rest of my life on this side. Nothing was perfect. Not machines. Not love. Not people. Not dreams. Not hopes. But things were better here. That much I knew. Sometimes at night, I could still hear the drones from so long ago looking for us, coming to take us to the bad place where the woman with crazy eyes would hurt us. I pushed away those thoughts. They did no one any good.

As the years went on, the ships making it through the hole were more and more destitute. The last few had really sick people aboard, people who had eventually started to behave not like people at all. They wanted to eat human flesh. Uncle Dane, who headed up the medical unions, had them locked in cells in the bottom of the station as he studied them and tried to help. Uncle Dane had never seen anything like them. He called them Zombies and the name stuck.

Zombies couldn't be allowed to come through or, worse, couldn't be allowed to not be caught before they spread their condition. There was even talk of closing the hole altogether so we could stop the creatures from coming through at all.

My mother didn't want a permanent closure, but she didn't have the votes. She could have them ... if only I'd agree to let Argus Lapidus court me. Or so Uncle Nolan had said to my father two weeks ago. They didn't know I'd heard them, and it was better they didn't. I might have to address the issue verbally if they learned I knew the truth.

Not that I was at all surprised.

Argus and his three brothers wanted me. I'd have to be an idiot to not know. His gaze followed me whenever I passed him from where he sat by O'Grady's pub, the king on his perch. I was no great beauty like my mother. His craving wasn't for my body, although there were so few women in the universe I'm sure he wouldn't complain about getting to see me naked. That wasn't, however, his main concern. No, he wanted the power that an alliance with the Alexander crew would give him on the Mars Station. The same alliance would get my mother what she wanted. He'd vote the way she wanted if she gave him her daughter. She'd never brought up the idea to me directly. My mother didn't take threats and ultimatums well. She might tell him to go fuck himself on principal alone.

I leaned my head against the wall. I didn't think I could handle one husband, let alone the four I would get with Lapidus. Maybe a single husband I could deal with—if he didn't want to talk too much at night. If he understood my brain allotted me a certain amount of words per week, and if I used them all up on a Monday, I was done until they circled back around the following week.

Who was I kidding? I couldn't have a husband. I was twenty-two, and I knew I wasn't marriage material. Why didn't everyone else?

The alarm on Artemis went off, jarring me from my thoughts. It wasn't the beacons setting the alert off. The one I worked on was perfectly fine. I ran from the room to check the sensor in the corridor. *Oh no.* I took a deep breath to swallow. It was the Sandler Cartel. They were here. And before I could even digest that startling notion, one of their ships fired at us. Artemis jerked starboard.

Our ship was old. Decades past being able to handle this kind of battle. And I was alone onboard with my twelve-year-old brother.

"Diana." Asher rushed into the hall and grabbed me. "What's going on?"

The boy had never seen battle off of the station where we had sub-routines after sub-routines to protect us if our own security forces failed. Utter terror crossed his face and made me focus. I took his hand then ran with him to the control room so I could see a live view beyond the basic run down the computer outside the engine room relayed.

The ship jolted again. The one good thing Artemis had going for her was that her shields could take some pretty good hits before they got into trouble. My Uncle C.J. had done a great job back in the day with making the armor strong. Still, the scene in front of me did nothing to make me feel any better. We weren't just facing one ship attacking us. No, there were four.

"What's happening?" Asher's voice shook, and his hand in mine was ice cold.

I didn't want to talk. I wanted to think. I had to figure out how ...

"Diana." He jarred my arm. My brother needed me. I had to reassure him even though there was no easing statement I could say to make this better.

I pulled him against me. "If Sandler has come with this many ships just to the black hole, then he has ten times that many aimed at the station. Don't be scared. Uncle Nolan loves a good battle. He's been prepping for this kind of assault a long time. Sandler Cartel might finally get it through their thick heads they aren't ever getting Mars Station from us." I forced more words from my mouth. My tongue felt heavy, itchy. I hated when this happened. The alarms going off were playing havoc with my nervous system. We never knew why I reacted the way I did to things. There was no medical reason to be found. Yet here it was again. My voice threatened to stop working.

I kept talking, pushing through. I'd fall apart later. For now, Asher needed me to communicate, not just act. "We have to get safe. Come."

I pulled him along. The weapons were not as great as the shields. To protect the station, my father had taken most of his bombs off Artemis and put them on the station where his family lived so he could shoot them off as he saw fit. We weren't entirely without resources on Artemis, but getting away would be better. Artemis couldn't run away. She was too big, too bulky, and Sandler had us blocked. There were, however, escape pods. Tiny enough not to be noticed on their own, they had the right kind of alloy to distract the other ships' sensors and let us make a go for it.

They fit one person each. Ash was going to hate it. I didn't care. Alive was better than dead or captured by Sandler.

I shuddered at the thought.

The escape pod room had once been the hydroponics bay. I remembered growing vegetables with Cooper, learning how every small detail played a part when you made something from scratch. When we'd gotten to Earth and then promptly left it to go to Mars Station, my Uncles redesigned the ship. Food wasn't as much of an issue as getting away. The Station, Mars itself, and Earth grew enough food so that Cooper moved his design off Artemis and C.J. and Wes installed the pods.

"Hold onto the wall in case we jar again." I turned on the computers and quickly typed the pass codes to turn on the escape ships. One immediately lit up, but the other nine remained off. I hit the trigger again. They were broken. I couldn't understand how this happened. Uncle C.J. would never have let Artemis remain damaged like this. He would have at least sent me to fix them, and he ran periodic scans of the ship to check her maintenance. We still used Artemis regularly for small things like beacon repairs.

The ship got slammed into, veering portside. Okay, we didn't have a lot of time. Sandler wanted Artemis dead in space. Or they at least wanted us away from the black hole. I couldn't worry about why the pods didn't activate. I had to deal with now.

"Diana," Asher cried in heaving sobs. I squeezed his hand. There wasn't any time. We only had one escape pod, and there wouldn't be enough air in it to let both of us breathe. I had no time to alter the settings.

I pushed him into the pod. The second it registered in his brain what was happening, he fought me. Fortunately, I was still bigger than him, although not by much.

"What are you doing? There's only one. We can't both go in this."

I kissed his forehead. "I know. Be good. Be safe. Be brave. I love you."

I shut the pod and turned on the gas. It wouldn't put him to sleep, but it would make him loopy and relaxed. With a button on the ship's computer, I sent him out into space. He'd be okay. It was programmed to take him home. For good measure and to calm my beating heart, I checked the screen. He made it past the ships without any indication they saw him.

I rushed to the com and dialed Mars. Artemis was going to break soon. I could feel it start to rattle. My Uncle Wes picked up. My family had to know what was going on. "Diana? All okay?"

"No. We're under attack."

His eyes got wide, and he poked at his monitors. "I don't see that."

"Somethings wrong with your monitors then. Only one pod worked. I sent Asher in it. He's on his way to you."

Artemis groaned, and Wes heard the sound. He stood from his seat. "Tell me what's happening. Nolan, Geoff, I need you now."

"Too late." I shook my head. Only minutes had passed since the first explosion, and they felt like hours. "I have one shot left. I'm going to push into the black hole. Maybe they won't follow me."

"Baby." My father rushed into the screen. "What's happening?"

They all spoke off screen, and I ignored them. Taking control of the ship from the pod bay, I maneuvered it as best I could. It wasn't enough. My propulsion engines were broken.

"Diana," my father shouted. "Report."

"Engines are down."

He pointed at me. "Use the bomb. The one left. It'll push you. Check your com. I'm sending the directions for where to aim it and when to tell it to blow. It'll move you. We'll come get you from the hole, tug you out. Do it. Now."

I couldn't think about what I was doing. Bombs terrified me. Even using them from the computer made me want to puke. Still, I had no time to worry. I had to get it done. The Station alarms went off. My family would have no time to hold my hand through this.

I did as he wanted, and the force of the explosion pushed me into the hole. I watched as the view changed on the monitors. The black hole seemed thicker than normal space. I couldn't reconcile what I saw with any science I understood. Maybe I was losing my mind. Soon I couldn't see much of what was on the other side. Wes shouted something to me, but he looked like a talking head. The view screen went black. I sat back in my chair. All I had to do was wait. I'd sit on the edge of the black hole, and when they were done with their battle, they'd come and get me and ...

No.

With what little stellar cartography I had available in the thick black nothingness, I could see two of the Sandler ships fire. I wouldn't be able to withstand a direct hit. The shields were down. I didn't want to die. I wanted to live. I wanted more out of life than I'd had. But I wasn't surprised it would end this way. My whole life had been surviving one disaster after another. It had always been a matter of time until it all went to complete hell. I braced, ready for it. Somehow, I'd always known I would die in violence and not old in my bed with loved ones around me. I'd been born in an explosion, and apparently that was how I would go out too.

Except Sandler wasn't firing at me. A bright white light burst into my vision, and then the entrance to hole closed. I was stuck inside the black hole with no way to get out the way I came in. Artemis rolled, and I hit my head on the floor. Pain overwhelmed me. Finally, everything went black.

I woke to the sound of Artemis' alarm blaring. Every single part of my body hurt and tears pooled in my eyes. I rubbed my temple. Even that small movement hurt like hell. I was probably concussed, and when I tried to pull myself upwards, I threw up. Yes, I was certain about the concussion. Damn it. Finally, I managed the task. I made my way over to the comm. I was fully in the black hole. Closing the other side created some kind of vacuum, sucking Artemis toward the other exit. I wished I'd studied more black hole physics. I'd always sworn I wouldn't find myself back inside of the passage and had no need for the material. What did it matter if I understood the specifics, really? The laws of space and time didn't work the same in the hole. End of story.

Even in the fog of my pain I knew one thing, I would eventually come out the other side whether I wanted to or not.

The machine in the medical bay would fix my head. Then I could think things through. I wasn't dead, and if there was a chance in any universe of getting me home, my family would figure out how to do it. Assuming they weren't dead. Why had none of the monitors in the station worked?

Sabotage ...

I hated the idea.

Days turned into weeks. Weeks into months. All things considered, Artemis moved pretty quickly through the hole. It had taken her eight years under the direction of my Uncle Wes to get to my mother and me the last time he'd taken the ship through. Then again, he hadn't had the benefit of what seemed like a wind tunnel pulling me along. If I was correct, I'd be through the other side any day. Of course I might be wrong. I was wrong about a lot of stuff.

Five years passed on our side of the black hole when they'd come to their eight-year journey. Trying to understand the Space-Time-Continuum sucked big monkey balls.

I laughed at my own joke and planted another small orange tree. Artemis still had seeds galore in her storage units. Some of the plantings were dead, but some had been salvageable, and a little know how—thank you Uncle Cooper—had allowed me to get to work at feeding myself. It was a really good thing I liked kale. Or I could, at least, pretend to.

"Okay, Diana. Time to run the ship." I talked to myself as much as I could. Lately, it was less and less. The first days I'd been temporarily mute; violence always did that to me. I'd come around to speaking to myself quite a bit. The Artemis computer had an extensive reading library, and I read aloud anything and everything I could find.

I spoke to myself about everything before I did it. And then how it went after.

I was sick of the sound of my own voice.

Jogging the halls was the best exercise I could do, and I forced myself to do it every day. When I wasn't working on feeding myself and staying healthy, I fixed Artemis. Machine by machine, room by room. The fuel cells were holding up beautifully, and as long as I didn't tax her too badly, I could make things run smoothly.

The only things I couldn't create were bombs. I'd set off the last one, and I didn't know how to make more because I'd downright refused to learn.

I put the music Asher had scribbled on the day we'd been attacked into the computer and I let it play. The sound had become an old friend keeping me company.

Finally, the ship and I came through the hole with a giant groan. The thick space shot us out and into a spiral. I wasn't going to hit my head again and stayed put in my chair, holding on for dear life until the ship righted itself. I sat an extra minute just to be sure and then laughed at my ridiculousness. The computer showed no ships around, and even stretching the scan I couldn't find any.

Space was really dead out here.

I didn't want to hide by the black hole forever. Like it or not, at some point I was going to need more fuel if I kept flying. I wasn't sure where to even begin to find any. With no other choice but to figure out my surroundings and how to survive, I'd set Artemis down on a remote planet, set the beacon on the ship to transmit a signal my father would think to look for, and wait.

I even had an alarm to tell me when it was most likely that my family would come for me. I'd done all kinds of calculating in my head and confirmed with the ship's computers that I wasn't entirely off base in my math. How long the battle would take. How long it would take Wes to reopen the hole. How long the ships would need to get through. Time moved slower over there than it did over here. I needed to account for the difference. All in all, I'd decided six months. In six months, assuming they didn't hurry and surprise me, they'd be here.

We came for each other.

Two planets looked promising, but I quickly narrowed that down to one. I wasn't sure what happened with the atmosphere on the one I'd almost picked, but it kept changing. Weird. I'd never seen anything like that before. I made a note in the log. But the second one had the right breathable air and almost no population. Five souls seemed to be making home in a large pod which occupied miles in the most landable area. Otherwise there were hordes of some kind of wildlife moving here, there, and everywhere. The temperature itself was unappealing. Most of the planet remained in a constantly iced-over state. Still, it would be okay. I'd stay on Artemis, and she'd keep me warm until my family came.

I smiled at the thought as I set her down, keeping the shielding up so the pod population wouldn't notice me. I was a woman alone. That wasn't a great state to be in on my side of the universe. I really didn't want to be found on this end where, from all accounts, it was much worse. I wasn't my mother. I'd never make it through.

The landing went smoothly, and I cloaked the ship in the base of a mountain range where I would hopefully not be seen. The ship's computer, still loaded with data from when it had been used here, said the planet was some place called Orion. Once upon a time it had been an oil haven for Ochoa, the ruling planet where my Uncle Cooper's family had reigned over the populace. That had all gone to hell, and we'd left.

What had happened to the population of Orion? The cities were gone.

Who were the five people in their pod?

I would probably not find out, ever. Six months to hide, and then my family would come for me.

Chapter Two

Greetings.

The animal life I'd thought I'd seen on Orion before I landed proved to be not animal at all. A few days of studying and running tests from the computers confirmed what I'd suspected from the first minutes on the planet—the Zombie virus Uncle Dane was trying to treat on the other side of the black hole was rampant on the cold planet where I now hid in my spaceship. The animals were people, or they used to be. They were now Zombies.

I chewed on my carrot stick and made notes. The scary, infected souls made me nervous, and I rubbed the goosebumps on my arms. I didn't know what I'd do if they overtook my ship. The good news was they roamed in large groups, almost herds. So far, not one of their gatherings had moved anywhere near the mountainous location where I'd set down Artemis.

The other surprise for me was how vastly cold Orion was. The computer had underestimated exactly how low the outside temperature got, particularly at night. I didn't have any gear that would let me go outside. I was going to have to stay in the ship and hope the fuel cells held on long enough for me not to need to exit. Otherwise I was royally screwed.

I turned on my microphone. "This is Diana Mallory. Day 21 on planet Orion. So far, so good. The Zombies are three clicks away at least and headed in the other direction from me. Good news, indeed." I cleared my throat. I would be lucky if I managed to talk for ten minutes today. "As for the other inhabitants, they also seem unaware I'm here. I continue to believe there are five other human souls here. Well, alive ones. That's it. I'm going to see if I can get some of the armor fixed."

It wasn't really broken, but I needed tasks. "That's it. Thanks. That's all for today."

Not even ten.

I walked to my comm, finishing the carrot. Once a day— okay maybe three to four times a day—I checked on the others who lived here with me. They didn't know I existed, thanks to the armor, but I knew them quite well. Or at least bits and pieces of their routine. At first I thought there were only two of them and that the computer had miscalculated like it had the planet temperature. But as time moved, I'd gotten glimpses of the other three. Artemis hadn't totally misread everything. Something with the atmosphere seemed to really throw off her sensors. I needed to investigate more.

I'd think about it after I did my daily observation. I'd given the souls I silently watched code words so I could keep them straight in my head.

At nine in the morning, the one I thought of as *Black Coat* always came outside dragging double bagged garbage with him. I could see the two bags as one of them always stuck out higher than the other one. Not that the garbage particularly mattered. He was meticulous in bringing it out and didn't let his gun wielding companions fool with his task, even shoving the other men's hands off the garbage once when they had tried to help.

Black Coat was called Black Coat in my mind because he wore a different coat than the others, a black one. I might not be particularly creative. All of the men wore thick fabric masks to block the cold. I pushed my video feed in closer so I could see Black Coat better. Unless something really changed, he wouldn't come out again today, so I needed to catch sight of him when I could.

He wasn't as tall as the others, but his shoulders were broad and he moved with the grace and steps of a man who knew where he was going. Well, I was ninety-nine percent sure he was a man. I was pretty convinced they all were. I'd spent my youth watching men and women walk around the promenade on the space station. These people moved like men.

Black Coat paused today after he dumped his bags into the compactor outside of their pod. The machine turned on, and he looked up to watch the smoke as whatever was in the machine turned into ash in front of them. He usually stomped back inside but not today. I wondered what he thought about. Why did he stare at today's discarded pile?

He didn't have the same partners every day, but he always had one with him. Seemed obvious he'd need backup with the Zombies on the planet.

Today, his cohort was the man I thought of as the *Tall One*. None of them were exactly short. Or at least as far as my stalking them from a distance could make out. Tall One could be goofy. Sometimes, while Black Coat unloaded his bags, Tall One danced around on the ice and snow. He'd fallen once and turned the whole experience into a game, actually throwing snowballs at Black Coat, who had not picked them up and chucked them back.

I wanted to. I'd never made a snowball.

Sometimes Tall One came out by himself or with some of the others. He'd carry a weapon slung over his right shoulder. He'd check the perimeter. Sometimes he ran the distance. Actually, he had been present during one of the stranger events I witnessed.

Two weeks earlier, around lunch time, Tall One and *Bouncy Guy*, whom I'd not seen before then, came out of the pod and started throwing a ball around together. I'd almost jumped out of my skin. First, who wanted to throw a ball with gloves and snow gear on? Second, the Zombies were ridiculously close. If I had been them, I would have been hiding. Instead, they seemed to want to draw them in. The more they threw, the closer the hoard got to the pod. That was when *Two Weapons* arrived. He stepped out of the pod, unzipped a side of it, and started dodging around until the Zombies made their way inside the pod.

They were either helping the creatures, experimenting on them, or doing something really nefarious to the Zombies. Why else would they bring the beings into their housing unit on purpose? Bouncy Guy and Tall One hadn't stopped playing their ball game, and eventually Two Weapons had come out and said something that got their attention. He'd flayed his arms around in the air for a whole minute, and they'd followed him back inside the pod.

Orange Hat had been in view the least amount of any of them, and I'd witnessed him the first time with Two Weapons and Black Coat. The group had come out together one morning, following Black Coat. Orange Hat said something to Black Coat, and they'd almost come to blows about it. I think. I'm not always clear on these things, but Black Coat waved his finger in Orange Hat's face, and eventually Two Weapons came between them. Black Coat stomped back inside, and Orange Hat stormed to the other side of the pod and re-entered there. Two Weapons remained by himself for some time outside. Before he came back in, he'd done a complete 360, checking out everywhere he could see.

I worried he might spot me but luckily the armor kept me hidden and the mountains blocked sight too. He'd have to have super vision to see Artemis.

Today, Black Coat shoved his garbage into the compactor and followed Tall One back to the pod. I slumped down in my seat. Some days they didn't do much. Today was one of those days. I turned off the view screen, setting it up to beep me if any serious movement took place anywhere, and I got busy being busy. Six months to kill in one spot was a long while. It was good to have chores.

Or so I kept telling myself.

The days blended together. Excitement came in the completion of small tasks and sometimes fixing potential problems before they became bigger ones. I'd always wondered if I could truly go without human interaction. It turned out I could; I just hated it.

The tears I started shedding one month after I landed on Orion shattered me. I didn't see them coming, I didn't know I was so upset, and when I was through weeping, I fell into such a deep sleep I almost missed my daily watching of Black Coat. I scurried to the view screen and tried to make my blurry eyes work. I needed to see them like I required air. He had Two Weapons with him. They stopped for a bit after the garbage dump to chat about something. Two Weapons threw his head back and laughed. I would have loved to hear what they'd said.

When they left, I tried to figure out if I could make the lighting function in the hydroponics bay work better. When Uncle Cooper had run the room, it had been a growing haven. I could get it back there. I just knew I could.

The buzzing of the fire alarm startled me, and I rushed out to the main room. Something—probably my messing with the power supply across the ship—had shorted out the fuse for the star maps system. It wasn't a real fire, just some smoke. I ran to it and quickly turned off the alarm before I got the alarm all fixed up again. The alarm was loud in the quiet of Orion, and I'd never been so grateful to shut off a noise in my life.

I sunk down on the floor to drink my protein shake. Artemis was old. I loved her. She'd been my savior when I'd been five. The ship had meant as much to me as the men who steered it, maintained it, and brought me home in it. But she *was* old. I had to remember maintenance was the name of the game and not innovation. I couldn't mess with her so much simply to give myself something to do.

It wasn't like I was much of an innovator anyway. I could fix things, sort of, when I wasn't making things worse and getting sucked into black holes.

I had my worst nightmare ever that night. In it, Asher didn't make it back to Mars Station. Sandler Cartel blew him from the sky. He cried for me, big ugly tears, and I tried to get to him, only I couldn't. My family—Mom, Dad, Uncle Wes, Uncle Cooper, Uncle C.J., Uncle Nolan, Uncle Dane, and all my brothers and sisters—rounded on me with hate in their eyes. I was responsible for Asher's death. He'd been smart, talented, and perfect. They never wanted to see me again. They were glad I was stuck on a frozen planet where they never had to see me again.

I jerked upright in the bed, sweat dripping all over my body. I'd kicked the covers off sometime during my dream, and now I was freezing. Artemis' computers kept insisting this was summer, but the planet could have fooled me. How bad would winter be if this was summer?

The view screen beeped, and I walked over to look. It was the middle of the night, usually a quiet time on Orion and the Zombies were moving, creating quite a commotion as they did. They were coming straight at me. Ah, hell. I wasn't sure what I should do and stood silently watching, as if I could will them away with the force of my thoughts alone. Finally, I snapped out of it. I had no weapons. None, whatsoever. I'd used the last bomb following my dad's instructions.

If the Zombies suddenly became super strong and broke through, I was seriously screwed. Where could I lock myself up to hide? Would the compartments under the floor fool them? Could they smell me?

I never got the chance to think about it. Banging started on the outer hull followed by the sound of scraping. Seeing was, in this case, better than hearing. I turned on the ship's outside monitors and watched in horror as one Zombie after another came and banged on Artemis. I guess once one Zombie found something, they all did?

The doors would hold. I knew they would. You couldn't scratch your way onto Artemis. I sunk to the floor watching the view screen. *I'd be fine. I'd be fine. I'd be fine.* I repeated the mantra over and over again hoping at some point I'd believe it.

Eventually I had such a crowd of Zombies right outside my door I couldn't see anything else through the monitors. I shut off the view screen. I'd probably miss seeing whatever Black Coat did with the garbage.

At some point the pounding became white noise. They were there, but they were distant. Artemis was real. Everything else was ... just somewhere else. I dozed off on the floor for a while, hearing the sound of the Zombies outside, when a siren outside the ship made me dash to my feet. The noise wasn't somewhere else. That was close. And what the hell was it? I turned on the screen, but I still couldn't see anything except the Zombies. The pounding and scratching stopped abruptly. What the heck was ...

The hatch to the ship flew open, and a burst of the coldest air I'd ever felt slammed into me, stealing the breath from my lungs. I first fell backwards and then down onto the floor, gasping. I hadn't known you could feel the cold so utterly and completely inside your very soul. Cold burned.

My days spent on climate controlled ships and stations hadn't prepared me for this. I'd lived on a cold planet before we'd been rescued. I must have forgotten how horrific an experience it was, or it hadn't been as bad as this.

The hatch closed with a loud bang, and if I could have lifted my head to see which Zombie made it in, I would have done so. All I could manage was to breathe.

There was a rustling sound and then a hiss as two sets of feet abruptly stopped. "Shit, Damian. It's a girl."

A warm hand touched my arm, only the touch scalded. I was so cold that everything else was too hot. Gasping, I raised my eyes to see the kindest eyes I'd ever gazed upon staring down at me. Dressed from neck to feet in snow gear, he'd thrown his mask and hat to the side where it lay pooled to my left. I blinked rapidly. He was really, really tall. I had to stretch my neck a bit to look at him until he squatted in front of me. Could this be the Tall One? I still couldn't breathe without gasping. My chest burned, and I couldn't think clearly.

He was blond, blue-eyed, and buff. I couldn't make out more than that in the pain I endured. If I had to guess, he was around the same age as me.

"I can see that, Sterling," a low, deep voice responded to him. "Her gender changes nothing. Girl or no girl, I'm not going to put up with corporate espionage. It would be just like Archibald Corporation to send a girl to distract us from our mission. Theft is theft, and espionage is espionage. All of it is illegal. And I'm not putting up with any of it."

Damian was dark-haired with chocolate brown eyes that might be warm if he wasn't so angry and spitting a venomous gaze from his eyes to mine. He didn't look much older than Sterling.

People confused me on a good day, and I was too cold—burning cold—to manage any of this right now. I shivered, hard. Was it possible to die from seconds of exposure?

"I don't think she's okay." The one called Sterling put his hand on my arm. "We busted open the door. She's not dressed for this weather, not even to be inside. We hurt her."

Damian chewed on his lower lip. "I think you're right. Why would she be so not prepared? Who doesn't bundle up for Orion exposure?"

Sterling stood. "Look at this place. It's old. I think we've misjudged. This is not Archibald. We've interfered in something else. We need to help her. Now."

Two Weapons—he had two attached to his back—Damian—picked me up in his arms. His hands on my skin hurt, and I cried out. He yelled over his shoulder. "Give me your coat. I'll wrap her in it. I'm going to shove her in the carrier. Then I'll come back and get this ship. We'll tow it in. Get some answers, one way or another. Signal Lewis and Cash. Tell them she needs help. We really blew this. Bad."

Sterling tore off his coat and wrapped me in it. "Don't open the door when you come back for me. I'll be as ill-prepared as she was for the burst of cold, even built as I am. Hey, miss, you're going to be okay. I swear it. Okay? We're so sorry we hurt you."

He seemed sweet, but he had a gun strapped to his back, and he'd busted open my ship hatch without one thought about any consequences. I really couldn't breathe. I tried; air felt like it stuck in my lungs.

"She's not vaccinated to it, either. She's not adjusting to the air change." Damian shouted. "Call it in."

I passed out.

I wasn't a fainter, usually. If I couldn't deal with something, I tended to simply check out vocally until I could manage again. Or, at least, that was the best way I could explain it. I opened my eyes, hearing the sounds of beeping around me. I was inside a cylinder with red and green lights flashing this way and that way. I hissed in my breath. I hated medical machines. They were lifesavers, but claustrophobia had never been my friend.

Outside the tube, hushed conversation filled the space.

"Vitals are good. Once we sucked the radiation out, she healed the way she should. You can stop fussing. We don't even know this girl yet." The man's voice was deep and controlled. He spoke as though he meant to be obeyed. I could listen to him speak all day. He could read me instruction manuals for food processors and I'd be fascinated.

"I know quite a bit about her now. Her ship was a plethora of information. She came through the black hole ..."

The first voice interrupted the second one. "I know. We've been over this about a hundred times in the last two days. It's fascinating she came through the black hole. That doesn't mean you know her, Judge. Her ship can't tell us if she's the biggest bitch that side of the black hole."

I laughed. I couldn't help myself. He was funny and for that matter, right. They didn't know me. Maybe I was a big bitch. I didn't think I was, but who really knew how others perceived me?

Movement toward the dark cylinder told me they'd heard my outburst. A loud beep sounded, and the cylinder around me buzzed before it detached in the center and was pulled downwards into the medical table.

Two men stared down at me, and neither were the men who'd burst into Artemis and destroyed my routine. The one on the left wore a white lab coat, which at least gave the impression he was a doctor. His features reminded me of those from a place on Earth called Asia. High cheekbones framed his face and thick almost black hair stuck up in every direction as though he'd not taken the time to brush it.

Next to him, the man to his right had lighter brown hair and green eyes. He widened them when I met his gaze. Neither of them smiled, and I suddenly felt like an exhibit at the zoo.

"Judge, go get Cash. I'm told his bedside manner is better than my own."

"Right." Judge seemed to do a double take. "His bedside manner is nowhere near as good as yours."

"Just go get him."

Judge nodded once before he reached out to touch my arm. "Everything is going to be okay, miss. You're safe here."

I took a deep breath. He turned to leave, a bounce in his step. If the man staring down at me hadn't seemed so intense, I might have smiled. I'd bet money the guy leaving was Bouncy One. Whether or not I was safe certainly remained to be seen.

Chapter Three

Same planet, different world

The man whose name I didn't know approached me cautiously. Up close, I could see his features were hard, and a scar marred his face, one long mark from his ear to his left eye. He turned his head to the side slightly as he regarded me. I was flat on my back on the table. I wasn't going to hurt him. Why did he seem so ... wary?

He took my hand in his and then slipped his other hand behind my head. "Let's sit you up slowly. I don't want you getting dizzy. It can be tough coming out of the machine after being in there for an extended time."

I processed his words. "How long was I in there?"

No-named man didn't let go of me, even once I was up. "Two days. You had to be treated on multiple levels. You weren't vaccinated for the radiation in the atmosphere, and you weren't prepared for the cold. Both had to be handled. The first was a slow process of removing the radiation from your blood stream. The second was just a matter of warming you up. Then the computer vaccinated you. The radiation shouldn't be a problem again. You could, however, freeze to death."

He'd given me a ton of information. Radiation. Vaccinations. Freezing. All things I was really, really glad not to die from. In the corner of my vision I saw a black coat hanging on the back of the door. Black coat? This was Black Coat. I let myself stare at him, desperately wanting to ask him what he took out every morning and disposed of outside the complex. Except it would be weird to do so, and I didn't want to admit to spying on him and the others so regularly.

"Thank you for your help. I'm sorry to have been so much trouble. I wasn't ... doing any of the things the other two thought I was. I'm just waiting until my people come to get me. I'm Diana Mallory."

"You have people?" He raised a dark eyebrow. "Must be nice. You came from the black hole. That's what your ship's logs tell us, and our engineer, Judge, has been obsessing about that for days. The black hole is one of his fascinations. Your people are going to come through the black hole for you?"

It seemed really odd to be talking to this man about this and still not know his name. "What should I call you?"

He scrunched up his face. "Sorry. This is why I told Judge to go get Cash. I'm terrible at bedside talk. I'm Dr. Lewis Hurst. I only bring up the doctor part so you know I'm not some random person poking at you. I'm going to shine this light in your eyes."

I was struck, rather unusually for me, with how really, truly cute Lewis was. He seemed nervous and competent at the same time. He shined a bright light in my eye. It was blinding, which made me want to rear back; only his hand on the back of my head kept me steady.

"I just want to check your vision. If the machine is lacking anything, it's a full on study of the human eye. Sometimes it misses things. I've got to do this the old fashioned way. Look left for me, in the corner of the room."

I did as he said. Did our machine at home have a problem with eyes? I'd never heard it did. Maybe I'd never had a reason to know ...

"Right. Other corner." I did as he said and then jolted when Judge and another man in a lab coat burst through the door. The second lab coat guy—Cash, I think they'd called him, stood next to Lewis. I couldn't see him through the blinding white light in my eye.

Lewis pulled back. "Your corneas seem fine. Want to look Cash?"

"No. I'm sure you did fine." My eyes cleared enough I could see the second lab coat guy was tall, dark-haired with olive skin and nearly black eyes. His hair was straight and fell just below his ears. Underneath his white coat, he wore dark pants and a green collared shirt. "Judge said you needed me."

"I'm bumbling the bedside talk." Black Coat—Lewis—looked at the floor.

I placed my hand on his arm. If anyone knew how awful it was to feel like you had to communicate and couldn't, it was me. "You're doing just fine. You told me what I wanted to know, quickly. And you haven't been unkind."

Lewis' eyes flared with happiness for a second. "Thank you, Diana. I appreciate that you're not a hysterical patient."

I smiled and dropped my hand. No, I didn't particularly get hysterical. I got ... quiet. But these guys never needed to know anything about my issues. I'd be gone before it ever became a problem.

I extended my hand toward the second doctor, Cash. "I'm Diana Mallory."

He took my fingers and squeezed them in his own. "Cash Wilder. I'm a doctor like Lewis, here. Dizzy?"

It took me a second to realize he'd asked me a question. The tone of it stayed the same as his initial introduction. "No."

"Headache?" Same intonation. Next to him, Lewis rocked forward on his feet and then back again.

"No."

"Nausea?"

I replied the same as I had.

He nodded once. "Great. Then the machine really did its job. I wasn't sure when Damian ran you in here if we'd gotten to you in time. What were you doing sitting in a ship on this planet, wearing no protective gear?"

I had to take a moment before I answered him. He shifted gears so quickly. "Well, I wasn't exactly expecting to come here. I crashed. Well, I set it down, but with little other choice. I'm waiting for my people to come get me. Are you all wearing protective gear inside?"

"Yes." The third man who had thus remained quiet rushed forward. "Sorry to interrupt but that's more my realm than medical. I'm Judge Tomlinson."

I quietly regarded him. He'd heard my name, and if what I overheard before proved true, he'd been through my records and knew who I was. Judge had brown hair and green eyes. He was tall, like Cash. Whiskers covered his face and his smile seemed genuine, and sweet. He seemed like he was full of energy, not fully staying still even when he stood in front of me. He was definitely the Bouncy One. And like Lewis, I found him seriously cute. What was the matter with me? I didn't spend time worrying about whether or not men were attractive.

Now I couldn't control thinking about two of them. Oh heck, if I was being honest, Cash was pretty spectacular on the eyes too. Maybe the medical machine had done something to me.

"The clothes you're wearing are made of a synthetic that keeps out the cold."

My clothes? I looked down at myself. I'd never even considered I was out of my usual attire. I was in a uniform that looked like a jump suit. Over my heart was embroidery with the word *Evander* on it. I touched the patch quickly, feeling the fabric.

"You can't feel it." Judge continued on. "But it's there. Like a coating. Keeps us warm all the time."

Lewis smiled, his eyes travelling to the floor. "Judge helped make the coating. He's right to be proud of it."

"Well, it's nice to meet you." I was fairly certain I'd now met everyone. The two who'd busted onto my ship were Tall One

and Two Weapons. Then Lewis was Black Coat, and Judge was
Bouncy One, which made Cash Orange Hat. I could now put
names to descriptions. "I'm sorry to have been trouble. If you
let me get back to my ship, I promise that you won't have to
put up with me again. My family will come get me, and then I'll
be gone."

Cash and Lewis made silent eye contact I didn't understand.
Judge furrowed his brows. Finally, he spoke. "I'm afraid we
can't let you do that."

What? My heart rate kicked up. "Why not?" They couldn't
keep me here against my will. Could they? Would they?

Judge answered. "Your ship was damaged pretty badly. The
Zombies did a job on the hull. Another day and it would have
ruptured. You'd have been really screwed then. I can fix it. But
I can't let you back over there until then. Well, I mean, you
could get in it now if you wanted since it's inside our pod.
You'd be fine now. But if you tried to take it out there ..."

"Not to mention," a new voice caught my attention from
the doorway. Damian—one of the two who had busted my
hatch—sauntered forward. He wasn't carrying two weapons
currently. Unarmed, and not terrifying me to death, I could
officially say he was the fourth handsome man in the area. I
took a better look at him. He had brown hair and brown eyes
but lighter than both Cash's and Judge's, with light, chestnut
brown eyes. His skin was pale, his face narrow, and his physique
lean but strong. I quickly categorized him as I did everyone and
then put the information away. Usually, what people looked
like had no bearing on me at all. Except I'd clearly experienced
some sort of issue when I'd been unconscious and now couldn't
stop noticing these things.

"Yes?" I answered his unfinished statement and hoped I
simply hadn't missed the rest of it when I was otherwise
absorbed.

"We don't know what we can do with you yet. Letting you go may not be an option. We have to hear what Evander wants us to do."

Lewis' gaze hit the floor before he walked left, and Cash turned around fast before he made it to the back of the medical bay, suddenly preoccupied with something in a cabinet back there. Judge stopped moving altogether.

My tongue felt itchy. Whoever this Evander person was, he made the others nervous. Was he the Tall One—Sterling—who'd told Damian to take me here? Damian had listened to him after a bit. "Who is Evander, and why does he get a say in what happens to me?"

Nolan had taught me to fight. I'd never used the skills. Hiding and waiting out the battle was the best course for me, so I didn't get in anyone's way. Still, I knew a bit, and I could probably get out of this room if I had to. What I did next would be the question.

"Evander's not a someone; it's a corporation. I guess you wouldn't know that from being on the other side of the black hole. We all work for Evander. We live off their good graces and do their work. They give our lives meaning and teach us to survive, even when other things are awful." He said the last bit in a monotone, and I wondered if he was reciting something memorized. "When I busted through your door, I assumed you were from a rival corporation, come to steal our research and trade secrets. You have my apology for that."

I slid down onto the floor, my feet bare but warm. I wondered if Judge had sprayed me down with the synthetic he used on the clothes or if their floors were simply heated. "I may not have been clear; I frequently am not." Lewis' head shot up when I made my statement. Was he concerned I was going to not make sense? "Evander gets a say about me, why?"

"Because they own this planet, and you landed here without permission. Generally speaking, that would mean paying a fine.

We'd have to figure out how many days you were here, and they'd calculate accordingly. But you're a girl. And women are scarce. There's a price for that too."

Judge rounded on Damian. "By hells bells, Damian. What is the matter with you? You tell it to her like that? And you know you wouldn't sell her off any more than I would."

"Listen ..."

Judge pointed at him. "She's our guest. We found her. We made her life harder. We're going to fix it. End of story."

I wasn't going to argue with them. I'd never make it through the verbal onslaught. My body already wanted to shut down. What I was going to do—what I think my mother would tell me to do—was survive. They were coming for me. If I had to abandon Artemis to them, then I would. I'd bide my time, do as they asked, and then steal their shuttle. Evander wouldn't sell me off. I'd reset the signal to another frequency and wait somewhere else.

Keeping my face serene proved harder than I thought it would. I did my best. "Okay. I think I can grasp some of this. Forgive me; things are different where I grew up. We've heard about your corporations from people who come through the other side of the hole. I know there are several, and loyalty is given to whichever corporation acquires your services." My mother had once called it barbaric, although I wasn't certain we were much better. Was anything? "How long will it be until you hear back from Evander about what to do with me?"

Damian's brown eyes met my own. There was something about him which seemed strangely familiar. I couldn't put my finger on it and didn't plan to try to figure it out until I was alone. He reminded me of something.

"I haven't sent them any information yet. When I do, it'll be six months to a year until we hear from them. We're on the outskirts here."

Judge moved left until he hoisted himself onto the table next to me. "Don't worry."

"Would you like a tour?" Damian extended his hand toward the door. "Since you're going to be with us for a bit, would you like to see where you're going to live? We're working out where to put you to sleep right now."

I took a deep breath. "Artemis is here, right? I mean you said she's safe in the pod here? So couldn't I sleep there?"

"Oh," Damian nodded fast. "We didn't think about that. I mean, yes. That'll work."

"You'll be alone. All alone." Cash spoke from the back of the medical bay. "Our living stations are on the other side. "

I wiggled my bare toes. Before I went on any tour, I was going to need shoes. "I'm always alone. Don't worry about that."

He sucked in his breath. "Are there so many women on the other side of the black hole they let you be by yourself?"

"No one really lets me do anything. I do things because I do them. When my mother established herself over there, that was the kind of rule of law she put into play. It's always the woman's choice. Marriage. Work. Spiritual deprivation. Whatever happens, it's her choice. The men have choices too. They can decide they don't want to be in a marriage with one woman and multiple men. They can say no. Or the opposite. They can say they want that, and she only wants one on one. Or they can say no to it all. Some men like other men." I rambled. I had to stop. "Anyway, everyone gets a choice, a say."

Lewis looked at Damian. "Sounds like the old rebels. One woman, many men. Her choice. No politics, no fighting."

Damian didn't respond but his jaw hardened. After a moment, Judge jumped down. "Come on. Let's show you around."

"Can I do that without shoes?" I lifted a leg to show him.

"Oh," He whirled toward Lewis. "Got any of those slippers from when we came out of hyperspace?"

"Yep. Sorry I didn't think of it, Diana." Lewis ran toward a cubby and pulled out white slippers. "These will do for now, and we'll fire up the replicator tomorrow and make you sturdy real ones. Sound okay?"

A burst of speed came through the door, and Tall One, Sterling—I had to remember their names—appeared. "Did I miss everything? Hi, I'm Sterling Whitworth. I'm sorry we made you sick."

"That's okay." His smile was infectious, as were his blue eyes. "Nice to meet you Sterling."

"I'm sorry I didn't introduce myself. I'm Damian Osborne." Then now introduced Damian shifted uncomfortably. "I do have manners. I swear."

Sterling punched him in the arm. "No, he doesn't. Don't believe him. Damian's got no class at all. We're all just total goofs here. Good thing we've got a purpose or we'd be of no use at all."

They were big on those ideas—purpose and usefulness. I stored that information for another time, when I was alone. Lewis came over and knelt down, holding the shoes out in front of him. There was something so sweet about the gesture. I smiled at him, and his guarded eyes showed happiness for a second. I slipped my feet into the soft shoes. The whole exchange took seconds, and yet I felt like time slowed to a crawl where it was only the two of us in the universe.

I blinked rapidly. Had I hit my head?

Judge laced his fingers through mine. "Come on?"

"Sure."

There were several kinds of people. Some of them were the type to hold hands; some of them weren't. Other than my siblings, I was a not holding hands kind of a person. Yet I didn't pull out of his touch. He'd been kind, and I thought it possible, considering his reaction to Damian's proclamations, he might even let me leave in Artemis after we fixed her. I wasn't sure. There was a lot left to figure out about my circumstances and the five guys I'd watched intently for months and didn't know at all.

We rounded the corner, and I heard voices spark up behind me, although I couldn't make out what they said. Whatever it was, the four others in the room were speaking passionately.

"So this is the main hallway. The whole pod is electronically maintained and controlled. Which means, of course, I maintain the electronics and the controls." He shrugged and grinned.

The hallways were brightly lit, with something resembling plastic being used for walls. The floors and ceilings were metal. "This is really impressive. I grew up on Mars Space Station. To maintain something this size, they'd have five or six engineers."

His eyes widened. "You grew up on a station? Wow. The stations on this side of the hole are not someplace anyone who isn't breaking the law wants to be. I don't think they have kids there."

"I bet they do. I've never been anywhere—beautiful or horrible—that there weren't children. The roughest ships have families. The most overrun places on Earth. People make families; they survive." I was suddenly really uncomfortable that I'd spoken so freely. "But what do I know? I haven't been on this side of the hole since I was five. Ignore me."

He stopped walking. "You lived here? And then you went over there? And now you're back?"

"Yes."

"That's so ... amazing." He tugged me further down the hallway. "We have everything you could want, I think. I mean, you're a girl. We don't really know girls. Women. Sorry."

Other people got hung up on words carrying all these connotations. I'd never, ever be okay with hate speech. But that wasn't what I was getting from Judge. He just seemed a little giddy to be showing off his place. I was lucky if I could form sentences. "Don't worry."

"Anyway, in here is the recreation facility. Game room. Gym. Entertainment center. Every six months to a year, Evander sends us new stuff to watch. Well, new to us. It's old in the cluster of planets where there are more people. We try to spread it out. We watch movies on Friday. And then usually we can last till the new burst comes in."

He walked me inside the room, and I almost flinched from the burst of color. Unlike the sterility of the hallway, the game room wasn't one bland utilitarian bunch of nothing shades. I could tell they all spent actual time in here. He'd described the gym—and I recognized the equipment as being close to what I used—and the movie screen on the wall. There were video game consuls like the ones my ten-year-old brother Colin, Dane's son, played on. There was also artwork all over the walls. Someone was a painter. A piano and, to my astonishment, a hot tub.

My mom had one in her bathroom on Mars Station. It was an excessive luxury for any space station, that all had to watch their power. My Uncle Wes insisted she have it, and he paid the extra credits for it by working eight extra hours a month on the station to facilitate the electricity the spa used up. How were they running it here?

I pointed to the water. "How do you run this?"

He scratched his head. "We've never used it. The idea is, I guess, to relax if you overdo it at the gym. What we'd have to do is pump in the water. That's not a problem ... with all of Orion's ice. Filter it. Clean it. Add the requisite chemicals and draw power from another system. The manuals suggest food source area, but I've reworked things so many times these computers are really mine more than the company's now—at least in how I think of them. I think the laundry facility is where I'd draw power."

"I tried to draw power on Artemis to facilitate the hydroponics bay, and I ended up setting off an alarm and a minor smoke incident. I think that's how the Zombies found me."

He rocked on his feet. "Zombies? Is that what you call them? I could see that. Sure, old Earth literature. Pulp stuff. From before. Oh, but you've been to Earth. That's so cool. Anyhow, yeah, we call them the Infected. They did hear the sound. So did we. Our computers missed your landing—good job with the stealth—but the burst of sound triggered our security alert."

Good to know. When I escaped and had to hide elsewhere, I'd keep that in mind. No alarms. No noise.

"This is a great room. I'm impressed. Evander must want you comfortable."

He nodded fast. "We're going to be out here for two decades at least. They have to keep us happy so the brains of the operation can keep doing their work and they don't have to change the rest of us up too much. Retraining delays profit."

This was such a different world. I was afraid it might open up and swallow me. "Right. Profit?"

"From the Infected? Oh, didn't we say? That's what we're doing. Cash and Lewis are going to cure them."

I'd never heard of a more worthwhile endeavor. Still, I wasn't sure I understood. "How will that make profit for Evander?"

"Once they're better, they'll be customers. They'll need to start from square one." Judge looked over his shoulder. "Look, it's better if we don't talk about this part. Okay? Damian's an incredible guy. We've all been together five years, and he lets a whole lot slide. He's become like a brother to me. But, in addition to security, he and Sterling are both company men.

We all are. But their sole purpose here is to protect the company's investment in Cash and Lewis. I know this must be foreign. They're all like my family now. Yet there's always going to be this thing ..."

I squeezed his hand. "I'm not going to make trouble."

But I'd certainly stumbled into some. Leave it to Diana Mallory to walk away from one sort of politics into another entirely.

Chapter Four

The machine does what?

I followed Judge through the hallways, and certain things did start to become familiar. In a lot of ways, a computer was a computer. I fixed them regularly, and I figured I could help while I was here. The more easygoing I was, the less likely they were to discover I planned to get away as fast as I could.

I'd never had to manipulate anyone before, and now I had five souls to trick. I had no idea if I'd be any good at it.

They had a hydroponics bay, that Cooper would envy for its space, and an actual farming area where they had livestock—chickens, lambs, and cows. They'd been put in stasis during the trip to the planet. Someone had to take care of them.

"This is the weapons area. You have to have a code to get in. I can't give that to you. Not unless Damian says ..."

Every time Judge hedged on something, he wore such a look of guilt on his face I couldn't help but feel sorry for him. I didn't want their weapons. "Don't worry. I can't imagine why I would need one here. You've all assured me I'm safe." Except for the chance Evander would come and sell me. I pushed away the thought. They had to believe I was willing to go along ...

"Right," he brightened up, and we walked together in companionable silence. He pointed down the hall to the left. "That's where Artemis is. And if you go past it, quite a distance, that's where the Infected are kept. Come on; I'll show you."

He wasn't kidding when he said it was quite a distance. We didn't stop where they'd stored Artemis. I planned to get to Artemis as quickly as I could when my introduction to this new place finished. It took twenty minutes to reach the Infected.

Once I got there, I could see them through a one-way mirror, but they couldn't see us.

"They can smell us, though." Judge's statement caught my attention, and I watched as the thirty infected souls started pounding on walls as soon as we came close. "In five years, I haven't gotten used to them."

I couldn't imagine ever being used to them either. "The Zombies came through the black hole on a ship. We don't really understand how. Their ship had a homing device set to find the closest populated area. They got all the way to my family's station on autopilot. They managed to bite three people before they were restrained. It was, unfortunately, a month before the security guards who'd been bitten showed signs. My Uncle, he's one of the doctors on the station, he had almost decided to let them out of containment—the security people. Big giant mess. He's working on a cure, too."

Judge stared at me when I talked, and I lowered my eyes. I didn't like being the center of attention in a crowd and avoided those kinds of places or scenes. I wasn't asked to be on much. No one really wanted to talk to me, and I was better off for it. Still, the way Judge regarded me made me feel like I was on stage with all my clothes off. My cheeks heated up.

"Do I have something on my face?"

He rubbed his chin. "No. Why do you ask?"

"You're staring at me."

Judge laughed, a low sound. "Come on. You must be used to men staring at you. You're gorgeous."

"Oh." I stepped away. The woman problem. "I'm nothing to look at really. Trust me. I've seen beautiful women. I was raised by one. I'm kind of small and uninspiring. I'm not looking for flattery either. I am good at seeing things as they are. It's just you don't see many women. So they all look good."

He outright laughed, a loud bang of a sound that startled me into taking another step back. "No, don't be afraid. I'm sorry. That's ridiculous. I've seen beautiful women. Evander always has some they're negotiating off in marriage. It's been five years, but I've seen them. And the Ultra-System takes care of me. I'm safe to be around. I would never have hurt you before the US –ah, that's what we call the Ultra System either. You're safe. Even if you're wrong about how beautiful you are."

"Um." I huffed out my breath. "Maybe you need glasses. Lewis said the medical machine isn't good with eyes."

"You're funny, too."

I was? I'd never thought so, and certainly no one in my life found me amusing. "What's the US?" I needed to change the subject.

He held out his hand, and despite my moment of discomfort, I took it. "I'll show you the holding room."

It took us the same amount of time to get back from the Infected area to the center of the holding room. Six machines lined the walls. Five of them were space pods, like the ones I sent Asher off in. Thinking of him panged my heart. Emotional pain hurt me more than physical sometimes. I made myself examine the machines. Unlike the ones on Artemis, which didn't work but that was a whole other problem, these had a rocket launcher on them. They could push off into orbit before they travelled through space. The residents here said something earlier about hyperspace. These must have been what they slept in. Five modules for the five guys. They'd been asleep for their long journey to the edge of their universe. And woken up here.

The final machine was something different. It almost looked like a bed with a lid. There was motor attached to it, so it was clearly not meant for travel. The letters U and S were on the front.

I pointed to it. "The Ultra-System?"

"Correct. I guess you guys don't have anything like it. Look, um, our corporation doesn't want us to go sexually mad. There are no women. The five of us are likely never to have a wife. We're not high enough up. Damian could, but he didn't take an assignment important enough for Evander to warrant that treatment. I guess if Cash and Lewis are successful, they might get one ..."

I held up my hand. "You're avoiding, right? You don't want to tell me? This has something to do with sex."

His cheeks got red. "Once a month, sometimes more if we need it, we each take a night in the US. The machine reads our likes, our dislikes, and it makes us a vivid dream where we have sex with a partner designed for our needs at that moment. It can change. The computer taps into our sexual fantasies right then. We experience the dream in first person. It satisfies us, and while we sleep, the machine also administers a hormone, a sort of alteration on melatonin, that keeps the urge at bay until we go back in the machine again. We have sensors on the back of our necks." Judge pointed to his. "If we get out of whack, Cash and Lewis can either order us into the machine or administer the drug themselves."

I touched the side of the machine. "Does it work for women too?"

"I ... I," he cleared his throat. "Honestly, Diana, I have no idea. The subject has never come up. I'll look it up."

"I was just curious."

On one hand, I was glad to know about the system. What a beautiful idea. Why make people go through deprivation? On the other, I wanted out of this conversation immediately.

"And obviously, these are the hyperspace pods you came in?"

"Yes." He touched the side of one of them. "This one was mine. They're really advanced. If the Zombies get out and we can't contain them, the computer will sense the distress and literally magnetize us into the pods before knocking us out and sending us home." He touched the back of his neck again. "The same device that monitors us would send us here. It's like a giant magnet. We can't control it. Boom. In here. Gas to knock us out. Launch."

Wow. I touched his sleeping module. "That is some impressive tech."

"That's why Sterling and Damian busted through your door. The other companies would love this stuff, and they don't have anything like it."

Technology wasn't proprietary where I lived. If someone had something, pretty soon we all had it. "Why can't they invent it too?"

He leaned against his pod. "Because they don't have me."

The comm system turned on, and Damian's voice travelled down to us. "Could you bring Diana to the dining room? We need to have a meeting."

"Sure." He replied and grinned at me. "Come on. Lewis cooked. He's really good. Unlike when Sterling cooks, and then it's a disaster."

His easy grin did make me feel like all might be okay. But I wouldn't—couldn't—let my guard down. Judge was nice, and his background in engineering made me understand him completely. The others? I wasn't sure, and even when I was, I still had to get out of here. My family would come for me. I didn't belong on this side of the black hole.

We walked side-by-side to the dining area. We'd glanced at it earlier but not gone inside. It should be around the next corner. "Judge." A thought dawned on me. "When you took Artemis, did you turn off my signal?"

He shook his head. "I didn't. It's such a low subspace frequency I didn't consider it a risk. The other corporations know we're here. It's not like it's a secret. Is that how you plan to alert your family where you are?"

"Yes," I took a deep breath. At least that wouldn't be a fight. "Thanks. I figured they'll be here in six months. Or around then."

He quirked his head to the side. "Really? That's fast. Want me to look at your math?"

"No, that's right. Trust me. We always come for each other. As fast as we can."

He nodded once, his eyes hooded. I wasn't sure he believed me. Only, he didn't know my family. They'd never leave me here a minute more than they could get to me. I steeled my shoulders. I had to believe. I was their problem, but they loved me just the same.

Dinner turned out to be vegetables with a light sauce made out of some kind of oil and vinegar. They also had potatoes, grown in the pod, and chicken. I tried not to picture the chickens in the farm section. Chicken was delicious. I wasn't going to obsess about how it ended up on my plate. Much. Which one of them was responsible for killing it? I rubbed the back of my neck and took a deep breath.

"This is delicious. Thank you." It had been a long time since I'd eaten anything other than synthetic protein. Real food after all this time was a true treat. "Thank you for letting me eat your food."

Cash sipped his tea. "As long as you're living with us, it'll be our pleasure to feed you."

"Thank you." He spoke so formally. I wondered if, on the planet he came from, speaking like he did was common. "But I would like to carry my weight. I realize your corporation allots you a certain amount of food. I must be taxing on your budget."

Damian quickly shook his head. "Don't worry on that subject. We are a self-sufficient group. Our farming unit produces quite enough for our food intake. You shouldn't be a problem. Unless you eat half your body weight."

"Damian." Sterling set down his water. "Even I know women don't like to talk about their weight."

I smirked. I couldn't help myself. Damian and Cash were serious. Sterling seemed to like to make jokes. Judge had energy to spare, and while he could fall into seriousness, he was mostly funny. And Lewis hadn't uttered a word since we'd sat down.

Damian shot Sterling a look before he spoke again. "I need to ask you some questions, Diana. I'm sorry to sound so investigatory. The circumstances of your joining us are unusual, to say the least. I need a thorough report. I have to get some information about who you are, where you came from. And Evander may have their own questions."

I braced myself. I had to get through the time I would spend with these men, fix Artemis, and figure out how to leave without them stopping me. Evander had questions? Fine. They could have answers. I wouldn't be here when they came to collect me.

Damian cleared his throat. "You're from the other side of the galaxy."

"No. I was born here. On a space station. The day Olivia Jackson took control of the galaxy with the nuclear bombs. She attacked my grandmother's ship, the Bridge, and my mother gave birth during the attack."

They were all silent, staring at me like I'd spoken a foreign language.

Finally, Lewis said something. "That's not possible."

Cash finished. "Fifty years ago."

Judge grinned. "Space-time continuum is a real bitch. The black hole isn't a set figure. We can do guesswork for math, but who knows, really? Ten years. Eighty. All the same in that hole."

My heart pounded so fiercely against my ribs I thought it would explode. "I don't understand."

"Black hole physics doesn't work like regular physics. The same trip that once takes one year, can take eight the next time or one hundred. We really don't know. It never makes sense. Vacuums don't hold up to scrutiny."

If his words were true ... when was my family coming?

"You could be our mom." Sterling grinned. "Hottest mom I've ever seen."

"Sterling." Cash rolled his eyes.

Sterling shrugged. "What? She is."

Damian played with his pencil, moving it along his fingers. "How old are you chronologically?"

"Twenty-two. What month is it? Year?" I suddenly didn't know anything, understand anything. And I was stuck. On this side of the galaxy, at least until I got Artemis fixed. How long would that take? And then how much time would pass in the hole? Would my family even be alive? Remember me?

Lewis, who sat to my left, touched my hand, saying nothing else. Immediately, some of my panic cooled. I could breathe. I could think. I nodded to him to say thank you, and he quietly winked.

"It's September," Cash finally answered.

"Then I'm still twenty-two. For another month."

It wasn't quite my birthday yet. I hadn't missed out on Uncle Nolan singing, my mother trying to bake a cake, and my dad telling me I was the best thing he'd ever done in his whole life. I breathed through my threatening tears. I didn't know these guys yet. They couldn't see me cry. That was too much vulnerability.

They had basically told me I had to be here, whether I wanted to or not. That was some form of kidnapping.

Damian nodded. "Okay. You were born on the day Olivia Jackson destroyed everything. On a ship called The Bridge. The famous one?"

"Is it famous?" I didn't know. My parents, especially my mom, didn't like to talk too much about that time. "We moved around a lot after. My father and uncles had been sent through the hole right before Olivia closed it with the bombs. They managed to get back through and find us on a cold planet, although not as bad as this one. They were involved in the ending of Olivia, although I don't have all those details, and then we went through the hole again. I was six."

Silence was thick, like the air when it was too hard to breathe. Cash spoke in a low voice. "Damian?"

"I know," the man who spoke for the company answered. His voice was low, and his neck muscles strained. Something I said had upset him. "What's your mom's name?"

"Melissa Alexander." The president of the Mars Company, a living legend wherever she went. A woman who had her mind messed with twice and still came out a superstar. Unlike her daughter who some days ...

"Then your father is Cooper Jackson?" Damian spoke the words hard, like if they had substance he'd have thrown them at me.

I shook my head. "Coop's my uncle. I'm Diana Mallory. My father is Geoff Mallory. Cooper is my brother Asher's father."

Was he still famous? They'd just told me fifty years had passed here. Why did anyone know his name? He'd be horrified if he knew people still knew thought of him. Cooper enjoyed the world better when no one knew his identity used to include the word *Prince*. Asher certainly didn't act like royalty.

"Cooper is my Uncle." Damian glanced away when he spoke, as though the wall was really interesting.

I didn't know everything about my uncle's family history, but the last thing I ever expected was to run into his family my first stop after coming out of the black hole. "How?"

"My father was his older brother. Not the one who was going to rule, but one of the ones who got locked up in the cage for the years Olivia was in charge. He fled Ochoa with my mother and raised me on a small farm two planets away. We used her last name because of the hatred for the Jackson last name. Cooper is something of a family legend. The man who killed my aunt to set the people free and then ran from the fallout."

I had to catch my breath. The air coming out of my lungs after his statement felt more akin to running a race than sitting still. "He didn't kill Olivia. My Uncle C.J. did. And he left because my mother wanted to, and there's nothing more important to him in the universe than my mom's happiness."

"Even more than that of the entire universe."

I nodded. "She is his *entire universe*."

Damian scooted back his chair. "Sterling, would you mind finishing? I need a walk. A fast one."

Sterling took a tablet out of his coat pocket. "Sure thing. I'll take notes."

I'd managed to make an enemy out of Damian simply by standing up for my uncle. What else was I going to bumble?

Judge took a long pull from his ginger soda. "Damian is sensitive about the Jackson story. He's lived with a lot of abuse. When people find out, they immediately associate him with Olivia, even though all of that was before he was born."

"I am sorry it causes him so much pain." No one should have to suffer for their family. We all had our own stories to write, our own mistakes to live with. Like getting sucked into a hole ...

Sterling drummed his fingers on the table. "Do you have any reason to want to overthrow the Evander Corporation?"

I shook my head; exhaustion suddenly rode me hard. "No."

"Will you sign a document expressly promising to not share any intellectual property with competing corporations, even under the pressure of torture?"

I sucked in my breath. What the hell? "What kind of torture?"

Cash shook his head. "We're not asking her that. If Evander wants that answered, they can come ask it."

Sterling set down the tablet. "Guess we're done."

"Great." Cash smiled. "Is there anything you want to ask us?"

"Yes." I had a whole slew of questions. I wouldn't ask them all, but some I wanted answers to right away. "Just to clarify, you—Cash and Lewis—you're the doctors."

"We hold different degrees in medicine, but yes, we're both doctors. Sterling and Damian are company security. Judge is our tech god."

I cleared my throat. "I could help you. While I'm here. I'm an engineer. Not like Judge is. But I can fix things, and you could point me at the things you can't get to. I'll get them done. That's what I do at home."

Cash and Judge looked at each other before looking at me. Finally, Cash spoke. "You want to work?"

"I want to do something. I know perhaps it's unusual for women or whatever. But I'm used to holding my own."

Lewis answered, "I'm sure Judge can use the help. He's always said this place really had enough work to warrant a head engineer and an assistant. Looks like you came right in time. He has to redesign the storage unit to hold more Infected. Project might take a year."

I played with my fork. I'd help Judge up until the point I got out of this place and found somewhere I wouldn't be held prisoner myself. "If Judge is willing, I am."

Judge nodded fast. "Don't get me wrong, it'll be weird for me. I never thought of a woman as being an engineer. But as long as you think you can keep up, I'm game."

Cash laughed, throwing back his head. "No one can keep up with you. You move a hundred times a minute. Give the girl a break. How about if she's smart and competent? Good enough?"

Judge's cheeks turned red, but then he howled right along with Cash. "All right, fair enough."

I was so relieved. The idea of not being busy while I bided my time made me feel slightly ill. I had to keep my hands occupied and my thoughts to myself. I never wanted to be a lady of leisure.

"One more thing." This was hard, but the sad fact was it might happen and so better to address it now than later. "I have a problem. Kind of a glitch in my internal programming." The description had always worked in the past. Four sets of eyes on me didn't blink while they waited for me to continue speaking. I took a deep breath. "Look, um, sometimes if I get really stressed, I quit talking. I can't help it. There's nothing physically wrong me," I made sure to make eye contact with Cash and Lewis when I delivered this fact. "I've been checked over and over. It happened right after my third birthday. I talked just fine, and then I quit. There had been some distress with my mom right around then. Then I started up again, right before I was six, like the whole thing never happened. Over the years, there would be occurrences of it—a few days here or there—until I was sixteen. Then after a bad attack on my home, I lost the use of my voice again for a year. It came back. I don't know what would have happened with this most recent incident getting myself thrown through the black hole. I was alone. I know Judge went through my logs. The days I didn't record were hard ones for me. I can't help it. I can't control it. I wish I could."

There. I'd laid it out to them. Lest they think they'd gotten a real prize to sell to Evander—of course Damian wasn't in the room, but presumably Sterling would tell him. For good measure, I added, "I can still think during the time I'm silent. I can do jobs. Follow directions. Sometimes I can write. Sometimes I lose that too. I'm not comatose or anything. I just can't find my voice."

Lewis furrowed his brows. "These times that you lose your voice come after stress. Presumably a psychological trigger. No amount of therapy worked? Behavioral or otherwise?"

"I went through it all. I'm just ... glitchy."

A muscle ticked in Sterling's jaw. "I hate that word for this. Who called you that, and why did you adopt it as your own?"

"I came up with it alone. Seems fitting."

He shook his head. "The people with you should be ashamed they didn't stop you from saying it. You're not glitchy. You're not a computer on the fritz."

So far, I'd ticked off Damian, and he'd stormed from the room. Now I'd upset Sterling. I was two for two and not surprised. I had to get Artemis fixed as soon as possible. I wasn't good with people. Voice or no voice.

Chapter Five

The cold, cold, nasty wind and how it blows.

Lewis walked me to Artemis as though I needed an escort. I wasn't unaccustomed to the way some men felt around women. On the station, a lot of the regular residents had to get used to the idea that both my mother and I would walk alone as we saw fit and not blink an eye.

I could have argued with the doctor, but I didn't want to. It was nice to have someone to walk the halls with. I hadn't yet figured out where everything was and getting lost wasn't in my game plan for the evening. I needed sleep, to be back on Artemis, and to get my head straight.

"Damian can be sensitive about his family. His story to tell. I doubt he even knows how rude he was. And Sterling has his reasons, too. We're a rough bunch here, although I suppose it could be argued the whole universe is a rough patch, made only for those who can survive the onslaught." We got to the outside of Artemis. She looked pretty good to me, but I could see what Judge meant when he'd said she wouldn't survive much longer. The door needed to be entirely replaced. I'd get to work on it in the morning in between working on whatever Judge wanted. I'd play the game, as my mother would say.

I regarded Lewis' strong profile. He implied something he wanted me to understand beyond what he said. I could make out that much. But reading subtlety wasn't my forte. I could tell him as much or pretend I'd gotten what he said to me.

I had to say something. "I'm not good with people. I tend to step on their toes without having any idea I've done so. I tend to speak my mind. I never mean to be unkind. But my existence has always been riddled with me screwing up, badly. I'm sorry that my uncle upset Damian and my speech issue bothered Sterling the way it did."

He shook his head. "It was how you referred to it that upset Sterling, not that you have the problem."

I didn't really see how my own personal experience would make someone else so completely upset. Truth was, I didn't want to get into it with Lewis right then. "Thanks for walking me back."

He nodded once. "You're welcome." He pointed to Artemis "I never saw it. I stayed with you. The others came and examined it, but I didn't. She doesn't look too badly damaged."

"I think we can get her fixed. She's been through a lot. Somehow, she survives again and again."

He licked his lips before he answered. "The best ships are like people, right? They can come out of a fight damaged but fixable."

I extended my hand toward Artemis. "Would you like to come inside?"

"Not tonight, but soon maybe. Thanks for asking."

"You're welcome." I stepped toward Artemis when his voice stopped me.

"Don't run away, Diana. Don't take her out before she's ready and get into worse trouble. People have a tendency to surprise us. Don't run tonight in a ship with a hull which might fall apart."

I touched the side of the ship, putting my hands on her. I could feel where they had scratched her nearly apart. "I'd have to be really foolish to run with the ship like this. I am many things; foolish has never been one of them."

"Sometime, would you tell me about Earth? The others all have their interests. If you tell Judge about the black hole, you may never get to stop talking about it. Despite his hurt tonight, I suspect Damian is going to want to hear about his missing uncle at length. I want to know about Earth. I've dreamed about her ..." His voice faded off. "Sometime. If you would."

"I ..." He sounded so wistful I couldn't help but respond to it. "I only lived on Earth a few months. I know what I remember and what I've heard from the constant comings and goings of people on Mars Station who travel frequently to earth. I'd be happy to talk to you about it."

His grin could have lit up the night. "Thank you, Diana. Sleep well. I presume Judge showed you our living quarters."

"He did."

"Then find us if you need us. Also, you can always try the comm. One of us stays awake most of the time. We don't have to. Sleep sometimes eludes."

I should go, but I didn't move. I wanted to ask him something, too. "What do you bring out every morning into the trash compactor?"

His eyebrows shot up. "You were watching." He didn't ask a question, so I didn't answer one. Instead, I waited to see what he'd say. "How did you know it was me? We're all covered head to toe when we leave the compound. Height?"

"Height was a factor, but I became convinced when I saw your black coat. That's how I identified you, the coat."

He grinned. "It's just a better coat than the ones they gave us. I don't care what they say. I'm warmer in it." He groaned and shook his head. "Okay, well. We don't like to dispose of the body parts of the Infected inside the compound. It's an extra measure we probably don't need to take, but I feel better for having done. I take them outside and burn them in the compactor we set out there."

Every so often, I wished I hadn't asked a question. My mind could get me into trouble. This was one of those times. Did I understand reality? Sure. Did dead Zombies have to be disposed of in specific places? Absolutely. Did I wish I could stop picturing dead body parts? Yes.

"Have I grossed you out?" He looked down at the floor. In the short time I'd been around him, I'd seen Lewis look away quite a bit. Did he have a problem with eye contact?

I crossed over toward him until I was near him. Gently, I placed a hand on his arm. "I'm not meant to be a doctor. I'm glad you are and others like you. Thanks for doing what you do."

He didn't speak, his gaze rising to meet mine. His other hand pressed against mine, squeezing. We stood like that for a second. "Sleep well, Diana."

There were only the two of us here. He liked to say my name. I smiled. "You too, Lewis."

With a nod, he dropped my hand and walked from the bay where Artemis and I would spend the night. I didn't like how off-balance I felt with Lewis gone. I stood too long, not moving. These guys had a way of throwing me so off-balance.

Judge, with the way he bounced and watched me like I was actually something to look at. Lewis, who seemed to see right through me even though he barely regarded me head on at all. Damian, with his accusing eyes and hot temper. Sterling, who somehow I had hurt by simply being me. And Cash ... I couldn't get a read on him yet. He seemed withdrawn, yet he seemed to know everything around him.

Strangers, I knew how to handle. What was I to do with such intensity around me all of the time?

I climbed the steps Judge must have left and made my way through the hatch into Artemis. She smelled like home. Clean with a touch of vinegar in the air. I'd had to make do with what cleaning products were available. Vinegar had become a scent I liked.

As fast as I could, I got to my bedroom. It had been my mother's room when we'd lived on the ship. Her decorations were gone. A white sheet from storage and a brown blanket plus one pillow was how I slept every night. I stripped out of my jumpsuit and put on my pajamas. They weren't coated in the substance Judge used to keep us warm, and I immediately noticed the difference. I wouldn't be freezing, but I was certainly cold.

I hadn't asked Judge about washing the outfit. Thinking I'd better be safe than sorry, I hung it up carefully and scurried to the bed.

"Artemis, lights. Off." I wrapped myself in the blanket and tried to close my eyes. Sleep was sometimes hard for me. I lay still for a while and tried to doze. When I didn't manage to bring on dreamland, I spoke to Artemis again. "Artemis, family picture. July. Last year."

A shot of my family at my Uncle Nolan's birthday party flipped onto the screen. We'd been on the station in Nolan's favorite restaurant, where they served breakfast all day. Every one of us had been there. My mother, my father, Uncle Nolan, Uncle Wes, Uncle C.J., Uncle Cooper, Uncle Dane, and all the kids. Asher—*Cooper's son*—Colin—*Dane's son*—Edward—*C.J.'s son*—John—*Wes' son*—and my twin baby sisters Iris and Felicity—*Nolan's daughters*. When my mom announced she wanted a child from each husband, they'd all agreed right off except for Uncle Nolan. He'd finally given in, and in turn had two kids to obsess over instead of just one. And girls to boot. Standing next to my father, Geoff, was me. Smiling from ear-to-ear.

I looked so out of place with the group, so much older than my siblings yet not aged enough to be considered an equal to my parents. Still, I loved them, and we'd been happy in that moment. People sometimes stared when we went out in public all together. No one had as many kids as they did. I'd never really cared.

They were somewhere, and they would come for me. I had to believe.

I fell asleep staring at their faces.

I didn't sleep long. A loud wailing sound startled me awake, and I grabbed the blanket around me, my heart in my throat. Had the Zombies gotten in? What was happening?

It took me a second to realize I heard wind. It was wind. In the lower parts of the space station, we could hear a faint sound of it. Particularly in some of the engineering ducts. But I'd never heard anything like this before. Why was it so loud? I hadn't heard the wind when I'd been alone on Artemis when I'd been in hiding. The walls were still thick. Inside the bay, it should be even more secure.

Tears threatened, and I pushed them back. I didn't get to be weak. I couldn't be. I hid under the covers and pretended I was fine. Maybe I would believe it soon.

A noise inside Artemis caught my attention. Footsteps. Oh, no. It was the Zombies. They'd gotten out and ...

"Diana?" Damian's voice startled me, and I yelped, my heart so loud I could hear it. "Are you okay?"

I tried to speak. "D-D-Damian? What are you doing here?"

His footsteps were steady while he walked toward me. "Judge realized he didn't give you any other clothes. I brought them. I figured if you were awake, I owed you an apology. If you were asleep, I'd have left them and gone."

I pulled the blanket down and stared up at Damian. In the dark room, I couldn't see his face. "Artemis, lights. Two degrees."

A dull glow entered the bedroom. Damian continued to regard me, his eyebrows sloped down. He chewed on his bottom lip. "Are you okay? What's wrong?"

"That noise. What's going on?"

It took him a second to respond. "Do you mean the wind? Oh, you've not heard it before. I didn't think .... summer winds. They come toward the end of every season on Orion. Loud, but spring and winter will be louder. I hardly hear them anymore. Don't be afraid. You're safe here."

"Th-Thanks." I wanted to burrow down into my blanket again but couldn't as long as he was here. Damian wasn't someone I wanted to show any weakness to. Maybe ever.

He set down the aforementioned clothes on a chair next to the bed and then sat back down next to me. "I owe you an apology."

"Accepted." I never held onto anger, and he needed to go.

He sucked in his breath. "Just like that?"

"Sure."

"You're really afraid right now. Is it just the wind or me too?"

Him? No, I wasn't afraid of him. Maybe I should be. He was still a stranger—and one who wanted to turn me over to his corporation. He hated my uncle. Snapped at me. Still, I didn't feel fear when it came to him. "The wind. I don't do fear well. Better for me to hunker down and wait it out."

"Damn. Um." He stood and took off his shoes. Why did he do that? "The wind is going to last days and days, and then it'll be Fall. Not that we humans, feel much of a difference between the temperatures. But our computers will note it. I'm going to climb in there, unless you tell me not to, and lay down with you. I hate being scared. Company helps. I'll keep to the other side of this big bed."

I'd never slept with anyone, not since I'd been twelve, anyway. When Asher was born, the baby needed that kind of attention, and I'd suddenly found myself being called things like young lady and grown-up girl. I was smart. It meant, among other things, I couldn't go running into my mom's bed at night and curl up with her and whichever husband she was with. They were busy with the baby.

"Okay." I couldn't believe I uttered the word even as I said it.

Damian pointed at the lights. "Turn them back down? Will the computer take direction from me?"

"Artemis will take direction from anyone who wants to give it to her. Artemis, lights off."

Damian scooted into the other side of the bed. With the lights off, my family's picture was much better illuminated again. "Artemis, screen off."

"Was that your family?" Damian asked as soon as I shut down the screen. "Lots of siblings."

One of them was his cousin. Since we lay in the dark together and already his presence in the bed had warmed me considerably, I decided not to mention Asher right then. I made a sound somewhere close to a, "Hmm."

The wind blew around us, not lessening but seeming to get louder. "You took my apology really quickly. I was rude to you. Make me work at saying sorry."

"I ..." I sighed. "I've never seen the point. Life moves on whether I accept your apology or not. I've always found it easier to simply get back on pleasant terms with whoever dished out the insult, intended or not, and get on with getting on."

He turned on his side, leaning on his elbow. I couldn't see him in the dark, just the outline of his body. "What about how whatever that person did had made you feel? Sometimes they should have to feel badly for a length of time to learn not to do it again."

"Did you feel badly already? You trekked over here to bring me the clothes and apologize. If you didn't care, you wouldn't have bothered."

"Diana." The sound of my name was soft. "Tell me off. Okay? If I ever do something rude again, tell me off. You deserve to really nail whoever is rude to you."

"That's not my way." A thought dawned on me. "Sometimes I'm rude. I don't usually mean to be. Are you going to tell me off?"

"Um." He actually laughed, a hard sound which surprised me and made me clutch the blanket tighter. "No, I don't know.

I haven't spent enough time around women to know. Just my mom. I never told her off. Her last name was Osborne. That's what I use now. Special woman. I miss her. I don't know if I'm going to tell you off or not. I'm not really a yeller usually."

I supposed his words made sense. "Then we'll figure it out and hope I don't make you mad."

He lay on his back. I closed my eyes. I'd never in a million years have guessed I'd end up in bed with Damian. Eventually, his breathing evened and then slowed. He snored, a low sound in his throat that didn't bother me. It was more like knowing he was there than anything else. I let myself drift into the sound of it. Damian's breaths, as low and soft as they were, drowned out the wind and even my own thoughts into nothingness. I fell into sleep.

Sometime in the middle of the night, we must have moved toward each other. I woke up with his arm slung over my body and my legs twisted up in his. He wasn't snoring anymore but breathing lightly, his eyes closed. I clung to his shirt and quickly let go. I didn't want to be inappropriate. I wondered if I'd bothered him with how I gripped him while he slept.

Instead of moving away, he pulled me closer and muttered something unintelligible. The wind blew loudly. In the hallway, Artemis had started the daytime routine with the lights. In space, it was always dark. I determined day from night based on the ship's routine, which kept us in steady awake/sleep cycles. The light outside said it was early morning. Probably not time to be awake yet.

I rolled over, which was hard with his arm around me, but he didn't let go. I didn't want to be caught staring at Damian when he opened his eyes. His head dipped down; his nose pressed against my hair. I wasn't getting back to sleep. Not with the way his holding me brought my body awake. I wanted him. I'd never had sex, the idea sometimes terrifying me. Would I have to speak to the guy afterward for a long length of time? I had urges just like everyone else, although they passed quickly. I didn't harp on good looks or let myself daydream.

Paloma, my best friend on Mars Station before she'd been sent off to the Sisters for getting into trouble, and I used to talk about boys. She'd point at some she liked; I'd mention others. We never liked the same guys. It had been harmless. Then she'd been caught kissing a station engineer. Her parents were way stricter than mine. My own mother might have been relieved. But her father was a council member back then, and he'd shipped her to a life of meditation until he and the Sisters deemed her ready for the world again. We still wrote once a week.

She was investing in people's lives and doing good works while I obsessed on the station.

I wanted Damian. Badly. It would pass, I was sure. When he got of bed and I could reclaim my headspace. But right then, I wanted to feel alive with him in a way I never had before.

He moved slightly, and I felt his hips close to mine. He wasn't hard. I wasn't well-versed in everything, but the basics didn't elude me. He sucked in a long breath, and I knew he'd be waking up any second. I closed my eyes. I would pretend to be asleep. Sometimes I had no options except bad ones. Pretending to be asleep was my best out.

His hand flexed against my stomach, and he groaned slightly. He didn't let go and instead rubbed his forehead against the back of my head. Then he fell silent again. He wasn't back to sleep. I knew the difference in his breathing.

He didn't move, and neither did I. Minutes passed.

Finally, he let go of me, and I immediately missed his warmth. He sat up, the covers moving slightly when he did. I decided it was a good time to wake up. I stretched my arms over my head and sat.

He rubbed his eyes and looked at me. "Hi."

"Good morning." I sat upright until we were shoulder to shoulder on the bed. "Did you sleep okay?"

"Honestly"—half his mouth rose in a smile—"never better in my entire life. Not even when I was out cold in hyperspace."

Maybe he needed company sometimes, too. "Once I fell asleep I was out like that too. Thanks for coming and making last night okay."

His eyes flared before they hooded into an unreadable gaze again. "Thank you for accepting my apology and letting me sleep in your bed."

"Knock-knock." Judge rounded the corner. "I brought coffee. Let's work on your ship before we ... Oh, sorry. Excuse me." He backed up but didn't leave the room, his eyes huge as he stared at us. I saw a million emotions cross his face.

"No." Damian jumped to his feet. "It's absolutely not what you're thinking. I brought her the clothes. I apologized. She forgave me. She was terrified of the wind. I stayed here so she wouldn't be alone in fear. End of story."

Maybe that was the end of the story for him. I put on my best smile. He'd clearly not been as taken with me as I was with him. Not wanting to be any more uncomfortable, I got out of the bed. Judge's face seemed more relaxed.

"I'll get dressed fast and come. What's the deal with washing the clothes? Is it just normal? Or do I have to take care of the substance?"

"Normal wash. Use the laundry facility. I did the best I could for sizes. Everything is going to be too big for you. Only the jump suit is one size fits all."

I touched his shoulder. "I appreciate you even thinking of it. You're so kind to me."

"Well, you know, beautiful girl practically falls into our pad, and I'm not going to be a jackass."

I rolled my eyes. "I told you ..."

"Judge." Damian padded toward him. "Don't talk to her like that. It's not appropriate."

With laughter, Judge responded, "I told her yesterday that she was beautiful, and she didn't faint at my feet. She doesn't believe me. Told me I was wrong, and I don't think she's just saying that. So I'm going to keep telling her until she says, 'Thank you, Judge,' and knows I only ever speak the truth."

Damian rounded on me. "Do you seriously not think you're beautiful?"

It was too early for this. "I'm going to take a quick shower."

I fled into the bathroom.

Chapter Six

Repairing what's broken

The clothes I chose didn't fit well, unsurprisingly. I had to roll the sleeves and the pants and then pin everything together. Being five feet tall, I was way shorter than any of them. My underwear was going to tear sooner or later. I might have to figure out how to sew. I was sure Artemis could give me instructions. Lewis had offered to replicate some shoes for me. My own were not going to be great for withstanding the cold. For now, they would do. I left the slippers he'd given me on the side of my bed.

If I'd had any shoes on when they'd taken me, I'd never have gotten my slippers. I smiled down at them. I don't know why I liked them so much. But I did, and unless they asked me for them back, I was going to keep them.

I hurried outside, hoping Judge hadn't left. He'd wanted to work on Artemis, and that's what I really desired, too. I had to get her fixed before Damian sent for Evander. Damian ... who had held me so close ... was going to give me away to his corporation.

Outside Artemis, Judge waited for me. He stared at the ship with his head tilted.

"Ah, Diana." He grinned. "I think we need to take more than this section off. I walked the side. I'm concerned about some of the bulking I see."

Bulking? "Where? Show me?"

Together we walked around the outside of the ship. He pointed out various parts that caused him concern. I wasn't surprised. We'd been attacked by Sandler, and then I'd not been able to get outside to fix her because of the weather. In retrospect, I was glad it hadn't fallen apart in route. Not that I'd exactly planned my trip.

"Tell me the truth. I'm in over my head. Is she salvageable?" If she wasn't, I needed to start accepting my fate. Or stealing one of their shuttles, which I really hated the thought of. I didn't want to be a thief. Then again, I preferred to be a thief than a piece of chattel.

He knocked his shoulder into mine gently. "Are you kidding? Piece of cake."

"I don't think that phrase actually applies here. In no way will it be a piece of cake. We have no idea how damaged the ship is beneath the bulge."

He shrugged. "That's the fun stuff."

"I'm a different kind of engineer. I want to know what's wrong before I start to fix it. I can allot a proper amount of time and be sure I'm ready to do the job. I'm not an innovator. I'm a fixer." My uncles could invent things. I never wanted to have to.

Judge banged on the side of Artemis. "Takes all types, Di. I hate the minutia of keeping up systems when I could be planning how to make them better. If I'm not wrong, you fixed up Artemis a bit. I saw your upgrades."

"Yes, but I hated it."

He'd called me Di. My family sometimes did that. It rolled off his tongue like we were long-term friends. My heart jumped, and I made myself breathe to calm down. I couldn't have a repeat of the day before, when everything they did made my hormones go crazy.

He shrugged. "Yeah, but you did it." He banged the hull again. "Come on. Let's get busy."

His energy was up again. Judge had been relatively still this morning. Not anymore. He burst toward the ship, pulling a monitor out of his pocket. "We'll start by checking on the pressure. Can you go measure where the outside is buckling up?"

"I can do that." I'd always taken direction really, really well.

We worked for two hours and hadn't taken any of the siding off the ship yet. Judge examined everything. He gave me polite orders, and I took them without complaint. I didn't even understand why he wanted to know some of the things he did. From experience working with C.J., Wes, and even my father, I knew I shouldn't interrupt with questions when engineers were busy. Even Dane, when he was busy, could snap. Cooper was a bear in his hydroponics bay. Only Nolan took the time to explain. Mostly, it was better to wait.

Judge blew out a loud breath. "I think that's it for today. Still have to work on the regular stuff I do." He grinned at me. "Was that awful?"

I stretched my arms over my head. "Not even a little bit. You give clear-cut instructions."

"Really? Most people find me confusing. Thanks, I'll take the compliment. Di, um, listen. I'm sorry I didn't tell you about the wind. I should have thought of it."

"Oh." His apology surprised me. I'd moved on. Working the last two hours, I hadn't heard the sound at all. Since he'd brought it up, the noise whooshed back into my consciousness. I didn't react. Judge, I was pretty sure, was being kind. Should I say something else? Sometimes it was hard to know.

He nodded once. "Well, I can stay with you if you get scared. Or you could come to me. Okay? You don't have to be alone. Damian showed up, and that's good. He's a great guy. Like a brother to me. You never have to be scared. You're safe here."

"Thank you, Judge." I couldn't imagine crossing the long distance of the pod to find him. By the time I got there, I'd be utterly humiliated from needing to be comforted. I'd have made it through the night under my covers. Not as warm as having Damian. I would have made it.

He brightened at my thanks and nodded toward the hallway before he took my hand. "Let's go."

I could walk by myself. I didn't need him to hold my hand. Only, I didn't pull away. Judge was nice, and I wouldn't mind having a friend. I had to try to not make things weird or uncomfortable. Not until I ran away.

"What's the pressure gauge say over there, Di?"

I stared down at the number on the device I held while I knelt next to the two-way window where we could see the Infected. They couldn't see us ... but they could smell us. I shuddered. "The same as before. Within normal limits."

"I believe you that it says that, but it's wrong."

He knew the pressure in the window better than the gauge?

"Don't mind him. He's a perfectionist." Sterling knelt next to me, seemingly coming out of nowhere. "Just keep telling him what it says, and he'll eventually work out in his head what's bothering him and fix it, or he'll get over it. I've been the one holding the gauge. I give you credit. Most of us lose it a lot earlier than you have." He held out a bar. "Lunch?"

I took it from him, grateful for the offering. My stomach growled. "Thank you. I guess I'm hungry."

"Forget to eat?" His blond hair fell over his eyes, and I had the strangest urge to reach out and push it off his baby blues.

"Not usually," I shook my head. "Guess I'm just distracted on my first day."

He sat stretching his long legs out in front of him. "You can sit. He'll never know you sat if you pop into a squat when he calls instead of already being there."

Judge worked two rooms over. He spoke into a mic when he wanted my attention, and I answered the same way.

"He told me to squat here and be ready. I don't want to start breaking rules right away." Not when I was lying to all of them right off the bat by planning an escape while acting compliant. I had to be myself as much as I could, and I was a rule follower.

Sterling lay flat on his back. "Suit yourself. My knees hurt looking at you."

I doubted that entirely. Sterling was a giant muscle. I could see them through his pants and his shirt. He could probably squat for hours and never notice. He seemed different than last night, easier-going, and not angry anymore. Still, what I'd said to Damian remained true. Anger eventually went away. To make things hurry up and get back to pleasant times, I let things go. It appeared Sterling did too.

Still, an apology might help. I was sorry I'd upset him right off the bat. "Last night, I made you angry. That was not my intention. I'm sorry."

I went back to looking at the gauge as the number stayed exactly where it was, not budging at all. I felt more than saw Sterling lean up on his elbows.

"I'm touchy. It's one of my worst flaws." He lightly nudged me with his foot. "I'm sorry, too. I don't want you to think I'm not approachable or you can't touch me. We're all like family here."

I was getting that impression. They all said it. Even as Judge worried about Sterling and Damian being company men, he cared about them. These guys were on the edge of their universe, doing good work and getting through every day laughing together. It was, in its own way, enviable.

Sterling hadn't explained why he got so upset, and I wasn't going to ask. They were family. I wasn't. I wasn't going to pry to satisfy my own curiosity.

He rolled over until his head was on his elbow, and he stared at me. I finally had to look at him. "What?"

"Tell me about Mars Station where you grew up. Is it really exciting?"

He looked like a little boy, his eyes bright and questioning. I smiled, his enthusiasm enticing. "I grew up there, so I don't know if it's exciting or not. It was a good option, considering the other places we could have ended up. My mom immediately got elected into politics, so we were treated well by everyone there."

"Were there lots of kids?"

I nodded. "Yes, a big school and an indoor playground. I was never much into socialization, and I tended to stick by myself."

"You can't eat and squat. Seriously." He grabbed the mic from my hand. "You're going to give yourself indigestion. Judge, Diana is going to eat. She's taking twenty minutes."

A moment later, Judge answered. "Sounds good. Have a good lunch."

"See?" He shook his head. "He'd never expect you to eat like that." Sterling patted the floor next to him, and I sat down.

My legs immediately thanked me for stretching them out. I took a bite of my bar. It was sweet and tangy. The side of the wrapping said *Protein* and I was glad for some. I needed to keep my strength up.

Sterling tapped his foot. "How many floors is your station?" He watched me chew, and I wished he was eating something too. Consuming food when no one else ate always made me feel like I was eating really loudly.

"Twenty." I swallowed the last bit and rumpled up the wrapper in my hand. I didn't see a garbage can in the room.

Sterling extended his hand and took the wrapper from me before putting it back in his pocket. He furrowed his eyebrows. "Hard to keep order on a place that big."

"There is lots of help. Well, there's external, space, security, and internal, station, security. Keeping an eye on the ships coming and going is a different thing entirely. Inside? They have hundreds of officers."

Sterling whistled through his teeth. "That's too many. I mean, ignore me, I'm not there. I'd rather have a smaller amount of well-trained people who can cover large distances. Easier to run, better to quality control. If eighty of those guys can barely fire their weapons, it's a total waste of time. You spend more time worrying about getting shot by the guy next to you."

Okay, I could mind my own business, but if he was going to say something that interesting, I needed more information. "Do you have experience in a scenario like that?"

He let out a loud breath. "Walked right into that one." His grin was huge. "Yes, I've been in many battles. I grew up in Evander Corporation. I was bred to be a soldier. A fighter. I am what I am."

"Bred?" What did he mean by that?

"Evander thought for a while they could solve the 'girl problem' by making babies in labs. The girl babies never lived long. They couldn't make that work. Then they decided maybe they didn't have to entirely lose money. They made really strong boys with high likelihoods of turning out to be aggressive and war-like. We were their perfect security force."

I touched his arm and tried not to overthink my action. He didn't flinch or push my hand away, so I left it where it was. "Excuse me for saying so, but you don't seem overly war-like."

He smirked and shook his head. "I can be. I'll just say, maybe you aren't the only one who's glitchy."

The wind let out a loud burst, and I jumped. It sounded like thunder. My heart leaped into my throat, and Sterling yanked me against him, embracing me in his strong arms.

"I—I'm not usually afraid."

"Don't worry. The winds are really horrendous. They don't last forever. Couple weeks. We forget them. They start again. It's like ... life. I don't know. Ignore me." He tightened his hold. Sterling smelled like soap, clean and fresh. "Sometimes thunder rocks through the wind."

As my heart stilled, my current foolishness made my cheeks heat up. I pulled back a little and rubbed my eyes. "I'm sorry."

"Don't be. I got to protect you for three seconds. Did my ego a world of good."

I snorted, which quickly turned into outright laughter. Soon he joined me, and we were both belly-laughing. When we finally stopped, it was to see Cash standing in the doorway, staring at us with his mouth open. "I've clearly missed something."

Sterling wiped at his eyes; he'd laughed so hard tears had started. He stood. "Yeah ... hard to explain."

"I ..." Cash grinned. "I was wondering if I could borrow Diana. I need some repairs on my console. It keeps shutting off and on. Judge is so preoccupied with window pressure he can hardly hear me when I ask. He finally said Diana could fix it. So can you come take a look?"

"If Judge is okay with it, then yes, I can." I rose and crossed to him. "Are we going to your lab?"

Sterling shook his head. "I'm going to go check on our Infected brethren. They'll roar at me. But it'll be okay today because I haven't laughed that hard, well, maybe ever."

"Me neither. I'm not really a laugher."

Sterling's face fell. "We'll change that. You weren't a laugher. Now you are."

"I don't find I can change much. I kind of am what I am."

He leaned forward. "Then you are a laugher."

Cash took my arm. "Much as this is a fascinating argument, I have a console that needs fixing. You can argue with her about her personality attributes later."

"Always in charge, Cash?" Sterling winked at me before he walked toward the window to stare down at the Zombies.

Cash and I walked together, and after a moment he spoke. "I'm not always in charge. I have no interest whatsoever in running things around here. I'm sorry if I interrupted some fun. I ..."

I interrupted him. "It's fine. We're working right now, aren't we? Fun later? Or at specific times? I shouldn't have been fooling around in the middle of the day."

Cash sighed. "We tend to have fun when it comes. Out here in the middle of nowhere? Some days we have to be off schedule. I do tend to want what I want when I want it. Sterling's right."

"I don't think he meant to hurt you. I think he was teasing you, like he was me. I'd had a freak out a second before because of the thunder and the wind. He hugged me till I calmed and then joked me out of my scared mood."

He stopped moving. "Has anyone explained to you about the winds?"

"Three people. I'm having an unusual reaction to the wind. I'll get over it. I think through my fears eventually."

He started moving again, this time more slowly. "What you say, about thinking through the fear, I get it. I do the same myself."

We walked together until we reached his office. I could see what he meant about the console. The second I walked in the room, I could see the console blinking on and off. I put my hands on my hips. "This is a power surge."

The console was wireless, which meant it was its own malfunctioning power source. Unless ...

"Do even the wireless devices draw power from the central power source? Pull from it wirelessly, too?"

Cash laughed. "I think so. Don't hate me. I'm really stupid about engineering."

"I can't save anyone's life, so we'll call it even."

A sound caught me up short. A roar. Like the ones I'd heard with the other Infected. I jumped back, and Cash placed a hand on my back. "He's secured. Don't worry."

A smaller version of the containment center was attached to the back wall of the lab. A man—or at least he used to be—banged on the glass. Unlike with the other containment center, I was quite certain this one could see me. It wasn't two-way glass. He banged on the glass, his eyes red, his face grotesque. How long had he been this way?

I inched toward him. The longer I stayed in this place with these five men, the more I'd get used to them, I supposed. I wasn't sure I should. They were dangerous. I should never stop being afraid of what was genuinely scary.

"How did this happen? How did it get this bad?" I forgot about the console for a minute. The Infected took all my attention. He looked at me like he wanted to eat me, and I believed he would if he actually got the chance. Starting with my brain.

Cash, who clearly didn't share my terror of him, strode until he stood right in front of the glass. He placed a gentle hand on it. "I don't know when this one changed. From the look of the decomposition, this could have been thirty years ago. Although some of them go faster than others. It depends on the planet, too. Orion keeps them looking human longer. The cold weather. To answer your question, from what I understand, when that mad, mad woman set off those bombs, she meant to take over everything. What she did was destroy most of the livable planets and leave them uninhabitable. Slowly, some of the people who survived the blast mutated. By the time anyone realized what happened, we were behind the eight ball." He shook his head. "Now it spreads with a bite. Or a scratch. It can't be contained. Some of the planets simply can't be managed, even by corporations. We have to cure it. Or vaccinate for it. I can't fail."

"You won't then." I could hear it in his voice. He wasn't the type to lose his way. If he declared he would do this, he would. I knew what drive could do; I'd seen it my whole life. Drive opened black holes after they'd been sealed.

He didn't turn around. "I wish I had your certainty."

"Why are you unsure?" I found the courage to stand next to him against the sealed off enclosure.

"Because they keep dying. Nothing I've done so far has worked. Lewis is the smartest doctor I know. He's as confused as me."

"You only have to be right once. Failure just means you haven't gotten your one-off correct yet."

The room looked just like Lewis' had. The labs had been built to look the same. The only difference as far as I could see, was Cash was less orderly than Lewis. He had things strewn everywhere, and yet I could see the room remained clean. He was disorganized, not dirty.

I walked over and picked up his orange hat, which sat on a chair in the corner of the room. "This is the hat I saw you in outside. I used to think of you as Orange Hat."

He turned, an eyebrow raised. "It's so much warmer than the other stuff. I don't care that it's not protocol. I like it better."

"Right." I set down the hat. I'd told Lewis, too, about my personal nicknames. What was the matter with me? Why was I talking so much?

I made my way over to the console. Cash was right. The power source came from the same place as the wired in machines. I stared at the wires on the ceiling. It would just be a question of finding the power source itself. I could easily find where I needed to go.

I turned on my heel, and, staring up the ceiling, I made my way out of the lab in the direction of the wiring.

"Diana!" A shout behind me made me stop short. Cash ran to catch up with me. What was wrong? "Where did you go?"

I pointed at the wires. "Going to find the power source. And I can also check to make sure there aren't any breaks on the way, too."

"I turned around, and you were gone." He took my arm like before. "Come on; we'll go together. I can show you where the power comes from. That much I know. We'll check the line together."

His words confused me. He had a lot to do. "Is there a reason you were worried about me doing this alone?"

"No, not particularly. It's just that ... I don't know. You were there, and then you weren't."

Okay, I wasn't going to make sense of this until I was alone. Cash was really handsome; his olive skin and piercing eyes reminded me of the romance novels I used to sneak sometimes when I'd finished work. Eventually, I'd stopped reading them. I wasn't going to have that kind of love. Why break my heart over and over with fiction?

Like Sterling, he smelled like soap. Only the scent was different on him—darker, spicier. Different scents worked differently on other people.

"Maybe I'm an idiot. I'm not used to women. I think I might be a little nervous around you. Don't worry. I'll think through my fear."

I laughed, covering my mouth, and he grinned like he'd won a prize. "Ah, there." I pointed at the ceiling. Smallest hole. No one will see it if they're not looking for it, and Judge is so busy. I can fix it." I pulled my wrench out of my back pocket. With a press to the button on the side, the wrench elongated. We didn't have this tech at home. Judge had loaned it to me. I hated to ever have to give it back. Between the slippers and the wrench, it was like my birthday. Even if I could only have them temporarily.

"We're lucky your console is so finicky. It likes its power streamed in a steady line. Something like oxygen support could have shut off, and we'd have been screwed." Or the safety lines that kept the Zombies where they were. Although those systems had redundancy after redundancy. Judge would have noticed that problem. His focus seemed to be on security measures, and I appreciated that.

I looked around. I didn't have a ladder. But a chair would do. I grabbed one from the laundry room next door and dragged it into the hall.

"Diana?" Cash questioned what I was doing with just my name stated.

"Gotta get up there." I climbed onto the chair and started twisting one of the electrode mechanisms to get it off. Our tech wasn't that different at home than here. So much time had passed, but then again, they'd been nearly destroyed and had to come back from that. It would make a difference.

"Don't fall. I don't want you to hurt yourself." He gripped the side of my chair, holding it steady.

"I won't, but even if I did, you'd fix me up, right?"

He didn't answer instantly, but when he did it was with a low voice. "I would."

Chapter Seven

Game Night

I was pretty exhausted. I'd never anticipated I'd need to fix so many small things going wrong at the station. After Cash's console, I worked on the heat in Lewis' lab, which had for some reason started acting up; Damian's device, which automatically closed the weapons closet, needed fixing; and I eventually ended up in Sterling's room trying to make the water in his shower spray harder. I'd gotten them all done.

Now, I sat across from the others while they chatted. Judge elbowed me gently. "You okay?"

"I am." The steak was delicious. I still didn't know which one of them was responsible for killing the animals. Or how they stored food so it didn't go bad. Those were things I had to learn.

"You're quiet." He side-eyed me. "Something go wrong today?"

"I talked more today—a lot more than I'm used to. I think I need to be quiet for a bit."

Under the table his foot met mine. "Of course. I'll leave you be. Just promise to tell me if something goes wrong. Okay?"

"Um, okay." I wasn't used to so much attention, and they were all staring at me now. "I'm okay."

"Something wrong?" Lewis sat forward. "You can tell us."

"She doesn't talk this much usually, and she needs to be quiet." Judge responded for me. "Let's give her a break."

Damian motioned with his fork. "You were the one who brought it up. I noticed she was quiet, and I left her alone."

"Congratulations on being so smart, Damian. Would you like a medal?" Cash responded, and Sterling dropped his knife, loudly.

They were fighting. I looked between them. Why were they fighting? All I had done was not want to talk during dinner. My uncles and my father never fought. Sometimes they debated, but it always ended with my mother's opinion and everyone doing what she wanted, even if they grumbled about it. Years earlier there had been times they'd disagreed and taken matters into their own hands. But not lately. I didn't know what to do when people fought.

My tongue itched. When people fought, everything went sideways. Stability disappeared. Things erupted. Chaos. No. I pulled it back. I wasn't in the middle of an ice planet with no protection and drones above my head. I was at a dinner. They were arguing. That was it.

"Stop," I managed to spit out. They all silenced immediately. "Don't fight. Please."

Judge's foot, still touching mine, pressed harder. "We fight sometimes. Bicker. Don't worry. We've all been together a long time. It's normal."

"I don't like it." I was done eating. "I'm sorry. I think I need to go now. I must be tired. It's very rude to eat and run. I know. Only ..."

Damian reached across the table to grab my hand. "Don't go yet. We'll behave. I swear we can. It'll be fun. Game night. We do it every Thursday if not more often. Nice routine. You'll love it."

I breathed through my nose. Judge's foot. Damian's hand. All of their eyes pleading with me. "Okay."

Cash grinned first, and the rest of them followed. Game night might be just what was needed. Fun and games. No more fighting. We ended up cleaning up dinner together, which gave me the chance to see how they saved their food—freeze dried. I washed the dishes.

"When should I cook?"

Lewis knocked his shoulder into mine gently. "You don't have to."

"I'm not great but functional. I'd like to contribute."

He shook his head. "You totally are."

"How so? I'm not pulling nearly my weight here. You're using your supplies to feed me. You've given me clothes and safety." I grimaced when I said the word. Damian's looming threat of sending me away never left me. I wondered if I could manage to fix Artemis at night so I could hurry the process along. "I can cook."

"Damian does all the cooking. He likes it. Calls it soothing."

Judge came up behind me, tugging me into his arms, which made Lewis frown. "You give us something beautiful to look at, and you fix our stuff. I can't believe how many things broke today."

My cheeks heated. The fixing I would take a nod for. "If I am beautiful, and I've never thought I am, I'm too small, my hair hangs limp on my shoulders, and I'm not well endowed." Judge let me go. I think he would have interrupted, but I didn't care. "Let's say I'm wrong. I'm beautiful. Who cares? It matters so little to who I am. Tell me I'm smart, helpful, interesting, worthwhile. Tell me I made your day better somehow. Tell me just about anything else. Beauty is a commodity. If I'm beautiful, then I'll be worth more to your corporation when Damian sends me to them."

Judge leaned forward. "You're all those things. I can tell, and I've only known you such a little time. You're also beautiful."

I pointed my finger at him. "You're going to make me mad if you keep that up."

"What happens when I make you mad?"

I shrugged. "I get over it, and I move on. I have six brothers and sisters. I'm not interested in holding on to anger. But I wouldn't push it because my father makes bombs and weapons. We know how to explode in my family."

My throat ached, and I stormed from the kitchen into the game room. Damian was spreading out cards on a table. Every card had a symbol. I didn't recognize the game. I knew poker and black jack. And a game called holler that they played on the casino in the station. I didn't know this.

"Everything okay?" Damian looked up.

"I just yelled at Judge." And felt a little shaky for having done so.

Damian raised a dark eyebrow, one side of his mouth going crooked in a smile. "I thought you didn't yell."

"He pushed a button."

"Oh yeah?" He sat back in his chair. "What is the button? I won't push it."

Judge and Cash entered the room, and Judge answered for me. "I keep telling her she's beautiful."

Cash finished, "She doesn't like it."

"I see." Damian stretched his arms over his head. "Sterling and Lewis will be here any second. Do you know how to play Puff?"

I shook my head. I appreciated Damian dropping the subject. I already sort of thought he wasn't attracted to me even if he thought I was pretty. We'd been very close when we woke up and he hadn't seemed interested at all. Sheesh. What was wrong with me?

Judge took the seat next to me on the left. I was right across from Damian, and Cash sat to my right. Sterling and Lewis entered together and took the remaining seats.

"Tomorrow"—Cash cleared his throat—"everyone should go see Lewis and get their levels checked. Some of you are a due for a trip into the US."

The sex machine. I tried to stay cool. Nods around the table were the only response he got to his announcement. This must be a regular thing.

Judge pointed to me. "Diana asked me if the machine works for women, too. I didn't know. Meant to look that up."

Lewis and Cash made eye contact before Cash answered. They had such a secret code, where they didn't speak and I couldn't follow. "Yes. It'll work. There's never really a reason to. You're kind of a unique case. Women are never not able to get what they need."

"That's not true where I'm from. Not exactly."

Lewis raised his eyebrows. "You've mentioned it before. Feel up for telling us?"

"Are we having a talk fest or playing cards?" Damian held up three. "Diana, what you do is hold three cards together. If you think you've got a match ..."

He kept talking, and I watched his mouth move. I'd never been so keenly aware of people in the room. Every move any of them made moved through me like I might explode from it. And why had Damian cut me off? I was grateful for it. Sitting still and being silent worked for me.

Damian nodded. "Got it?"

Not even a little bit. I shook my head, and he grinned. "You'll catch on."

As the game moved on, it became clear I really wasn't going to. Usually I was good at this kind of thing, but I was exhausted and things that should make sense were not. I rubbed my eyes. When I spoke, my voice croaked a little bit. "I've got to go to bed, I think."

"Really?" Damian raised his eyebrows. "This is round three."

"I'm just exhausted." Achingly so.

"Do you think you'll be able to sleep?"

Cash cut in. "Did you not sleep last night?"

"She was scared by the wind. I stayed with her. She did eventually knock out for a while."

The others stared at him silently. They were definitely communicating again. Judge threw down his cards. "In her bed. He slept in her bed."

Damian held up his hands in defeat. "Totally platonic. Put down your pistols."

Sterling took my hand. "Come on. You're tired. I'll walk you back."

I went with him. His hand was huge in mine. I didn't know any of them well yet, but he seemed quiet for Sterling. He laughed a lot, kept up with conversations, and smiled frequently. His eyes were different, withdrawn.

"Have you ever gotten so used to doing something that you do it just because you always did?" He scratched his chin with his free hand. His long blond hair fell to his shoulders. It looked so soft. I wanted to touch it. To do so passed some sort of boundary for me. I wasn't ready to stroke someone's hair, and I had no idea if Sterling would even like that.

I kind of understood what he meant. "Yes, actually. I used to attend meetings with my family because I always had. We'd go someplace, all together. I have no idea why I did that after a time. When I was little, they had to bring me to keep me safe. Later? Why did I bother? I don't know."

His eyes widened. "Yes. Like that. And then maybe something changes, and it makes you question why you keep doing it. But then you think maybe the original reasons were important ones."

"Sterling." I was really done for the night. "I don't follow hypothetical questions that aren't math related. I'm sorry I can't be of more help."

He grinned at me. "You're so awesome. You don't lie much do you?"

I was lying to them every second I didn't tell them I intended to run. "I try not to. Sometimes it's necessary. Why lie when the truth would do?"

We reached Artemis and Sterling stared up at her. "When we busted open the hatch, I didn't think it would be you I'd be finding in there."

"Who were you expecting?" I remembered they said something about rival corporations.

He grinned. "Bunch of guys stealing our stuff."

"You ran in without worrying they would hurt you?"

"Honey." He touched the side of Artemis almost reverently. "No one hurts me."

Now that, I couldn't believe. He was big—of that there was no doubt. Apparently he'd also been made in an Evander laboratory. The man in front of me was flesh and bones. He could be hurt. It might be hard, yet I had no doubt it could happen.

I squeezed his fingers. "Be careful with yourself anyway."

I didn't see his kiss coming. One second he towered over me, the next he hauled me up, back against Artemis, his mouth meeting mine. I gasped against his mouth, and then I quit thinking. I had never been kissed before, by choice more than anything else. I hadn't wanted people near me. But I wanted Sterling.

I wrapped my arms around his neck and decided I didn't care that this was all new. His lips were firm and soft. He didn't push too hard, just tasted and let me kiss him back. My body came alive, every nerve ending in my body—some I didn't even know I had—and I wanted him. He backed off for a second and then kissed me again. I closed my eyes, letting Sterling become my whole universe.

He pushed my bangs off my forehead and cut off our kiss to stare me in the eyes. "I knew when I saw you I was getting a gift beyond measure. I know we have to know each other better.

I'm so glad you're here, darling. You came from the other side of the galaxy and landed here with us."

I didn't know what to say, and I didn't want to talk. I took the initiative—very un-me—and I kissed him again. He closed his eyes and let me push against him. I'd never had sex. That didn't mean I didn't know how. I did. The logistics of it I understood.

Yet after a few minutes of kissing him and really getting into it, I hadn't gotten anywhere with him. I had my legs wrapped around him, and he wasn't hard. Not even a little bit.

He finally stopped kissing me, and when I looked at him, his eyebrows were sloped downwards. I'd grabbed the back of his hair, and it was as soft as I'd thought. Gently, I ran my fingers through his hair. Shouldn't he be at least a little into this by now? Was I rushing things? Going too far?

"Are you okay?"

He pressed his forehead to mine. "I'm not sure."

"What's wrong? Am I pushing you?" I'd never done any of this before, and I might be breaking some kind of rule. It would be so Diana Mallory to blow turning on a man. Paloma used to be able to do it just by winking at them. I'd ground myself into Sterling, and nothing had happened.

His eyebrows shot up. He had such a long, strong face. Since I was touching him, I kept doing so, my finger stroking the slope of his nose. He shuddered in my embrace.

"There's something wrong."

"Oh." I wasn't even sure what to say. Humiliation burned, and the wind sounded louder than I'd heard it yet. "I'm sorry."

Of course there was something wrong. There always was when it came to me.

He sucked in his breath. "Don't be sorry. Um, I'm going to set you down."

"Okay. That's probably best." And then I would run away and sleep until I didn't remember I'd done this. He set me on my feet. I straightened my shirt. What the hell was I thinking? I couldn't throw myself at any of them. I wanted all five of them, and I didn't get the impression they were okay anymore on this side of the hole with the whole multiple husband concept. I needed to get myself under control. I was going to ask Cash or Lewis to put me in the machine. They'd make it all go back to normal for me.

I wasn't going to get through the next months until I could leave if I didn't.

"Thanks, Sterling. Goodnight." The wind howled, and I shivered.

He grabbed my arm. "I'm sorry. I don't know why ..."

"It's me. I get it. I pressed you for something you didn't want, and you're being nice about it. Trust me; it won't happen again. You were sweet, and I went too far."

"No." He grabbed my arms and picked me up again. Sterling was so big, and I was so tiny next to him. Still, he didn't scare me. His hands were gentle. "This is me. I want you. Are you kidding? I dream about you. But something is wrong with me. It's not you. I have to go talk to the doctors. I'm ... defunct. This isn't you. Don't think that."

Oh. I had completely misread this situation. "It's not me?"

He hugged me really tightly. "Don't ever think it's you."

"Okay. Can I help you? Are you in pain?"

He closed his eyes and rubbed his nose in my hair. "I'm numb. I can't explain it."

I let him walk me inside into the bedroom. Tiredness weighed on me. I'd even put up with the wind to close my eyes. I needed release—for the first time in my life—and I wasn't going to get any. Sleep had to help. I might have face-planted on the bed. I don't know. When I woke up, I was still in my clothes with my shoes off and a warm Sterling half covering my body with his own. He didn't snore but breathed gently in my ear. His hand was on my ass, his legs entwined with my own.

We were both sleeping on our stomachs. He was also fully dressed without his shoes.

The light on Artemis showed it was morning. I moved slightly, and Sterling's fingers massaged my rear end. I blushed, my face getting really hot. Why had I behaved so badly last night? I'd totally lost my head. And what did he mean he was numb? Did he mean his penis area ...?

I shifted my hips, trying to move, and came in contact with the part of his body I'd been wondering about. He wasn't hard. Neither had Damian been the night before. I wasn't making the men around me particularly hot.

He thought there was something wrong ...

Sterling's eyes opened. "Hey, darling."

"Hi." His soft hair touched my neck when he raised his head to look at me. "You okay? You fell asleep so fast. I ... I hope it's okay I stayed. I was worried. You were breathing fine and everything. I wanted to hold you."

There were lots of things I wanted to ask him, and yet in the light of day those words were harder to say without the ease of exhaustion to make me brave. "Thank you."

"Are you? Okay?"

I sat up, stretching my arms over my head. I needed a shower and coffee in that order. "I'm not sure. I'm not behaving like myself. My thoughts are weird."

He fingered my arm, drawing a small circle on my skin. "I like you like this."

First step in reclaiming myself was to act the way I always did. "Truth of the matter is, I am the only girl here. You've been here a long time. If there were other women walking around, you wouldn't be so preoccupied with me. I get it. I've never been one hundred percent comfortable being a default choice based on being in the right vicinity."

Sterling's eyebrows rose slowly. "Did I give you the impression I liked you because you happened to be here?"

"No. Sterling, I know how these things work."

He rose from the bed and laced his shoes up. "I'm going to see the doctor, and then I'm going to show you how I want you, how it's not convenient."

"I ..."

I don't know what Sterling would have said because he stormed out like someone chased him. He was going to show me? I rubbed my face. Artemis needed to be fixed. Maybe it was better if I wasn't around people.

I had taken the second panel of the day off Artemis when Judge arrived. He looked pale, and I stopped what I was doing. I'd given him a horrible time the night before when he'd been trying to be nice. "Are you okay?"

"I ... Shit. We had a little talk this morning, the guys. The doctors thought we knew exactly how the US worked, but we didn't. It's startling. Going to take a little getting used to, and I'm not sure I can ever get in it again." He walked toward the ship. "I see you've been making progress without me."

He was pale because of the US machine? "What is it doing to you?"

"Temporary chemical castration every month." He cleared his throat. "The, ah, machine gives us some stimulating dreams and at the same time makes us not able to ... function properly. I guess no one thought it would be a problem. We were never going to have the chance with any girls. Better to get the once-a-month fun followed by the surety we'd never act up—being alone in space forever—never get so sexually frustrated we made bad decisions."

"Judge." This was hard. "I need to get in the machine."

He dropped his wrench. "What?"

"I want all five of you. Okay. I know it's weird for you. I come from a place where it's still normal. It can't work. I get it. So, the machine can make me not feel that way anymore. I've only been here days. You're all fighting, and I'm messing up everything." I handed him my hammer. "I'll go get in it now."

Judge blinked rapidly. "Hold on."

I didn't listen to him. I'd said the single most humiliating statement of my life. When I got out of the machine, I'd be in controlled. I wouldn't make Sterling feel like things were wrong with him. I wouldn't be flirting with guys who could physically not help me.

He grabbed the side of my arm. "Before you do that, I think we should have a meeting. All of us. Talk some things through."

"So I can humiliate myself with all of them instead of only you?"

"So they can tell you about the screaming fight we all had this morning—including Lewis, who never yells—about how we're all falling for you really fast, really hard, and not one of us wants back in that machine. Maybe we can work something out here."

His words stunned me. It took me a second to process them. The whole time I'd showered, drank coffee, and worked on Artemis they'd been fighting over me? They wanted me like I did them? What did any of this mean?

Still, I let him take my hand and lead me to the dining room table. It wasn't meal time; everyone seemed to have had breakfast on their own, and yet within minutes of Judge leaving me in there, they'd all taken their seats from the night before.

I rubbed the back of my neck. How did my mom manage this? How did she tell six men what she wanted all the time? How did she get out of her own head and do what she did? Why didn't I have any of those genes?

Judge sat last, directly next to me. "I asked you all to come here so we could talk."

Cash closed his eyes. "Tell me you didn't do what I think you did and actually share with her what we discussed this morning?"

Sterling groaned, and Lewis found something interesting on the floor. Cash stared down Judge, which left Damian regarding me with his calculating gaze.

Judge shook his head. "Only after she told me she wanted all of us, didn't think it could ever work, and was going to get in the machine herself."

All heads turned toward me. I think I might have been as red as a tomato. Was it possible to die from embarrassment?

Chapter Eight

Cruising

I cleared my throat. "Okay, let me explain. I realize this is really, really weird. Where I'm from, one woman with many men is still an okay thing to do. It's almost more normal. Has to do with my grandfather on Earth. Long story. Anyway, I am having feelings for all of you. I don't expect any of you to do anything about that."

Lewis looked up from the ground. "Why?"

"I have a number of reasons. Shall I list them? Okay. I'm going to." If I spoke fast, I could get through this quickly. "Number one, people aren't in relationships like the one I would need. I never thought I wanted any marriage. How was I going to get through having to talk at night? I thought, maybe, *one person* I could manage because I'd only have to handle that much conversation. I seem to have less trouble speaking with the five of you. I'm off track." I forced myself to breathe. "Anyway, it doesn't matter. It's not the thing to do here. Not allowed. So it's almost not important to list the rest."

Lewis raised a hand. "Sorry, but I have to interject. While it's true Evander doesn't allow for plural marriages, there are other corporations that do."

Damian jolted. "There are?"

"Yes. Seems that fact is hidden pretty well. I started researching it when she got here. Just ... well, I did. Carrey and Winsely both allow for it. If that's what people want."

"Well, we can't simply change allegiances to them. We have proprietary interests. They'll have us killed."

Lewis shook his head. "I'm not suggesting we do."

"Truth is"—Judge spoke slowly—"we're at the edge of space. No one has to know anything about what we do out here."

He'd given me a great opportunity to make my next point. "That's the problem. We aren't going to be hidden here forever. Damian has told them about me. We can't hide. They'll come and get me. Then what'll happen to me? I have to be self-preserving here." I didn't look at them. My hands were suddenly very interesting. "I have to go before your corporation comes for me. Don't hate me. I can't be hauled off to who knows where. I have to get Artemis fixed and go before that happens. I can't have the five of you in my life and then disappear. Why would you want that either? Sounds like a special kind of pain."

"Well," Damian was the first person to answer. "Diana, look at me please." I raised my eyes. He licked his bottom lip. "I didn't send the report. I never did. I almost did twice when you first got here. Then I deleted the whole thing after I spent the night. I felt ... I couldn't share you with them. You're none of their business. So if you think you have to run, to leave us, because I let them know, then let that go. You're safe here. You're hidden."

The others didn't look surprised. Had he told them? Or did they simply know Damian so well they'd understood what would happen? My shoulders slumped. Fear was a powerful burden to carry around all the time. It weighed on me even when I wasn't aware of it.

"Diana." Damian's voice was soft. "I'm sorry. I should have told you."

"Thank you for telling me now." I nodded. There weren't words for this, not language sufficient. "Thank you for not turning me in. There's still another reason. Similar to that one."

Cash answered me. "Go on."

"My family is going to come, and they're going to take me away. I have to go with them. I belong over there. That's my home." I'd only been here such a short period of time. I couldn't replace my entire existence there and turn my attention to being here for the rest of my life. They were coming for me. That's what we did for one another. I would go home. I would leave them.

Judge shook his head. "I don't think you should let that stop you from being with us."

"You think they're not coming. You think they're years and years away trapped in that black hole. Or fifty years passed over there already or here to their now. That the time differential means everything is screwed up. I should be an old woman here. I'm not. I get it. I ..."

Lewis jumped to his feet and walked over to me, placing his hand on mine. He knelt down next to me. "Don't get upset. Okay? Who knows what's going to happen with the black hole? I'm sure your family is doing all they can to get to you. Of course they are. Listen, and just consider this, okay?"

He was such a calming presence. I didn't know him well yet, although I admired him immensely. Lewis looked at the ground for a second in a way I'd seen him do so many times. He collected his thoughts that way. I don't know how I knew it so well already. I just did.

When he was ready, he met my eyes again. "The five of us are so taken with you. We've all been using that US machine since we were nineteen. Before that age, corporation gives you a chance to ... experience things if you can. Personally, I never got that chance. I was found when I was two on the streets of Ochoa. I'm not the kind of guy the women of this world are going to spend time with, at least not unless they get paid to do so. I didn't have any money. The US was it for me. I'm not talking about sex. At least, not only sex."

Sterling rose. "I think what Lewis is trying to say is we could, in the time you're with us, have something with you—if you're willing—that like Lewis, I've never had either. A chance to know you. To woo you. To make you ours. And if you go, then it'll be heartbreaking, yes. Hopefully, for you, too. It's something we haven't had before and never would have anyway."

His words banged around in my head. I had to think—to remember—what it was like to have multiple men with one woman. My mother managed them like she'd been born to do so. Could I? Even though they all seemed to be agreeing with this—for the moment—that didn't mean we were all going to be okay.

"We have to live here. In this pod. Until my ship is fixed, at least. If this falls apart, it will destroy everything."

Cash's voice was low, but I heard it. "You can't let the fear of a terrible thing stop you from embracing the possibility of greatness. This could be the best thing ever. I would trust these guys with my life. I'll trust them to do this with you."

I wanted what he said, I craved the ability to believe it too. Yet there were things I knew that they didn't.

I sat up straight. I didn't inherit anything from my mother, not really. She was strong, tough, passionate. She knew how to lead and how to tell someone to fuck off. I was much more my father's side of the family. Quiet. Behind the scenes. My father said I looked just as his mother had. I'd never seen her, not even in photos since there weren't any. I did resemble him, strongly.

Since there was no other choice, I was going to have to do my best to fake it. I'd be her daughter. I still had to be me, but I'd somehow pull off acting her like her when I had to.

"If you're serious about this, then there are conditions. Otherwise I get in the machine, and we'll all put this to rest." I steepled my fingers. This was hard. I didn't like telling people what to do. If I didn't, they'd all break apart. I was going to leave them. They couldn't be destroyed when I did.

Judge blinked. "Conditions?"

"That's right. I know how these things work. This was how I was raised. I've seen where it works, and I've seen how it doesn't. My family worked beautifully." At least as far as marriage went. "As far as I can tell, the way that multiple men can share one woman and not ultimately destroy each other with aggression and anger is: I'm in charge. I'll try to do what you want. Be there for all of you. Ultimately, I say yes; I say no. Or I walk away, and I'm done with it. Might seem cruel. I know that. What would be worse for me, for all of you, would be to end the years of friendship that the five of you share. You can't fight over me. That's my first rule. The most important one. Do this, and you'll survive this, whether it works or it doesn't. Second rule. Damian, you want to know why Cooper Jackson travelled across the universe, leaving his royal family and everything he knew? Because my mom wanted to. He doesn't take orders from anyone. Except her."

I wanted to throw up. I waited for a response. I'd clearly stunned them into silence. "Why don't you all think about it?" And since I still had to be me even though I was pretending ot be mother, I had to add more. I wasn't good at pretending. "I don't like giving rules. I'm not good at it. I hate it, in fact. I'll go. Back to my ship. I'll wait."

"Hold on." Damian rubbed his eyes. "Please."

I let out the breath I'd sucked in. "Okay."

"I ... I understand what you're saying and maybe even what you're not. I am personally willing to try. Some of these other guys take time to process. That's fine. We're not in a rush. The medicine the US has been giving us is, according to Cash, going to take a long time to run its course. He doesn't know exactly how long because no one quits taking it."

Cash interrupted, "It will go away. The chemistry indicates it. It's the timing I'm unsure of. Or exactly what the withdrawal will be like."

Damian finished. "Right. We'll feel the initial signals of it going away long before it's actually gone. I think that might be a good thing. We can get to know each other, without the sex, and see how this goes. If we like it. Without the physical getting in the way of the whole thing."

"Let me know when you all decide. I'll be on my ship."

Judge lifted a hand. "My turn to hold you off."

I took a deep breath. "Sure."

"I think right off the bat we need to, or you need to, make a sleep schedule. Sterling and Damian have both gotten to sleep with you. I want a turn. I imagine Lewis and Cash do, too. Can we do that? Even before sex?"

I actually liked the company in bed. "I'm fine with you making the schedule. I guess it could be the first test to see if you can manage not to fight."

I was making this up as I went along. Damian stared at Judge. "Would you like to go tonight? Have your turn? Unless you need to think on this."

Judge put his hands out in front of him. "I'm a yes."

"I think you need to all be agreed before we sign onto this. I don't want to presume I ..."

Sterling interrupted. They were hardly letting each other get a word in edgewise. "I'm a yes. Cash?"

"Yes." He looked at Lewis. "Well?"

"I'm a yes."

And just like that, plans were made.

I hoped I could be the woman I had to be to make this work. Otherwise we were royally screwed.

Judge walked me back to Artemis, a bundle of nervous energy. "I guess we're not getting a lot of work done today. Do you want to do something fun?"

"Is that allowed?"

"Oh, yeah. I mean, Damian might fuss if we did it too many days in a row. If something is going to break, I'll fix it. Until then, want to play?"

I grinned at him. My nerves had been frayed, yet he seemed so ... happy. "Sure. What did you have in mind?"

"Come on." He pulled me toward the Zombie holding facility. I spent as little time as possible in any room with the Zombies. They creeped me out.

I shivered. How long would I have to stay here before I got over it? When would they become commonplace? I swear one of them looked at me full on and *saw*. He roared at the ceiling, all animal-sounding. Was there any human left in him?

Judge fiddled with something in the corner. I wasn't sure what he was doing, but I hoped we weren't going to be playing in this room. All day. I shuddered.

When had I become such a coward?

"Judge." I turned to him, but he didn't answer. I tried again. "Judge."

Sterling stood in the doorway, one gun slung over his back. "Don't mind him, darling. He'll be lost till he gets this together. I know what he's going to show you. I think you might be the only person in any universe who will love it as much as he does."

He sauntered toward me and stuck out his hand. I let him link our fingers together. Touching them all, all the time, was going to be part of this now. I had to get used to it. Truth was, I started to like it.

"Sterling, I need you to promise me if something were to happen and I were to ever get bit or scratched or whatever by one of those things, you won't let me become one. If I can't be saved, don't let me become Infected. I hate to ask it, but put me down. Okay?"

Sterling was still as he spoke, and I noticed the lack of movement in the corner, too. Judge must have tuned in. He took slow steps toward us.

It was Sterling who answered. "Nothing is ever going to happen to you. I won't allow it. You're safe. Judge made these containers so safe for all of us. We have security measure after security measure in place. The Zombies aren't getting anywhere near you."

"I can show you the schematics. Maybe that'll make you more comfortable. It would take an incredible amount to go wrong all at once. I'd stop it before that happened," Judge added. He had a robot in his hand. A medium-sized toy robot and a remote.

Judge had momentarily distracted me with the toy. I found my words again. "All of that being said, promise me, okay? You won't let me be a Zombie."

Sterling nodded. "I promise."

"Me too." Judge nodded. "I'm sure the others will promise too. We'll tell them. Truth be told, I wouldn't let any of them become Infected. You're safe with us." He held up the robot. "Still want to check him out?"

"Does it involve the Zombies?"

He shook his head. Judge reminded me of my brothers or the kids on the station when they got a new toy they wanted to show off. "I built it to assist with the Zombies, but he does all kinds of things. I never get to show off the other things."

Sterling patted my cheek before continuing on his rounds. I'd have to ask him what he looked for and why, if we were so perfectly safe, did he and Damian carry three guns between them. I never accidently ran into Damian during the day. Where did he go?

Judge ended up bringing me to his bedroom. It was a ten-by-ten room that fit a bed, a dresser, and a small bookshelf that also seemed to double as a desk. He'd taped pieces of papers with equations all over his walls. He sat down on the floor and patted the spot next to him, which I took.

"Diana, this is Cruiser. Cruiser, say, 'Hi' to Diana."

As far as robots went, Cruiser was funny looking. The design made me smile, and from what I knew of Judge, I could see his handwork all over it. The robot had a mouth that was currently turned upwards in a smile, although I wouldn't be at all surprised if it had the ability to frown. He was multi-colored. Blue, red, green, yellow. If I stood, he'd come up to my waist, so right now I had to look up at him. His hands currently resembled human ones, yet the slider device on its wrist told me they could shift into other things if the user so wanted. I suspected that was what the remote was for since Judge talked to him instead of pressing buttons right now.

"Hello, Diana." Cruiser said to me. He had a pleasant voice, soothing, like a warm bath.

"Hi, Cruiser. How are you?" I didn't usually ask machines how they were doing. Although I thought of Artemis as alive plenty of times. What would Cruiser say? How far had Judge designed his programming?

"Better now that I have a pretty lady to play with me." The robot lifted his eyebrows.

I gasped and elbowed Judge. "Did you tell him to say that?"

"When would I have told him to?" His eyes sparkled with mischief.

"When you were fooling with him in the viewing area by the Infected."

Judge sighed dramatically. "What can I say? He has good taste. You told me I couldn't tell you that you were beautiful. You didn't say anything about Cruiser."

"You're sneaky. You know that?" I looked down at the floor. "It was never a factor in my life. I'm not sure how to ..." I didn't have the words. Process? Incorporate? Take it in? Make it mine? I didn't know. So I stopped.

Judge didn't push. I expected him to complain. He didn't. Instead he turned to Cruiser. "Cruiser, we're not going to do Infected work today. Diana, Cruiser does a lot of the interacting with the Infected. He sometimes sedates them for the doctors so they don't have to go near them while they are worked up. It's important work. What he was designed for. Or, at least, that's what I told Evander so they'd fund him. I couldn't very well suggest Cruiser needed to be made so he could juggle."

Saying the word, a compartment opened in Cruiser's stomach, and he pulled out some balls. Seconds later, he juggled them.

I giggled. It was one of the funniest things I'd seen. A sophisticated robot, designed to work in hazardous conditions, was juggling balls on the floor of Judge's room.

"Or do cartwheels."

As I watched trick after trick, I laughed more and more. Judge's smile grew wider while he showed off his robot. He scooted closer to me, and eventually I put my head on his shoulder. This was fun. He'd called it playing, and he was right. Cruiser was more than a functional tool in the fight to save the Zombies; he was a toy.

Judge didn't know the full extent of what Cruiser could do. He'd programmed him with circus tricks and games, yet he'd never had the time to check them all out. Sterling liked to watch him too, and the others were impressed, but he wasn't their cup of tea. We started testing him. I got him to hop on one foot and meow like a cat. He'd have been a great asset to have when I'd taken care of my siblings. We could have made hours pass this way when we had to be confined to our rooms for safety. Judge entwined our fingers. We'd missed lunch. I didn't care. I couldn't remember the last time I'd ever been so relaxed. Happiness trumped hungry for me. I'd eat dinner.

We were quiet. Judge shut Cruiser down for recharge. His power cells were big enough that he could last for days, but in the event of an emergency, it wouldn't do to have him at half power because we'd played too long and hard with him.

"Do you like comics?" He turned to me, an eyebrow raised.

"I don't know." We didn't have them where I was from. I knew what they were; sometimes C.J. lamented that he'd lost his from the time he was a boy, yet I'd never gazed on any myself.

Judge jumped up and grabbed a tablet. He sat back down and picked my hand up again, placing it where it had been on my thigh, and held my fingers with his own again. With his other hand, he pressed a button to turn on his tablet.

His fingers moved fast over the device. We had similar ones where I came from, personal storage centers where we kept books we were reading, messages sent to us, appointments. If we had bills due, they popped up there. In school, our tests were administered on the devices. My brother Colin had lost his twice already. That hadn't gone over well. I pushed thoughts of them aside. Thinking about my family wasn't making me happy, and today, with Judge, I was determined not to be dour.

Judge scanned through his device. "What kind of heroes do you like? Flying ones? Fast ones? Big ones? Scary anti-heroes?"

I shrugged. "Show me your favorite."

His eyes brightened. It was so easy to make Judge happy, and all I was doing was learning about him. Something I really wanted to do. He pulled up a comic of man who wore all black. Whoever drew him had made him seem ominous. They called him the Sewer Man. He lived on Ochoa. Judge continued to show me picture after picture. He knew everything about the fictional character—who wrote him, who drew him, when the artist had changed. I watched his mouth move, not hearing every word he said. I cared much more about Judge's telling of the story than anything to do with the comic itself.

"When Evander sends in reports—we get them about every six weeks, and Damian sends a carrier back—I get new ones delivered to the tablet. They like to keep us happy, keep us out here."

I had never been brave when it came to touching, and yet still I felt perfectly comfortable in his quiet room doing so. I ran my hands down the back of his hair. Judge kept his short, the dark strands off his face. His eyes widened when I first touched him, but then he settled into it, leaning back a bit so I'd have an easier time. He closed his eyes and sighed.

"And are you?" I asked it as a whisper. The moment felt special, like it should be heard by only us and not any other ears anywhere in the universe. Or maybe I had suddenly become sentimental.

He opened his dark lids. "Am I?"

"Happy?"

He cupped my cheek. "I was never unhappy. I'm a guy who can make myself okay just about anywhere you drop me. I'm twenty-three years old." A year older than me. I hadn't known exactly. "I've been without family since I was five."

I gasped, and he shook his head. "Don't be sad for me. People have it much worse."

"How did they die?"

He was quiet for a second. "They're not exactly dead. Somewhere in Evander they're kept locked away. They got Infected. They were in the wrong place at the wrong time. I was lucky. My father worked for Evander. He was pretty high up. So the corporation took me, evaluated me, and I found out early I had certain gifts when it came to tech and engineering. Someday, when Cash and Lewis solve their puzzle, there might be hope for my parents. To answer your question, I learned long ago to make myself happy wherever I landed. The corporation decided to send their two most brilliant minds to solve a problem, to stick them where no one could steal their work, where there were plenty of Infected to study. Cash doesn't work well with everyone. Large labs make him nuts. The psychologist determined this was the best place. I had to go. Keep everything working. Help where I can. I'm happy."

I didn't stop touching him. I got what he said. Happiness was found where it was found, and sometimes I had to make my own if there was none to find elsewhere. Sometimes, the right song playing on a speaker could change the day from bad to good. Judge knew how to make it work, how to stay upbeat and be happy.

"I'm glad."

He scooted slightly closer to me. "But I'm happier now."

"I think you're all crazy to want this with me, Judge." I spoke the words plaguing me. "You're all amazing guys. Brilliant and capable. Gorgeous to look at." He blushed, and I wasn't upset to give him a taste of his own medicine. Not always nice to be complimented. "I'm really an ordinary girl who got really unlucky and fell through a black hole."

He touched his forehead to mine. "I knew when Damian carried you in through the air lock that you are mine. I love these guys. I'll share you with them and be glad to. If they didn't want you like they did, that would be fine, too. He set you down on Lewis' table, and I knew—you are mine. Just like that." He snapped his fingers. "The universe changed."

Chapter Nine

Judge Tomlinson

His words moved through me like a sigh. I shivered from them. My whole body was aware of him. He thought the universe had changed when he saw me. I stroked my hand down the side of his face. "That's the most beautiful thing ... ever. I have a hard time believing it, hard time not wanting to say to you that if I were a girl in a crowd, and you had your choice—as you should have—you wouldn't look twice..."

Judge interrupted. "Di ..."

I placed my hands on his lips. "Don't. I'm explaining, not disagreeing. I'll tell you something. Where I'm from, I'm valued for how I can help us politically. No one has asked me to say yes to the three brothers who want me. I know doing so would make things better for a lot of people. I haven't ever wanted anyone, not really. I look away. I don't think about men. If I met you there, if *you* were somehow on my station, I'd have noticed you. Dreamed about you. You move me, Judge."

His mouth met mine gently. I expected Judge to push. He didn't. Light kisses over and over. I wanted more, but I didn't press. The drugs were still affecting him. He wasn't going to get worked up like I could, and maybe not getting too heated was actually nicer to me. I'd have no relief unless I gave it to myself.

Judge tugged me on top of him until I straddled his lap. He wasn't hard. I hadn't expected him to be. He wanted me closer, and I was glad to be.

Eventually, I had enough. If we couldn't do anything else, frustration was going to become my constant companion. I pulled back. I wasn't sure what emotions I saw in his eyes. "What are you thinking?"

"I'm so happy I can kiss you. For now, it has to do." He scooped me up and carried me over to the bed with him. "Dinner's in an hour. What would you like to do until then?"

"What other things would you like to show me? We're having a fun day, right? Show me."

He pulled me to his side before he grabbed his tablet off the floor. "We have a whole lot of stuff we can look at." Judge handed me the tablet. "Find anything on it."

"Really? You're letting me go through your tablet?" To do so, where I came from, constituted a really big deal. It was inviting someone into your absolute personal space.

He kissed my temple. "I feel like I've been through yours. I watched all the videos of you, listened to the logs, checked out things on Artemis while you were unconscious and they were desperately trying to save your life. I had to be busy. They wouldn't let me stand over you. You can go through mine."

I almost argued some more and then decided to take the offering as the gift it was. I flipped through, clicking on more comics. There were three folders to choose from. One said *Hero*, one said *Anti-Hero*, and the last one said *M*. I clicked on *M*. What comics were in *M*? The comic inside was called *Mercedes*.

Judge sucked in his breath. "Oh, you found that right off." He rubbed his eyes. "All right."

"What is it? Would you rather I not look?"

He shook his head. "It's a pet project of mine."

I stared at the screen. "Are you making this comic yourself?"

"The nights can be long here." He groaned. "It's terrible."

Except it really wasn't. I flipped through the pages he'd drawn. He must have done it with his art app, drawing with a stylus or his hands. The main character, Mercedes, was a woman lost. She only had one arm. She wandered streets looking for the man who'd killed her lover. She wanted revenge. The skyline was elaborately drawn—bleak, broken. In the fifth frame she looked straight at the audience. She had blond hair, green eyes, and the saddest eyes I'd ever seen on the page.

"She's beautiful. Why is she sad?"

He leaned up on his hand. "I don't think she's beautiful."

"But she is." I ran my finger over the screen. "Striking. Unforgettable. You made her. This is ... I mean, I guess I shouldn't be surprised. You made Cruiser. You fix ships. You run this place. You're ... astounding. When you start writing more of this, can I read it?"

His face was totally serious when he nodded. "Absolutely. Tell me about you. I want ... all of it. What's your favorite color?"

I almost made one up simply to answer the question. "I never saw the point of having a favorite color. I'm not ..." What was the word? I didn't know.

"All right." He sat up. "Do you not have favorite things then? At all?"

I chewed on my lip. "At home, I had a favorite wrench. A favorite pair of shoes. A favorite blanket. Practical things, I guess."

"Favorite memory?"

That was a good question. A picture of Asher laughing as a baby while I twirled him in the air flashed through my mind. His baby face. His chubby cheeks. His little smile. The way he giggled and smelled. I loved babies.

I shook my head, clearing it. "When my brother was born, I was twelve. They had seven kids. Boom, boom, boom after Asher. But he was the first. I loved him. He used to stay with me a lot. After his birth, before Colin's, they found paid help. They didn't have any when they had Asher. I loved him. So much. And there was this one time when we were alone. He crawled around the floor picking up little toy shuttles. He'd hold them up, and I'd say, 'Shuttle,' and he'd laugh. We did that for hours. I think that's my favorite memory."

"I never had any siblings. That must be amazing."

If I had my tablet, I could show him their pictures. "I have some photos on Artemis' computer. Do you want to see them tonight? Assuming you still want to stay."

"I do." He brought my hand to his mouth and kissed it. "I really, really want the chemicals out of my body, Di. I want to kiss you and feel it everywhere, not just in my mind."

"What's it like in your mind?"

"Like heat that has nowhere to go." He scooted around me off the bed. "Come on. Let's put Cruiser back where he belongs, and then we can go see what Damian is cooking tonight."

He'd lain around too much. I could see it in the way he jumped from foot to foot. Judge had a lot of energy, and he'd been calm today. I wondered what a lack of activity did to him. I had to make sure to remember that about Judge. If this arrangement we'd all agreed to was going to work, I needed to keep their individual needs in line. I couldn't keep Judge cooped up all day doing nothing.

I took his hand and kept up with him as we practically jogged to the viewing room together. Sterling wasn't present— probably on his rounds somewhere else. Judge placed Cruiser back in his casing in the room.

The Zombies were pacing the room. They seemed more agitated than usual, pacing the room, moaning. "What's going on with them?"

"I call this time of day their witching hour. They get really upset. I don't know why. We're down to a low number of them. Cash will want us to go get more soon. Don't worry. It's safe."

I approached the glass and put my hands on it. "I'm not scared." Maybe if I said it, I'd mean it. "I saw you do it one day while I was hiding on Artemis."

"Oh yeah?" He leaned next to me. "What else did you see?"

"Lewis at the garbage every morning."

His eyes sparkled. "Exciting viewing."

"For me it was." I'd never imagined I'd be here now ... trying to figure out if I could ever be the woman I needed to be to make this work.

Dinner was fun, easy going. Damian had put together a stew with carrots and onions. The meat was so tender it practically fell off the fork. I'd never tasted anything like it and told him so. I sat next to Judge—it was his night with me. Lewis sat next to Cash, across from me. Tonight, Sterling and Damian took the ends of the table.

"Did you have a good day off?" Damian smirked at Judge and me. I shifted uncomfortably. I'd wondered if Damian was going to have a problem with our fooling around the way we had.

"Yep," Judge grinned. "Great day."

Damian nodded. "I think, considering this is our first week in our new arrangement, we're all going to take a day. Our first official day with her, we'll each take it off. Follow Judge's leadership on this."

Applause sounded through the room. Had they simply not had a lot of days off before?

I looked to each of them but didn't find an answer. Judge's foot played with mine under the table. This was as much, I decided, a result of his need to move as his wanting to touch me. How had he gotten through school?

A loud boom sounded, the lightning making itself known in an otherwise quiet night. They barely reacted, yet I jumped in my seat. "Sorry." I rubbed my neck. "Still getting used to it."

"You don't have weather on space stations," Cash said as an answer.

"No, but we had it when I was little on this side of the galaxy and the year we spent on Earth."

Lewis sat forward in his seat. "Why did you leave Earth?"

"My grandfather runs Earth, unofficially. There's a government, but they all answer to him. That pissed off my dad, my uncles, and my mom. They hadn't left one kind of hell to land in another. On Mars Station, it's not perfect. There's wheeling and dealing to be sure, but my mom could lose an election. It's not rigged. Nothing is ever perfect, but it was certainly better."

Damian had the next question. "Where would you go if your mom lost?"

"C.J. always said, somewhere far away, on the outskirts. There are planets being hydrated and terraformed all the time. They'd go there, get some land, use their skills, and live quietly. I personally don't know what I'd do there. I don't know a lot of people, but I like watching them. Having no one around for endless distances would be ... sad. Even here, I watched you guys in the morning. It was something. I can't go back to the way it was in the black hole. Not again."

Lewis nodded, turning his head to see me better. "You won't ever have to."

"Speaking of which, Sterling told us you are worried about being Infected. I won't let you be Infected. I'd cut out my right eye first," Damian pronounced.

Cash sucked in his breath. "Charming image over dinner, my friend. Diana, there's always the chance something can happen. I suspect you know this better than anyone. You got sucked into a black hole and thrown through time. If you were to be bitten, scratched, or scraped by the Infected, there is, initially, a way to stop the spread." He nodded toward Lewis. "Lewis over there invented it."

I touched Lewis' arm. "You did? That's amazing."

He shrugged. "Ten years ago. It's a little of, 'What have you done since?'"

"That would be enough for someone's lifetime."

Lewis rubbed his eyes. "Not mine."

Cash finally finished, "The point being, while I would never let you become Infected, were you to be bitten, we could stop Infection from happening within the first couple of minutes. So don't worry."

Lewis pointed at Cash. "What he said."

I should feel better. All five of them of them had assured me now that they wouldn't let anything happen to me. I was going to do my best to make sure I didn't encounter a Zombie. Still, a nagging worry plagued at me. I pushed it away, and the rest of dinner was filled with laughter. I stayed quiet, listening to them and feeling like I really started to gel with them. Even Sterling, who was naturally the quietest of the bunch, cut some jokes. I couldn't remember the last time I'd felt so relaxed.

We cleaned up together, and I hummed to myself while I wiped up the plates. Judge elbowed me. "One day with me and you're humming to yourself."

I shook my head, grinning. "I had fun today."

"Me, too." He nodded toward the game room. "Watch a movie tonight?"

"I love movies."

He patted the back of my head. "I'm going to go pick one out."

"Okay." He'd been in one place for too long. I shook my head. The guy needed to move. Was he going to be able to sit through the movie?

Cash hopped up on the counter. "I get you tomorrow. We drew straws, Lewis and I. I won. So I get to go first. He's the day after. Then you're back to Damian and then Sterling. We'll do that order from now on."

I smiled at him. "Sounds great."

He nodded. "Tell Judge I'm picking you up at eight."

That was early. We didn't start working until nine usually. I had no idea what Cash wanted to do first thing in the morning.

Cash raised his eyebrows. "Unless that's too early for you, Boo?"

I wondered if he knew he'd used a term of affection. He hadn't done so before. I liked it. *Boo*. It was sort of ... sweet. He'd also issued me a challenge I meant to meet. "I'm up for whatever, Champ."

I wasn't sure where I pulled out the nickname. He grinned from ear-to-ear, both from my agreement to be ready really early for our day and also from the term of endearment.

"Cool." Cash jumped off the counter. "I hope you like anime. I can guarantee we're watching one tonight. Judge loves them."

"I like all movies. I don't get to see too many of them. Any kind is a treat."

I put up my last dish and joined them in the game room.

Unlike the last time I'd hung out with them, I wasn't too tired to think. I could probably learn a card game if they wanted to teach me. However, a movie sounded like a great idea. They were setting up the couches in front of a big screen when I came in. Judge sat on the left side of one and extended his hand. "Di."

I took his offering and tucked in next to him. If I understood the scheduling of this, it was still his night. Cash took over in the morning. We could all hang out together although I should show them individual attention. I wished there was a handbook for this. We were such a family growing up I'd never really noticed what my mom did during her days with my father and uncles. They rotated at nights. Had she made the days special? The kids had changed things anyway. Babies needed attention, and whoever was with my mom had baby duty too. When Nolan's kids had been born, he'd been around a lot more at night than his usual turn on the schedule. That was how it worked.

I think the only one of them that got shafted on that regard was my father. He'd never had me as a baby. Nothing about my life had worked the way it should have.

Sterling sat on my other side, his foot touching mine. Cash plopped down on his other side. Lewis and Damian took the other couch. Soon the movie started, and I stopped caring about who sat where or how I behaved. Cash had been right. Judge picked an anime. That didn't, however, do the movie justice. The presentation was so extraordinary the images were practically real. The story was interesting, too. It was a love story and a trope I was familiar with. Girl from the right side of the world, boy from the wrong. But he rose up to be such an important man, he eventually earned the right to court her.

I didn't see the end coming. She died, mauled down on the streets trying to get to him to save his life. I gasped, tears coming from my eyes. Her lover eventually became king of the universe, better for having known her.

"Aww, Di." Judge pulled me even closer against him. "I'm sorry. I didn't know she died. I thought it was lightweight. They send us thousands of movies. I liked this director before."

I laughed, wiping at my eyes. "Sorry. Guess I got caught up."

I sat up while the lights in the room came back on. Five sets of eyes stared at me with various emotions quickly passing over their faces. It was too much. I couldn't deal with being stared at or even figure out, particularly, why they'd have such strong reactions to my being ridiculous over a movie.

"Sorry. Hope I didn't spoil the movie for everyone." Various *no*'s and denials sounded while I stood. "I should go to bed. I'm clearly all kinds of sappy."

Judge hopped to his feet. "Night everyone."

"Eight a.m.," Cash called over us. "If you're not up, Judge, I'm waking your ass."

We held hands as we walked. He'd been quiet and still while the movie was on and clearly needed to make up for the stillness now. I had a thought and almost dismissed it. But playfulness wasn't a side to my personality which came out often. I decided to embrace the urge.

I dropped his hand. "Race you." I took off running.

There was no way Judge wasn't going to beat me to Artemis. He was over six feet tall, and in my bare feet I was five feet exactly. Still, to hear him hoot with laughter behind me was worth the run. I'd made maybe one hundred yards before he scooped me up in his arms and flung me over his shoulder.

I squirmed until I managed to get onto his back, piggyback style, and I wrapped my arms around his neck. When I steadied, he took off running, me squealing the whole way. When we got to Artemis, he slowed then set me down. A second later, he pushed me against the ship, kissing me hard on the mouth, once.

He backed up to stare at me. "Caught you. I'll always catch you. You run, I follow. I'm never going to lose you, Di."

"Thank you for that promise." Why did I feel so free tonight? I wasn't going to overanalyze it when it would likely be gone soon. We walked together into the ship. Judge checked out some of Artemis' computers while I undressed in the bathroom. I needed to do laundry soon. My clothes were all so huge on me. I needed to get the one-sized outfit cleaned up so I could wear it again. When I came out, it was to find Judge in boxer shorts staring at my bedroom computer screen. I'd set it up so pictures of my family rotated through at night. I liked to see them before I went to bed, and when I turned off the light in the room, the wattage was low enough it didn't bother me.

I stopped short. Both Damian and Sterling had slept with their clothes on. This was a change. Not that I was complaining. Judge was gorgeous. I'd had no idea he had so many muscles hidden beneath his clothes. He was thin and lean yet at the same time one giant muscle. Also, somewhat shocking, was the giant spider tattooed on his back. I rocked back on my feet. If he could perform, I'd be more than willing. Still, it was probably best they were all incapable. We were getting to know each other before there was any sex because we had no other choice. If this blew up in our faces, there'd be no hurt from getting too close too soon. I supposed. Bitterly.

I shook my head. That was my constant state of lust thinking and not my better self.

He turned to grin at me. "Can we go over them sometime? I want to know your family."

"Sure." I pointed at his back. "That's an incredible piece of ink. A spider. Red, black, intense."

I wouldn't have pictured Judge with a tattoo. Damian and Sterling maybe. Judge surprised me.

"I hate spiders. They terrify me. Creepy things. I had that put there to remind me what scares us can remain behind us and not have to dictate our lives."

I walked toward the bed, expecting him to follow; when he didn't, I looked him square in the eyes. What I found there stopped me short. He was afraid. Right now. "What are you worried about? I can't imagine it would be sleeping with me. I don't think I take up the whole bed."

A bad joke, but I didn't know what else to say.

"I have to tell you something. I thought I didn't. Then Damian asked me if I had. Reminded me lying is not a good way to start things. I liked how you looked at me, how you seemed to think of me. I didn't want you to know I'd been in jail."

Jail? What had he done? Where I was from, prison was for murderers and people who had done things that could not be forgiven. I wasn't certain how the penal system worked here.

I crossed my hands over my chest. "What did you do?"

He took a deep breath.

Chapter Ten

The Spider on His Back

"When I was young, Evander would ask me to make something, and I'd make it. I never thought about the consequences of anything I did. They asked, I made. It was like a challenge. I could do things people twice my age couldn't manage. And fast."

I sat down on the bed. He stood in front of me in his black boxer shorts with his spider tattoo, looking at me as though he expected me to boot him from the room any second.

He ran his hands through his hair or rocked on his feet. Constant movement to go with what he had to tell me.

"What kinds of things were they asking you for?"

He took a second to answer. "Weapons. Bombs, mostly. I also made body armor. No one cared if I could build a holding facility for the Infected or transport ships that could get the sick to a hospital sooner."

"My father makes bombs. He was the best bomb maker the Nomads ever had." And I hated the bombs. I was always terrified one of them was about to go off. "He doesn't make them for anything but defense anymore."

Judge put his hands on his hips. "For real?"

"Yep."

He waited like he expected me to go on about something. Should I say something more? When I didn't, he continued. "Then one day, when I was about eighteen, I heard these two soldiers talking. They seemed pretty beat up. Covered in blood. Gook. Oil. I came out of the underground facility where we designed products. I needed some sunlight, and I wanted to read my comic. They were talking. One of them asked why they were getting sent out on so many missions. And the second one, he said it was because they had to try out the products the genius in the basement was making. The company needed to see if they worked. The soldiers employed by Evander were test dummies for Evander to sell the weaponry to militias. Their bodies, their lives were being destroyed."

His eyes were distant. "I found the nearest garbage can, and I threw up. How could I have been so stupid?" His voice cracked. "To me it had all been hypothetical. A challenge. Could I do it? I never stopped to ask, *should* I do it. I walked up to the soldiers. I asked them, how were they? Were the products holding up? Who were they fighting?"

I took his hand, but it stayed limp in mine. He talked, but he wasn't in the room with me, not mentally. "They told me. The last mission, my bombs had been great. They'd blown up another corporation's headquarters. They'd only lost five men. And they didn't know how many on the other side. The guy who told me, he looked kind of sick about it. Then he let me know that the mission before had not gone as well. They'd been nearly decimated by one of my air bombs. It detonated too quickly. I'd wondered about that one, if the timer was off. I'd told Evander. They took the product from me anyway. I could never understand why. The pursuit of profit is fine, only not at the expense of people's lives. I threw up again, right there behind where those two were talking. One of them was nice to me. He brought me a soda."

A thought dawned on me. "Who was the soldier?" I asked even though I knew. I could see it clearly in my mind's eye. I could picture the soda exchange.

"Sterling." He breathed in through his nose. "I promised this stranger that I was done making bombs. I don't think he believed me. I refused to work on any war-related products. Evander threw me in jail for failure to meet my obligations. I spent a year in jail, underground. Alone. They fed us three times a day. No one spoke to us. Some of the people there were very bad." He shook his head. "Then out of nowhere, Damian came. I'd never met him. He had a project he wanted me to sign on to. He'd convinced Evander I was worth more to them on a mission like this than in the cell. I didn't outright lie to you. I did sign on to help the Infected, like my parents. I am happy. I'm grateful. I'm lucky. Damian and Sterling, they've been friends for a while. Damian saved Sterling, too. Sterling told him about the engineer who refused to make any more bombs. That's how I'm here."

I stood then, like I'd been doing it for years, I threw my arms around him. "I'm so sorry you had to go through that. I don't have words."

He put his forehead on my shoulder. "When I think about the lives lost. Because I made the product."

I squeezed him tighter. "My father and my uncles, they've all done bad things. Every. Single. One. Of. Them. Guilt follows them, tied to their backs with a rope only they can see. I didn't know when I was little. I learned bit by bit. I can't make you forgive yourself. Maybe you're not supposed to. I don't know. I do think you were very young when you went to Evander, with no parents. You didn't have the context in which to understand what they wished of you. They fed you. They clothed you. They asked; you provided. They took advantage of your genius."

"I'm ..."

I didn't let him finish. "When you realized, you stopped. Not one person in a million would have the guts to do what you did. You have a conscience. A big one. I cannot discount those who died. If their memory makes you careful from now on, then that is a gift in a strange, sad way. You'll get no judgement from me."

Judge didn't cry in a big way. He didn't have heaps of sobs. Simple, long strains of tears left his eyes in silence. They hit my shoulder and travelled down my torso. I drew him toward the bed, not letting go of him. He was so much bigger than me. It had to hurt him to be so bent over. We lay together on top of my bedspread, just as we'd stood.

I rubbed his back, tracing the spider with my fingertips while he quietly cried. I'd never seen anyone weep so silently. Had someone told him he couldn't make noise? I took his cheeks in my hands, and I kissed him gently. "You can let it out. Don't hold it back. It won't scare me, and I won't leave."

As though my giving him permission to do so made it happen, his quiet crying turned into sobs. I held him while his body shook and the depth of regret inside of him rose to the surface. He'd told me he was a happy person, and he was. I didn't doubt him. Happy people could hold sadness inside too. I believed my family didn't understand or approve of me, yet they'd been there. Judge had been all alone. In a corporation. I hated Evander Corporation. I'd never tell my five that. I understood they had a sort of loyalty to them. As far as I was concerned, it sounded like they owned Cash's genius, Sterling's body, Damian's loyalty, and Judge's soul. I didn't know with Lewis yet, although I knew there would be something.

All in the pursuit of profit.

It was a long time before Judge quieted. My shoulder was soaked. I was going to need to change before I went to sleep. I wouldn't move until I was sure he was okay.

He hadn't moved in a few minutes, and I nudged away just a bit so I could see his face. His eyes were closed, and his breathing sounded even. He'd fallen asleep. I kissed his forehead. He was so beautiful. Even more so to me than I'd found him that morning. I didn't think it was possible he could get any more handsome. His mouth moved every once in a while like he was having a conversation in his dream.

Ever so slowly, I pulled away from him. His eyes shot open the second I got out of the bed. His arms darted outward like he sought me before he was even fully awake. "Diana? Where did you go?"

"I'm here." I leaned over to kiss him. "I'm going to the bathroom. Go back to sleep."

"No." He sat up slowly. "Did I ruin everything? I've never ... that is ... I'm not a crier. I ..."

I wagged my finger at him. "You stop that. You needed that cry. We all do sometimes. Even big, tough, geniusy alpha men. Okay? I'll never tell a soul. I'll be right back."

I came out of the bathroom, and he was still awake, sitting up next to the headboard. He patted the bed, and I slipped in next to him, pulling the blankets over both of us. He laid down on his side, looking at me, and after a second pulled me up against him until my head was on his arm.

"I cried myself asleep. I can honestly say I've never done that. Ever."

He was going to obsess over this. "For like thirty seconds."

Judge settled down, the smell of his soap and the essence that was Judge making the bed warm. The wind blew loudly. With everything happening, I'd forgotten about it. He pressed his forehead to mine again. "Did I blow tonight? Are you going to decide to take me off the schedule?"

I pinched his arm. "Don't be like that. I'm crazy about you. Way too soon to be as attached as I've gotten. How am I supposed to protect my heart from you?"

"You said that without a trace of irony."

"I have none."

He kissed my lips gently. "Today, before the weeping, was the best day of my life."

"I have a hard time ranking things outside of usefulness and productivity. I had a hard time with my favorite memory. I'm glitchy." He scowled at me, so I kept going. "I'll say simply that I loved today."

He was quiet for a long moment. "Sterling isn't the only one to not like that word."

"Tough. It's my word." I'd already decided to be careful using it around Sterling. I yawned. "Let's go to sleep."

He tugged me even closer. I wasn't sure I could breathe if we got any more pressed together. "I should warn you I don't sleep well, Di. My mind never turns off. I'm always solving problems or fixing things. I wake up usually twice a night at least. The second, or sometimes third time, I just get up and be done with it."

That wasn't going to work. I wanted him here. He needed sleep. We'd have to work this out so that he calmed down enough to make it through night, even if he rested in the bed instead of being outright asleep.

"Have you talked to Lewis about it?" This seemed more like a Lewis problem than a Cash. I might be wrong, but Cash came across as liking big, worldly issues and Lewis was more involved in the here and now. I reserved the right to be wrong about that.

Judge smirked. "He drugged me for a while. My brain wouldn't unfog. I couldn't work."

Well, so much for that. I yawned again. We couldn't solve everything right there in my bed. Maybe in the morning— which reminded me to set an alarm for Cash. "Do you have your tablet? Could you set the alarm for Cash?"

"What time did he say?" He got out of the bed slowly; I could see he dragged a little bit. The sobbing had taken such a toll on him. Judge grabbed his tablet out of his pants and came back to bed with it. "We need to get you one of these. I'll ask Damian if he'll be willing to pretend I lost mine and get you a new one from Evander."

I didn't want anything else from Evander. I'd taken their food, clothing, and lodging. It was hypocritical. I didn't want Judge giving them any more of his soul, not for me. I decided to change the subject. "We have similar tech at home. I didn't bring my tablet with me the day I ended up getting shot at and coming here. Cash said eight a.m."

His eyebrows rose. "What the hell is he going to do with you at eight?"

"He didn't tell me."

Judge set the alarm and lay down next to me, putting me back where he wanted me. "I would love to hear about your tech someday."

"I'll tell you another time." The wind blew in the distance, and Judge's racing heart told me he wasn't going to fall back asleep so quickly. I kissed a spot right below his neck. He responded really well to my touch. If I could calm him again, I would. He should never feel alone.

"You want to sleep, and I'm totally blathering on. I'm sorry. I'll be quiet."

That only made me feel much worse. I traced his spider again. "Tell me about what's specifically bugging your mind right now."

"The glass enclosures. It's not a new thing. They've bugged me from day one. Don't get me wrong. They're sturdy. I had Sterling throw things at it. The Infected are not getting through. I designed the enclosures. Evander had my specific instructions and sent the parts on the same ship they dropped us off on. I woke up, oriented, and built it from my own design."

I could picture him doing it. Probably still in his pajamas. "And?"

"They've never seemed right, and I can't pinpoint why. It's like they don't smell right." He groaned. "I'm possibly obsessive."

"You're definitely obsessive. That doesn't mean you're wrong."

He laughed, and I smiled. Finally, after a minute of considering his problem from all angles, I continued. "I see two suggestions I could make. Likely you've considered both."

Judge's eyes widened. "Hit me."

"Have you taken them apart and put them together again?"

He nodded once. "In the beginning. Since then, we've had the Infected. Cash isn't so anxious to let me fool with the holdings."

He'd done that. "Then is it possible they didn't send you the right materials? Even if they were packaged like they were? You asked for screws from one company; they sent it to you from another and packaged it as the first."

Judge jolted in bed. "Fuck." He covered his mouth. "Sorry. I never considered ..."

I patted his side. "I've heard curses before. They don't bother me. They're just language. Judge, are you considering running out there now to check the materials."

He nodded, so I kept talking. "Okay, go." If he needed to, he should. "Then don't come back here tonight. I'm not trying to be a bitch." I deliberately used a curse word. "I need to sleep. With the wind, I have a terrible time resting here as it is. If I hear you walking around at four in the morning I'll never get back to sleep, so please go back to your own room when you're done."

Judge didn't hesitate. He lay back down. I guessed staying with me now ranked as more important than checking the materials.

"There will come a time when I'll be able to distract you from work."

He turned on his side, and once again I found myself pressed to his chest. "How so?"

"Well, we'd have sex." I said it. I couldn't believe the words were out of my mouth the second I said them. "Then you wouldn't want to leave."

He traced my face, a slow grin appearing on his. "I ... I could make you feel good right now."

"How? You can't ..."

He cleared his throat. "In the US I really liked oral sex. I mean, I realize I won't get off on it this time. Only, I'd like to give you pleasure. That would be its own kind of reward. Not my pleasure. Not yet. Yours."

"I'm less experienced than you. I never had the US. That's not to say I haven't sometimes touched myself." Okay, this was too far for me. I had to stop talking about it now.

He leaned on his elbow. "Can I touch you?"

"Yes." My heart raced so fast. I couldn't believe this was happening. I'd told him one day I'd distract him, and I was apparently already doing it. He kissed down my body, pulling my oversized pajama pants off me and throwing them to the side.

"You smell really good, Di. I could just breathe you in all day." He kissed down my belly until he got to where he wanted to be. I didn't sleep in underpants. I simply didn't have enough of them. The pants covered me just fine.

Except now I was fully exposed, which I guessed was the point to begin with. He licked me from the bottom of my stomach until he reached inside of me and found my clit. He moaned, and I stole a look to see if anything was happening down there on him. Nothing. I laid my head back down.

"It's like I can feel what should be happening, and then it doesn't. Don't worry. It's not about me tonight. I love this. I'm right where I want to be, giving you pleasure. Always."

His tongue went back to work, licking at my most sensitive spot until it pulsed and swelled. I'd made myself come before, mostly in the shower. It always took me a really long time. His finger slipped deep inside of me. No one but myself had ever touched me there before. I closed my eyes, the feelings his maneuverings stirred inside of me nearly taking over me.

I really cared about Judge. It had been such a short amount of time, but he got me, and I'd really started to feel like I understood him, too. He could be deceptively bouncy. It just meant he concentrated really hard. Right now, all of that focus was on me. I didn't want to disappoint him and not be able to come. He'd take it personally as a failure.

"Get out of your own head, Di. I can feel you thinking. This is me showing you how much I care. Let me."

He'd read me perfectly. I made the thoughts go away; I made the worry, the stress, the freaking out all leave. There was only Judge. Only his mouth. Only the two of us and the things his tongue was doing to my clit. I moaned and covered my mouth with my hand, embarrassed.

His breathing quickened. "Don't take those sounds from me. Those are like gifts."

Judge's voice, his words were as much an aphrodisiac as anything else. I moved my hand from my mouth, and the next wave of pleasure that moved through me I let out. The more I let myself just go with the sensations, the more he got it right. *Oh yes, right there. Oh god, yes. That's the spot.* I was so wet. And then it all just exploded. My ears rang, and I buckled off the bed, steadied only by his hand on my knee. Colors crossed in front of my vision; for one second I knew the true joy of coming undone because someone cared enough to make you do so. I was so damned lucky. Tears streamed my face before I batted them away.

Judge grinned like a kid on Christmas. A second later he climbed further up the bed to my side and tugged me against him. "Thank you."

I managed to open my eyes. "That's my line."

There was such peace in his gaze. I gasped looking at it. He spoke slowly. "You're making everything right."

"That's too much pressure on me."

He tucked me against him. "No pressure, Di. Truth. Go to sleep. I'm not leaving. I'm even feeling tired myself."

I was dreaming about waterfalls. Judge chased me through a cave behind a waterfall. I laughed when I almost slipped, and he caught me. We stopped running, and hand-in-hand we stared down through the water to the lake below us. At some point, we were going to have to jump.

Judge's voice was low when he spoke. "You knew this couldn't last. I knew it too. At some point, we're both going to have to jump."

I don't know what he would have said next or how I would have responded. I woke up because Judge felt tense on the bed. His face looked strained, and his silent talking was back, his mouth moving quickly. He was going to burst awake any second. He'd told me he got up at least twice a night. Not much time had passed. I didn't feel stiff, and the hallway was dark. We'd never entirely extinguished the lights.

I didn't want to wake him, so I managed to touch the button to the side of the bed and get them off. It was easier to tell Artemis to do it, but I suspected one sound from my voice and the tentative hold Judge had on sleep would flee.

The room bathed in darkness, a calm one. With Judge in bed with me, I wasn't worried about the wind. I touched the side of his face and gently cupped his cheek. With my other hand, I held him close, drawing circles on his back. Tender signs that might lead the dark dream away and let him get some rest. I didn't know what his dream self had meant by "jumping." Still, the waterfall had been lovely. The real Judge should have something like that.

He squirmed for a second, and then his mouth stopped moving. He let out a long, deep breath and then his mood evened out into what looked like a deeper sleep. Assured he rested again, I fell back asleep. This time I didn't remember my dreams if I had any.

The next time he woke me, he'd made a noise. I had no question he was in the middle of a bad dream. He lay flat on his back, and his facial expression was that of pure pain. I moved until I fit against him again, flinging my arm across his chest. I laid gentle kisses to his shoulder while, as quietly as I could, I shushed him.

He settled again, his hand tightening on my back while his eyes remained closed, the movement of his eyeballs beneath his lids telling me he was deep in REM.

I pressed against him and closed my eyes. Keeping Judge asleep was going to be a process. I wanted this for him. I wanted to know I brought him comfort, that I wasn't another burden on a man who already had more than anyone should.

He lay quiet the rest of the night, and eventually I dozed off again. The alarm blaring to life woke me at seven, and I groaned. Judge hadn't moved since I hushed him back to sleep, and he still wasn't. I rolled over him and shut off the blare. He didn't move at all. I hated to rouse him when he looked so happy to be asleep.

Instead, I quietly made my way to the shower. My muscles were achy, and the warm water did wonders for them. I'd never needed a lot of sleep, and I'd quickly get over the lack of rest with Judge. He was amazing. He made me feel ... alive. I might even let him call me beautiful because I could see in his eyes he found me that way.

Judge made the world move. My heart fluttered. Cash was coming for me. I couldn't help but be really excited. He was so strong, brilliant, and mysterious in the things he said. I wanted to be a person he could trust, someone he knew he could open up to. He was also, to steal a phrase off the woman who sold baked goods on Mars Stations, handsome as sin. His olive skin and dark eyes were striking. He was tall and strong.

I finished cleaning off and dressed into a too-big-on-me pair of sweats and a t-shirt. Good thing we had nowhere to go. I'd be presentable for nothing.

Artemis' clock told me it was 7:50 when I got out, which meant I'd really dawdled under the hot water. I stepped out quietly. Judge was still out cold, and I made my way outside of Artemis to meet Cash.

He entered the hanger just as I got out of the ship.

"Hey, I was coming in to get you." He held out his hand, and I squeezed it in mine, which made him smile.

"Judge is still out cold."

He stared at the ship. "Is he sick?"

"I don't think so."

Cash put his arm around me and walked me slowly out of the hanger. "What did you do to him to get him to sleep? Have some secret from the other side of the hole?"

"No, I think he just needed a really good night's rest."

Chapter Eleven

Eggs a la Cash

What did Cash want to do at eight in the morning? He wanted to have breakfast with me alone. I kind of thought that was sweet. When we bypassed the kitchen, I became concerned.

"Where exactly are we going?"

He pointed at the ceiling. "Up."

"There's an up?"

Cash winked at me and didn't answer. I followed him into his office, staunchly refusing to look at the Zombie, and to the other end of the room where he tugged a rope that opened a hole in the ceiling and lowered a set of stairs. "How did I not notice this before?"

"You haven't spent that much time in this room. You weren't looking for it. The rope is pretty well camouflaged. And I guess you just didn't."

I grinned at him. "Thanks for the thorough answer."

"Anytime, Boo." There was the little nickname again. He gestured toward the stairs, and I followed him up them. Sure enough, there was an upstairs. It was an unfurnished, unfinished, wood-floored area that really must be the attic of the whole place. It stretched in every direction and, if I judged correctly, went the whole length of the giant enclosure where we lived.

I internally jolted at the thought. I didn't live here. I visited. My family was coming. Even if I wanted to stay here, eventually Evander would find out I was here and take me from them. Or try to. I didn't want that.

"So what do you think?" Cash gestured around him. "Technically, this is a storage area. We don't use it. I don't think Damian knows I come up here. So, if you wouldn't mind keeping this from him, I'd be ever so grateful."

"Sure." I didn't share secrets unless someone was going to get seriously hurt. Like the time Colin told me he'd electrified Asher's doorknob. That kid was too brilliant for his own good ... I shook my head. What the hell was the matter with me? "What do you do up here by yourself?"

He crooked his finger at me. "Come on."

I followed him. This was a side of Cash I hadn't expected. He was ... playful. With Judge, I'd seen it coming. Cash was so serious, so in charge. Eventually we came to a place where there was a break in the wall. The plastic coating of the rest of the area was still present; we weren't cold. We could, however, see outside.

I sucked in my breath. I'd only seen Orion from the view screen of Artemis. Everywhere I looked was white. He'd given me a window. My breath quickened, and my mind went into overdrive. I needed this, and I'd had no idea.

He came up behind me and wrapped his arms around me until I was drawn to his chest. "And what does my lady think?"

I gave him the first answer that came to my mind. "Like somehow the universe wanted to make everything new, and it carved out a space, and here it is. Beautiful. Untouched. Waiting for someone to draw on it." Then I felt stupid for speaking as I did. This was Cash. He was such a genius Evander had sent him out here to solve the unsolvable. He didn't want to hear about drawing on nonsense. "Of course, it's also a testament to, um, what happens after nuclear explosions when ..."

He interrupted me, whispering in my ear. "Shh. I liked the first one."

"I thought it might have sounded stupid."

"It sounded beautiful. I love beauty. I miss it. Everything here is cold and clinical. Or it was. Until Damian carried you into Lewis' lab, bellowing at the top of his lungs. You were pale, barely breathing. We thought we might lose you before we could get you in the machine. Even then the machine could only take you so far. You kept having to come in and out of it so we could treat you and put you back in. And I thought I must have gone crazy because you were the most beautiful—I know you hate that—girl I'd ever seen. I couldn't lose you."

I put my hands over his arms and squeezed him back. "Thank you for saving me."

"I think that was more Lewis than I. I helped, for sure. He's really the clinician. If life were fair, that's what he'd do, work with patients. I listened; I made a few suggestions. I was there. He told me what to do. He saved you. I obsessed."

I suspected Cash did quite a bit more. He didn't strike me as a stay-on-the-side kind of guy. I didn't want to argue. I wanted to stare at the white vastness. At the nothing waiting to be something.

"Thank you for this. Does it look better this time of day? Is that why you wanted to come here at eight?"

"No. Look to your left."

I did as he told me, and on the ground was a blanket with two plates covered up to keep the contents warm. A thermos had liquid in it. "I wanted to have breakfast with you. Right here. Where we could talk and look out the window."

I moved from his arms so I could stare at the picnic more closely. I knelt down. "I've always wanted to have a picnic. I did. I never dreamed I'd have one. Ever. This is literally a dream come true."

He motioned for me to sit, and I did, right next to him. "I've always wanted to make a beautiful woman's dream come true."

I elbowed him. "Stop it."

He opened the lids and presented eggs and bacon. They smelled like heaven. While I drooled over the food, he poured juice into small glasses. "You like eggs and bacon, right? I've seen you eat meat, so I know you're not a vegetarian."

"I love them. Did you make these?"

Cash raised an eyebrow. "I did. Damian does all the cooking because he's really good at it. However, I can manage some basics. This is one of them."

I took a bite and let the savory taste of hot scrambled eggs fill my mouth. This had always been my favorite breakfast. "A million thank yous."

"Never thank me. Ever. Okay?"

It seemed a strange request. "Really? It's basic manners; isn't it?

"All right. In public, thank me. Alone I'd rather you not. I'm hoping you'll come to understand that the things I do for you is my way of expressing my affection for you. All I want in return is to know you enjoy what I did. Maybe it doesn't make sense."

It didn't have to. He'd expressed a need. I was happy to give him what he asked. "Okay. These are the best eggs I've ever eaten."

We ate in companionable silence. When I was finished, I was full. Really full. I didn't usually eat much in the morning. I lay back on the ground. "I'm stuffed."

He moved until he lay next to me. "That's because you're so tiny."

"My father says my grandmother was tiny, too. My mom's medium-sized for a woman, and Dad is tall. I got the tiny genes."

"Whatever genes you got, they were the right ones."

The ceiling was made of the same plastic alkaline as the rest of the enclosure. It was translucent. I couldn't see through it, although it let some light through. "How did you guys put this place up?"

"We didn't. We were still out in our pods. You saw the pods right? The ones we'll get shoved into should the Zombies attack?" He snorted like the idea was ridiculous. I hoped he was right. "The ship landed, and the robots, probably designed by Judge, came out and put up the enclosure. We woke up in the pod room, shivering, disoriented, sick, and miserable. When we were finally able to think again, we went ahead and started undoing the boxes, fixing up the rooms. A second ship delivered the agriculture. We get periodic messages and shipments from Evander. All drones."

I rolled onto my stomach to look at him better. "I didn't know cryogenic sleep made you sick. We don't use that tech on our side. We have it. No one uses it. There's no need for us to sleep through travel. Aging is okay. Some people spend their whole lives on ships."

"They wanted us to basically be a day older than when we left. To answer your question, it feels like the worst flu you've ever had."

I shook my head. "Never had one."

"Then you're not going to be impressed I cured the Trinton Flu."

"That's amazing. For the record, just because I haven't had the flu, doesn't mean I don't know what it is and I'm not impressed by it. I am."

He pushed my bangs off my forehead. "Good."

"Can the Zombies do without you for a whole day?"

"Lewis will manage them today. They'll be fine." He rolled onto his stomach, too, entwining our legs. "What would you like to do? This was really what I wanted. You, alone with me in the morning light, eating a breakfast I provided for you, watching the whiteness waiting for color, and talking."

Now that I was full, I was sleepy. I needed to wake up. I wasn't going to spoil my day with Cash by falling asleep. "Make some suggestions."

"Let me think for a minute. If you want to doze off, you can. I can see you've got that I ate-a-lot tired thing going on."

I shook my head. "I don't want to fall asleep on our date. I want to get to know you. This is our time."

He liked what I'd said; I could tell by the way the color brightened in his cheeks. It was subtle, but it was there. "We'll have more time. Today isn't it."

"Don't try to lull me to sleep. I want to be up. Why don't you want Damian to know you come up here?"

He took a second to answer. "Because it's mine. It's not Damian specifically. I don't want any of them to know."

"Fair enough. You ask me something."

"Oh, what to pick." He laughed. "The pressure. All right. Fine. Um. I'm not used to so inorganically having to find a query. Let's see. Do you like living on Mars Station?"

I wouldn't have imagined that would be his first inquiry. "That's a complicated answer. I like it because my family is there. I've always gone with them, always. They said go, I went. I was a child. I'm a year from having to pick my own future. It's the law. I won't be able to stay with them forever. I can go and come back, but I must go in some fashion. The question is, where? I can get married. The only ones who want me desire the connection for political reasons. The way they look at me makes me want to vomit. I can get a job somewhere else. But where? Doing what? I'm a mid-level tech person. I can fix some things. So can a million others. Or I can go and spend five years with the Sisters of the Universe in mostly silence doing good deeds." I stopped rambling. "Sorry. That was more than you ever wanted to know."

"By contrast, I loved every second of your answer. Can I get some follow up questions?"

I giggled. "Funny man. This isn't a panel. Ask me anything you want. I'll do the same for you."

He inched closer to me, laying his head down by mine. Neither of us looked at each other, and yet I felt like Cash took up all the air in the room. I wasn't suffocated by him; instead, I felt enveloped in his being. I could get lost in him, and he'd take care of me. Of course, the risk was I'd be so happy letting him take hold of me that I'd never want to be on my own again. Could I come back from being close to so much ... power?

"There are always rules, Boo. Even when we don't know them. I'm feeling my way through this. I don't mind sharing you with the others. I respect them more than any other souls in the universe. They have become my family. I just have to understand how this works. I am a man who likes being in charge."

I rolled onto my side until he looked at me. "I don't want to be in control all the time. I think if we can manage to get through the no fighting rule—and the schedule—I'd be happy to let you all set terms and tell me what to do for the most part. I actually like knowing you can determine things. I don't want to be dictated to. I want to be part of things. Am I making any sense?"

"Tons. All right, what was that about a political marriage?" He said the words like they tasted bad.

"My mom is a politician on Mars Station. It would benefit her campaign and a lot of people if I let these three brothers court me. They'd vote with her, control the board. No one asked me to do it. Frankly, even though they make me sick, it might be the right thing to do."

"It's not." He stood and took my hand, bringing me up with him when he did. "They can't have you. I've seen political marriages. They kill the wife. Maybe that's sexist. I don't care. They kill the wife. My mother was eaten alive. No. Don't do that, Boo. Besides, as far as I'm concerned, you're mine. Sure, you're the other four of theirs too. But you're mine. I'm saying no."

I touched the side of his face. "You'd rather I took a job or went into meditation?"

"I'd rather you stayed here with me and let me take care of you for the rest of your life."

As if he'd said the final word on the subject, he locked our hands together, and we walked together back toward the ladder. Cash knew the truth of things. My family was coming back. He could want what he wanted. That didn't mean it would happen.

When we got down and he'd rehooked the ladder, he turned to me. "Like to dance?"

"I don't know if the spinning in a circle I do with my brothers and sisters qualifies."

"Are you trying to tell me you've never danced?" I nodded and he leaned forward. "Diana, the men around you are buffoons."

With that proclamation, we walked quickly together toward where the guys slept. I caught glimpses of the others. They were busy working or getting ready for their days. Lewis stared at what looked like DNA sequences on the screen that we'd watched the movie on the night before. Sterling did sit ups in the gym, shirtless. I didn't see Damian anywhere, but then again, I never did. It was like he appeared at meal times. If I hadn't seen him with his two guns when I'd watched from Artemis or slept with him the one night in my room, I'd have believed he didn't really exist at all.

Judge came out of his room while we passed by, his hair wet.

"Morning," he called out to me.

I waved back. "Morning."

Cash brought me into his room and shut the door behind him. "Sorry. If I let them all talk to you, I'd never have gotten you here."

I didn't remember my mother ever having to run down the hall to avoid the guys who weren't on the schedule that day. Okay. This was the first day. Actually, it was the second. There was going to be an adjustment period. Maybe I'd say something in a month if I still had to rush around.

Cash's room was much more decorated than Judge's had been. Although it was the same size, Cash had things up on the walls—posters of people I didn't know but, from the descriptions around them, I thought were probably artists. Models of aircrafts and places I'd seen covered his shelves. He had a screen on his wall.

He pressed a button on his tablet, and low music started in the room. I'd obviously never heard the song before, but I closed my eyes when it turned on so I could feel the melody. A woman and a man were singing about love. I smiled. The best songs always were.

"Diana." Cash's voice sounded melodic, like the music he'd played for us. I opened my eyes. He held out his hand. "Will you dance with me?"

"If you show me how and don't laugh at me while I do it wrong."

With our hands joined, he drew me to him. "I'd never laugh at you about anything, especially this. Maybe I'd laugh *with* you on another topic. Never *at* you. I promise."

He moved my hand until it was behind his neck, and took the other in his large, capable hand. "This isn't the right position. It's the way I want it."

We didn't have a huge amount of space to work with. That was okay. In the small distance between his bed and his desk, our bodies swayed together. Sometimes Cash would turn us or change how our feet moved. I stepped on his once, and he didn't blink an eye, just readjusted us a bit. Eventually, I stopped worrying. This was fun. I must have grinned because he did back.

The music moved through us, the song changing to something faster. Feeling brave, I let go of his hand and wrapped both of my arms around his neck—which was a stretch considering how much taller than me he was. He hoisted me up, my legs wrapping around him, and we swayed like that. I really didn't know how much time passed, nor did I care.

I'd always heard there were moments in life where you wished you could go on forever. Dancing with Cash became that for me. I think he must have felt it too. His gaze fell to my lips, and I knew he was going to kiss me. I closed my eyes and sighed when he did. His mouth was strong, firm, yet gentle with me. The kisses started out light, easy; however, that changed quickly. With a swing of his arms, he lay me down on bed, coming down on top of me.

"I know we're limited for now." His mouth met mine slowly, and his tongue licked my bottom lip. My body went on alert, and I sighed against him. He pulled back, his gaze holding my own. "I have some time right now to learn your body, to know it, so when the time comes, when I can actually slip myself inside of you and do what I really, really want to do, I'll know you so well it won't matter I have no experience with this outside of a machine."

I stroked the side of his face. I wasn't going to ruin the moment by asking him questions. I didn't always know when to say things and when not to. This time I knew better than to ask him about the US machine while we lay quietly kissing for the first time.

"What's on your mind?" He pushed my bangs off my head.

I shook my head. "It's nothing."

"Boo, when I ask you something, the only thing I require is you don't lie to me. If you don't want to tell me, say that. Don't tell me it's nothing when your brown depths are screaming at me that you have something on your mind."

They were big on truth, my five. Judge had needed to confess his year in jail, Damian had reminded him truth was pivotal, and now Cash demanded it from me.

"I am not used to people wanting to know everything I'm thinking. Most of the time they leave me alone to think my own thoughts."

He put his hands on the side of my head, stroking his fingers through my hair. "I want to know your thoughts, Diana."

"I'm afraid what I was questioning was going to ruin the mood. Seemed better to keep it to myself."

He breathed in through his nose, his nostrils flaring. "Now I really need to know."

"I wonder about the US machine. What that was like when you were in it. Not the whole giving you the medicine. I imagine it's administered through a needle?"

Cash cocked his head to the side. "Injection into our neck devices." He moved so I could see it. "Hits the central nervous system faster that way. This neck piece gives the medical machines quick access to us. And magnetizes us into the pods in the event of an emergency."

My finger hovered over the small metal piece on the back of his neck. What an amazing little computer.

"You can touch it, Boo."

I let the tip of my index finger stroke the top of the device. It was cool to the touch. For some reason I'd thought it would be warm—maybe because Cash's body was so hot. It didn't match the warmth of his skin.

"So you were asking about the US. I interrupted you. Go on." He sat, pulling me with him until I was on his lap.

"What's it like in there? Is it just a giant pornography video?"

"We don't generally discuss it with each other, so I can't tell you what it's like when say Sterling or Damian is in the device.

My understanding is it's different for each of us. The machine talks to us. Asks us some questions, reads some of our impulses, and then delivers whatever it is it thinks we need to get aroused. Then we go into a dream state. I've read the literature. Some people have elaborate scenarios. Spies running around. Cavemen. For me, the machine used to try to give me a storyline, but my brain wouldn't accept them. As though, even when I'm out of it, I know I'm in a machine having a functional experience I need to get through. The last few years, honestly, it's a faceless girl, and we get down to business. I don't really feel anything about it. I'm not in love with my US experience."

A functional experience. That was a funny way to put it, and yet I understood what he meant exactly. He didn't need a lot of show. Just what was real.

"Still, the machine knows exactly what to give you. When the time comes, I'm going to be really inexperienced."

He nodded. "Good."

"Good?" I coughed out my shock.

"I'd rather have your trembling hands and sweet kisses than any fake computer program in the universe."

Chapter Twelve

Cash Wilder

Cash ran out, telling me he'd be right back. I got off his bed and wandered the room a bit. I didn't want to snoop, just kind of look around. His model cars seemed glued together pretty well. Judge had told me sometimes the nights were long. Was this what Cash did to pass time?

The music still played softly, and I listened as a woman lamented the death of her lover. I rubbed my arms, trying not to feel all her pain. A strange memory hit me. When I'd been a little girl, Uncle Dane had told my mom he thought I felt everything acutely, much more than most people did. I remember that was the moment I'd realized how completely odd I was. I must have been about eight. We were on our way from Earth to Mars Station. I didn't want to feel everything, and I determined I'd somehow get it under control. I wouldn't let them all know how everything affected me all the time.

I rubbed my eyes. Was that when I'd shut my feelings off? Decided I could do without? At eight? Even when I hadn't talked between the ages of three and five, I'd apparently been a pretty happy child. My mom said I'd mostly seemed as content as I could possibly be.

I really didn't know. I wasn't set up for this kind of self-examination. Most of the time, I had to get through the day, and that took all my energy. Between Judge and Cash, I was having an awful lot of time to think.

On one of Cash's shelving units was a picture. I recognized Cash right away. He was young, maybe twelve years old. His mother and father stood behind him, his mom smiling. Cash got his good looks from his mother's side of the family. She was dark like him. His father wore glasses and had a serious expression on his face, as though he was at a different event than Cash and his mom.

The door opened and closed. I turned around to see Cash holding plates in his hands. I gawked at him. "You're serious? More food? You're going to make me fat."

"I doubt that." He rolled his eyes at me. "This is fruit and salad. It's lunch time. Three meals a day. Keeps the metabolism up."

Cash sat and patted the floor next to him. I sat and took the plate from his hands. He'd told me not to thank him, so I didn't. We ate together, and when I was done, I didn't feel overstuffed from the whole thing. He wanted to hear if I liked the things he did, and he also wanted the truth, which meant I couldn't simply lie and say I enjoyed something if I didn't. I chewed my bottom lip. It might get complicated keeping Cash happy.

Or maybe it was the easiest thing in the world.

"I overdid it with lunch, didn't I?" He smirked and shook his head. "I have this whole idea of how I want to take care of you."

I leaned my head on his shoulder. "It was yummy. After that breakfast, I wouldn't have eaten until dinner. Tell you what? How about if I promise to tell you if I'm hungry? I swear I can take care of myself."

He put my hand in his lap. "I know you can. Probably better than me. I've never had to live alone in a black hole, hide out in an old ship by myself, make it all okay. I've never done anything like what you've done. I thought maybe I could coddle you a little bit."

"No one ever has. Not since I was a little girl." I put his arm around me, and I found a place where I seemed to fit, with my head and arm on his chest. "Tell me about you. Where are you from? What have you done? How did you get here?"

"We're back to question time." He kissed the top of my head. "You smell so good. Like strawberries. All about me, huh? Okay. I saw you looking at that picture up there. So, my family is super-rich. We are a long line of doctors. Even during the days of Damian's crazy aunt and before that, we never had problems like the rest of the world. The men in my family have a history of being in the right place at the right time. My father got in with Evander early. My entrance was easy."

"That's great." I kissed his cheek. "And you wanted to be a doctor, too?"

"I did, actually. That was never the problem. Um, my father was a real asshole. He made a political marriage to my mother. Her father sat on Evander's board. The problem is, as far as I can figure it, she was in love with him. He didn't care for her all that much, and after I was born, he'd take his temper out on her pretty badly."

I was so close to him I could hear his breathing speed up. "By that, you mean he beat her?"

"Badly. All the time. Unless I was doing something spectacular to keep him happy. I did my best. I'm smart. I'm not going to lie. I'm good at medical research. I develop things. I save lives. I love it. Eventually, she died. About a year after that picture was taken. Not because of him. She was struck crossing the street. *Bam*. A transport bus took her right out." He pursed his lips for a second. "About six years ago, the old guy decided I needed to get married. He started presenting these potential brides to me. These women." He shook his head.

So Cash had had choices. He could've had a bride and happily lived out the rest of his life in civilization. I knew his work was important. Still, how had he ended up out here? "What was wrong with the women?"

"They knew exactly the right things to say at the right moments." He threw his hands in the air. "When to say yes, when to say no, like they'd been briefed on me. Maybe they had been. I don't think one of them spoke her mind, ever. I'd make these outrageous statements just to see, and they'd agree with me."

I tucked my knees up to my chest. I don't know why I suddenly became intimidated. Maybe it was seeing Cash as someone else, wealthy and in touch with a lot of girls. His genius hadn't intimidated me. So why did his connection to Evander make me suddenly feel small and insecure?

He continued. "One time I suggested the key to fixing the problems of the universe was to sterilize the rodent population on every planet. The woman agreed with me like I was some kind of genius for thinking of it. Hey, are you okay?"

"Yes." I didn't lie. I really was fine. He arched an eyebrow at my response. "Fine. I'm nervous all of a sudden."

His face fell. "With me? Why?"

"Because you're connected with Evander. I mean, I know you all are. But your corporation could ... try to send me away from here ... and they scare me, to be honest."

"Oh, no, Boo." He hugged me tightly. "Let me finish my story. I make Evander a lot of money. And they hate me. It's a mutual dislike society. I'm never going to ... what? Pick them over you? Send you to them? No."

"I got scared. I don't know why." It made little sense to me. I had to get control over whatever was happening with me. I was too open, too out there with my feelings. I needed the cover of ...

Cash kissed my cheek. "To make the rest of the story short, I ran for my life. Turned down all of their offers for jobs until I could get one all the way out here where I can really do some good. I love it. I'm using my brain. I wish it was going better. I begged Damian to bring me here. I wasn't his first choice. I know that. I basically sold him on taking me. I'd be okay without ever going back. My father died a year ago. There's all this money and property and just *stuff* out there waiting for me to do something with it. I won't touch it."

His whiskers rubbed my skin, and I loved the feeling. I sighed. "Forgive me for my little freak out. There's something wrong with me. I don't know what it is. I'm ... experiencing a ton of things emotionally. I didn't think of myself as being shut off before. For some reason, I'm ..."

Cash sighed in my ear. "You're letting yourself bond to us like we are to you. It couldn't have been easy to tell me you're scared of me. Thank you for your trust. I won't forget it."

He hauled me up. I wrapped my legs around him, assuming he wanted to kiss me again like he had before. Only nothing about this was like before. He laid me down on the bed, and his mouth was on me like he owned me and had the right to me exactly as he wanted me. I had no objections. I wanted him.

Crazy as it seemed, I wanted him to belong to me.

His tongue pushed through my lips, finding mine, and they danced together. I moaned against him. Frustration was my middle name. This wasn't going to end with his penis inside of me, no matter how much I wanted it.

His mouth moved down, kissing my neck, and one of his hands found my breast, messaging it through my shirt. I squirmed on the bed. God, this was really hard. Like sweet torture.

"Can I make you come?" His voice was low, his eyes hungry.

"Yes. I promise to return the favor when I can."

He grinned as he slid down my body. "I'll hold you to that."

Cash crawled down my body, kissing me while he removed my clothing. I was completely naked in front of him. His voice was low, and his eyes appreciated me. "Put your hands on the bars of my headboard and don't let go."

"Oh?" I slid up so I could do as he instructed. "This is how you like it?"

"When I'm in the fake space, in the US, it's the one thing I let the machine do for me. I do like it. There won't be any finishing today, obviously, for me. I'd still like to be able to close my eyes and think of you like this. Unless you detest the idea."

I gripped the headboard. "I have no idea what I like or what I don't like. I've never had sex. Let's give it a try. We'll see what I like. You and me."

"And just like that my heart ..." I don't know what he would have said because he didn't finish, and his finger massaging my clit. The bundle of nerves was swollen and ready for him. My hips bucked, and I held onto the headboard for dear life.

"So responsive." He kissed the inside of my thigh. "One might think you want me, Boo."

"Pretty much from the second I saw you. Well, maybe the second time. I was terrified the first time. Woke up in a strange place, and you came in kind of angry."

He shook his head, stroking me slowly. "Try, 'Terrified of the gorgeous girl with the eyes that saw right through me.'"

After that we were done talking, Cash played my body like it was an instrument he was learning. Eventually, he found a spot I couldn't get enough of. He seemed to get lost in what he was doing, and soon I shouted his name while my body exploded around his tongue.

I panted, and he moved until he held me close to him against his chest. Cash pulled the covers around us. I wasn't tired, just having a hard time getting my heart to slow down.

"Best moment of my life." He kissed the back of my neck over and over. "Thank you for coming here, Diana. Thank you for coming to this planet."

We spent the rest of the afternoon listening to music. He introduced me to this band or that one. Some of them I liked, some of them I didn't. When I told him I enjoyed one, we listened to more of them. We didn't move. Cash had me wrapped so close against him I could feel his heart beat.

"Not this one. Seems like the drummer is trying too hard. *Bang. Bang. Bang.*"

Cash didn't answer me, and I adjusted until I could see his face. He was asleep. Dark lashes covered his even darker eyes. He was beautiful and untroubled. We had an hour until dinnertime. I took the tablet from his hand, his fingers opening easily. He was lost to sleep. I turned down the music a little bit and hit the button to listen to the next song at a lower volume. I'd have loved to nap; my lack of sleep from the night before wore on me. If I understood the ways things worked, we needed to be at dinner as a group every night.

I didn't dare fall asleep and have both of us sleep through dinner. On my second day figuring this out, I wouldn't already screw up a routine that worked for them.

I got through about ten more songs before it was ten minutes until dinner time. I knew I didn't like to have to wake up and rush places, better to have a little time. I rolled over, stroking my hand down Cash's face. "Time to wake up, Champ."

He didn't move, and I pressed my lips to his. "We've got to go eat dinner."

His eyes fluttered open, and he took in a long gulp of air before a smile crossed his face. "Did I fall asleep?"

"You work really hard. I bet you never nap. You must have needed it."

Cash groaned. "I pass out on a first date."

"Yeah ... well. I liked being wrapped up in your arms. I thought about going to sleep, too."

He sat, stretching his arms over his head. "Why didn't you?"

"I was afraid we'd both sleep through dinner, and I wasn't sure, but I thought that might be a no-no."

"You're right." He rubbed his eye. "Damian takes a long time preparing the meal. Much more than he needs to. Truth is, the other four of us would eat just about anything. He says he likes doing it. I wouldn't want to hurt his feelings. He'd never say anything."

I got up, looking for my clothes that had been thrown to the side when Cash had been loving my body. His gaze followed me, and I tried not to indicate I'd notice. Nudity outside of the comfort of his bed was uncomfortable.

"Diana, Boo. Hold up." I'd almost stepped into my underpants. His arms came around me, hauling me against him. "I want to hold you for one more minute. Okay? In here? You and me, alone."

I didn't point out we'd have the whole night in my bed. I'd never say no to Cash holding me. He breathed me in deeply before he spoke. "Did you pick this song?"

It was operatic sounding. The last one I'd selected before I woke him up. "I did. I really like it. Do you?"

His grin was infectious. "My favorite, actually. I was getting to it. You found it on your own, and you like it."

I wondered if I'd passed some kind of test I knew nothing about.

Cash let me finish getting dressed.

Dinner tasted amazing. I sat with Cash on my. Lewis and Sterling sat across from me. Judge took the head of the table and Damian took his seat across from Judge. I went to serve myself, only Cash had already done it for me. He was big on food as a sign of affection. No one blinked at the action.

Damian hadn't used any meat for the evening's meal. He had pasta, butternut squash, zucchini and a red sauce he'd made from scratch. He'd also created a green salad.

"Damian, this is so good," I told him after my second bite. "I love this. I just adore it."

He steepled his hands and grinned. "Thanks. I actually made it thinking of you. I can see you like meat, but somehow I also thought you wouldn't object to a really good vegetarian meal."

"That's right."

Judge set down his fork. "I have to tell you all Diana was entirely right. She solved the glass problem."

Five gazes landed on me. Cash cleared his throat. "How could she have done that? She was with me all day. Unless you snuck out, Boo. Did you?"

"No." I kicked him lightly under the table, and he grinned.

Judge rolled his eyes. "Last night before we went to bed. And I slept all night. I didn't get up once."

Lewis sat back in his chair. "Did you drug him?"

"No." I wasn't going to tell any of them, not even Judge at this point, what I did to keep him asleep. It was personal, for now anyway.

"What was the problem with the window?" Sterling sipped his water.

"They didn't send me the right parts." He pointed the fork at Damian. "That's right. Evander wrapped the parts in the right packing. I thought I was getting what I asked for. I didn't. They faked it."

Damian held his hands up. "Going to stab me with that fork?"

Judge looked at the fork like he realized what he'd been doing. He set it down. "Sorry."

"First off." Damian set down his own silverware. "I didn't do that, know that, or even suspect that would happen. I hope you're not blaming me for it."

"I'm not." Judge shook his head. "Or I shouldn't be. I'm sorry. If Archie Peterson were here, I'd blame him directly."

Damian looked tired. I wasn't sure how I knew, only that I did. He was downright exhausted. "And since the head of Evander is so far away that news of our deaths would take six months at least to reach him, you thought you'd take it out on me since I'm the company guy. Is that it?"

Judge narrowed his eyes. "I pointed a fork at you. I didn't tie you up and beat you."

"Okay, I'm not even going down that road. You're worked up. I get it. For five years you've wanted to know what's wrong. I'm glad you figured it out. Are we still safe with what we have? Can you fix it? Shall I write to Evander and demand the right stuff immediately?"

Judge shrugged. "It's not as safe as I would have wanted it. The glass is still impossible for the Zombies to break. My preferred poly-glass would have taken a nuclear bomb to explode. This one will shatter under extreme conditions. I can't imagine having those conditions. Let's not worry. Don't bother Evander. I don't want them extra-poking into our business."

Wasn't anyone going to ask him? "What are the extreme conditions?"

"Lightning would have to hit it twice in a row. The first one to short out the secondary systems and the second to actually break through the three panels of glass." He laughed. "So we're good. The Infected can't break through, Di."

I knew so little about weather. "I grew up on a space station. Lightning doing that would be a weird thing, right?"

"Weird is a good word." Cash knocked his shoulder into mine gently. "Don't fret."

I helped Damian clean up dinner. We did so in silence, and when we were about halfway through, he smiled at me. "Thanks."

"You shouldn't be cleaning at all. You made it."

He shrugged. "I like to do it. I at least know where everything gets put away."

"Must be an ordeal finding everything you need every night."

Damian sighed. "After all this time, I kind of generally know there are three or four places where what I need is likely to be."

I put my hand on his arm. "Are you okay?"

"Why do you ask?" He stopped moving.

"You seem really exhausted, and Judge should not have acted like you knew about the glass. I don't know you well. You seem ... you seem like a person with a lot of integrity."

Damian leaned against the counter. "Thank you for saying that. You gave me maybe the best compliment of my whole life. I understand Judge. I always have. Does it feel good he took his fork and pointed it at me like he was accusing me of taking part in the great glass debacle? No. Will I get over it? Sure. Eventually. I am tired. I'm not sleeping well for some reason. I feel kind of ... out of sorts."

Cash leaned against the wall by the door. "We're all going to have that start to happen. Or we'll be overtired. I fell asleep for no good reason in the middle of the day today. The medicine is wearing off. We're going to have withdrawal symptoms. Like, maybe, Judge unreasonably blaming you for something we know you wouldn't do."

"Is going off the US machine going to make you all sick? I don't want you to be sick. I can ..."

Cash put his hand out in front of him. "Whatever you were about to say, please don't. I'll face whatever discomfort to have you. I think Judge would say the same thing for sure."

"Me too." Damian smiled. "I know Sterling's got no issues. How about Lewis?"

"He's good," Cash answered for him. "So forgive us if we all seem a little tired for a little while."

As long as that was all it involved. I wouldn't make them sick or risk them in any way.

That night, my five set out to teach me the card game again. This time I was able to follow them perfectly and even won a few rounds. My third time taking the pot, I looked around. I could see the exhaustion wearing on them. Sterling rubbed his eyes a lot. Lewis hadn't moved since he sat down, and even Judge seemed subdued.

If they weren't going to call it a night, I would. "We should all go to bed."

"Agreed." Cash nodded. "What time do you want her tomorrow, Lewis?"

The other doctor grinned. "Nine is fine."

"What? You don't want her as soon as the sun rises?" Judge snorted.

I put my hand on Cash's knee, hoping he'd not take the obvious bait. He didn't respond, standing up before he took my hand.

I looked around the group. "Goodnight everyone."

Later in Artemis, while Cash used the bathroom, I noticed a blinking light on the screen where my family's pictures flashed through. I touched the screen, and Judge's voice played lowly. "Hey, Di. I need to tell you that last night was the best of my whole life. I set up this frequency. No one uses it. It can be our thing. You leave me messages, and I'll get it on my computer. I'll leave you some. It's not breaking rules. Or maybe it's only bending them. Goodnight."

I smiled at the screen. He'd made us a frequency?

Cash came out the bathroom. "All okay?"

"Yeah. Give me a second. I'll get into my ridiculously big pajamas."

He laughed and climbed onto the bed. "Your bed is nicer than mine. Bigger. Comfy."

I hurried through my routine and came out half expecting to find him asleep. He sat on the bed, waiting for me. I crawled into his arms. "Artemis, lights out."

The room bathed in darkness. Cash kissed me on both cheeks. "Goodnight, Boo."

"Sleep well, Champ."

Chapter Thirteen

A Cave of Wonders

Cash was not a hard person to spend the night with. He barely moved, and he breathed in an even manner that made it easy for my own to match. We were wrapped up in each other the next morning when I woke up. He didn't move, even when I got out of the bed. Exhaustion from the withdrawal was going to be hard to watch.

I took a shower and grabbed all of my laundry. With a few minutes to spare before I had to meet Lewis, I got my laundry started.

"Hey." I looked up to see Sterling carrying his own basket of clothes. "We need to get you some more clothes. I'm going to tell Lewis to turn on the replicator."

"You guys wear the same uniform every day."

He nodded once. "Sure. But ours fit. You must burn calories just dragging around the clothing on your body."

I smiled at him. "How was your night?"

He yawned and jumped up on the dryer. "Not bad. I didn't sleep well. I guess that's going to be for a while. I've been through worse things. Sleep is a luxury. Important I never forget that."

There was one washer and one dryer. A thought dawned on me. "Do you do your wash at this time every week? Am I imposing on your washer time?"

He smiled, showing me one of his dimples. "You're so cute. No. We don't have set times. And even if we did, I'd give you mine if it would make you smile."

Sterling flirted with me. We hadn't had much to do with one another since the night he'd discovered he couldn't perform and I'd not had a clue what was going on.

"How have you been?"

He smiled. "Really? I've been okay. I'm tired but nothing I can't get over. Looking forward to my day with you. We agreed not to tell each other what we do with our alone time. I like the idea. I don't need images I don't want in my head." My cheeks heated, and if he noticed, he ignored the blush. "I only wish I knew if the others did the things I'm imagining so I wouldn't repeat. Don't want to bore you."

I walked until I stood between his knees. "Even if I'd done them, it would be a whole different experience because it's the first time with you."

He leaned forward and whispered, "Good answer. Even if that isn't entirely true. Seeing the same movie twice could be dull."

"Okay, I'll tell you if I've seen the movie."

He nodded fast. "Sounds like a plan. Now get out of here before I forget this isn't my day, and Lewis kills me in my sleep."

I pointed at the laundry. "I have to move them into the dryer."

"I'll do it for you when it stops, and I'll throw my own in. I'll even fold the monstrously large clothes for you and put them in your room."

"Sterling." Maybe small things like this shouldn't be bothering me anymore, considering I'd been naked with Cash and Judge, slept with Damian, and made out with Sterling. Still, it kind of did. "You're going to fold my underwear?"

I only had the one pair and one bra. Fortunately, I was covered in my uniform, and my breasts were small enough I could walk around without one reasonably well.

"Yep." He nodded. "Totally not a perv. Going to wash them and put them in your room. I'm not going to do anything weird with your undies." He winked at me. "Not unless you tell me someday you want me to."

I must have been a tomato because he roared with laughter. I fled the laundry room and ran into Lewis on my way back to Artemis.

"Hi." He grabbed me and tugged me into a tight hug by way of greeting. "I was coming for you."

I pointed at the laundry room. "I had to do wash."

"Oh, right. Of course. Do you want to wait until it's done?"

"No, thanks." I took his arm. "Sterling says he'll take care of it for me."

He nodded once and didn't show any outward sign of being bothered at all. "Great. Then let's go."

We walked the long path from Artemis to the main part of the enclosure. "Are you hungry?" He pulled out a protein bar, and I took it from him. These guys were preoccupied with me eating.

"Thanks."

He nodded once. "You're welcome. I thought we could go do something a little bit different today. Something I've been wanting to do for some time. None of the others want to do it, and it's not the kind of activity I want to do alone."

He had my attention. "What did you have in mind?"

"I thought maybe you'd like to leave the enclosure."

I stopped walking. "Is that possible?"

He grinned and then looked at the floor. "It is. If we have the right clothes and equipment, sure. We happen to have that stuff."

"Where did you want to go?" I had never considered leaving the enclosure. I figured the next time I went away would be when my family came for me. The thought panged my heart.

How was I going to leave these guys? But then how would I tell my family I wasn't coming back with them?

"Our equipment isn't perfect. We missed you for a while there, didn't we?" Lewis raised his head. "But it looks like there is somewhere with some heat readings. No life signs. It's a cave structure. I thought we'd take the truck and go look." He looked at me expectantly. I'd never explored anything in my life. I knew where I was going all the time, except for when I was in the black hole and then there was nothing particular to look at.

I touched his shoulder. "What about the Infected?" I was trying not to call them Zombies anymore. They were sick people. I needed to have more respect. Maybe I was finally getting used to them.

"That, our computers are good at. I've checked the scans. I see nothing but a few strays from here to where we're going. No hoards. And even if there were some, they can't get into our truck. We'd run them over if we had to."

I smiled. "Then let's do it."

"Okay, we'll suit up and go." Lewis put his arm around my shoulder. His touch was tentative. He didn't grab or pull. He questioned and asked. I wondered if he'd ever kiss me or if I'd have to initiate it. For now, I was happy to go exploring with him. He took me into the room with the pods and the US machine. They kept their outerwear in the pod room.

Lewis handed me a suit, which was going to be huge on me but would do. We needed to put it on directly over our skin. Clothing underneath would actually interfere with the warming process. I held it in my hands.

"This should go over my naked skin?"

Lewis was across the room, his back to me. I turned around in time to see the suit zipping up over the strong muscles of his back. He zipped from the front, so he had no idea I peeked. I felt like I'd broken a rule and quickly looked back forward. He'd given me privacy. What was the matter with me?

"Your underwear is fine."

"I, um, don't have any. I only have one pair. They're in the laundry room. I don't suppose it matters, right? I'm going to be keeping the suit on."

He was quiet for a moment. "I'm so sorry I didn't think about your needs. Stay here. For a second, okay?"

"Sure." I turned to watch him leave the room. I'd spent so little time in the pod room, not since Judge had shown it to me. They'd arrived in the pods, and some day they were supposed to leave in them. I touched the outside of one. I knew which one was Judge's—he'd shown me—but whose did I look at now?

The US machine buzzed in the corner of the room. I was ridiculously curious about it. Cash said it was a ritual for him that got the job done. He knew he liked her to hold the headboard. I'd liked that, too. What did it do for the rest of them? Big adventures or just-down-to-it sexual acts? Would they be satisfied with me when it came to it?

Lewis strode back into the room and handed me two pieces of clothing. A bra and a panty. He didn't look at me when he handed them to me. "I left the replicator on. It draws a lot of energy, and for some reason the guys decided I should be in charge of it. I have no idea why. Seems it should be more of Damian's thing. Anyway, I made you these. Left it on, so it would make six more pairs of, um, different covers. Then next week we'll get you some clothing that fits. Does that work? Forgive me for being thoughtless."

"Nothing to forgive. I'll put them on."

He nodded and looked at the floor. "I'll turn around."

I quickly took off my too-big indoor outfit and dropped it to the floor. The underwear he'd brought me fit perfectly, and it was so nice to have brand new clothing on my body. I wondered if he peeked at me changing like I had him. The thought made me hot, and I once again had to question my sanity. I'd had Cash, Judge, and Sterling all over me. Did I have to force my attentions on Lewis when he hadn't indicated to me in any fashion he wanted me yet?

I zipped myself into the outdoor outfit. When I was done, Lewis handed me his black coat. I grinned at it, and his smile back. "Thought you might like this one. I'll use one of the ones they issued us."

"Your black coat?" I put my arms through the sleeves, and Lewis zipped me the rest of the way in.

We finished getting ready, including the facemasks. I followed him out a door of the enclosure and into the truck that was going to take us wherever we explored. The bright, direct sunlight made me squint. I had so little experience with real, direct sunlight it hurt. I had to squint against the glare from the white ground. We clomped through the snow until we got into the truck.

I guess I'd been in it before although I didn't remember the trip with Damian that brought me to the enclosure. The truck was huge, with a large section in the back which presumably could move big pieces of machinery. Lewis turned on the vehicle, and we pulled into the snow on our way to wherever Lewis had seen on his computers.

"When I was little," he finally spoke after a few minutes of driving, "they found me on the side of the street on Ochoa. My family was gone. I was two. They can't tell me where I came from; no one knows. For years, they kept me in a small house with twenty-five other boys waiting to see if anyone would adopt us. I hated being cooped up. Eventually we took the achievement tests, and I must have scored high enough to get Evander's attention. Off I went. I could move around. Go outside."

I could picture him. Small, lost, and stuck in a house too tiny for the children running around it. Finally, getting some freedom. "I guess the obvious question is, why did you pick this assignment out here in the middle of nowhere where you're stuck in an enclosure?"

"I was hoping a really smart, beautiful girl would fall out of the sky and crash land nearby. It seemed a good plan."

I laughed, throwing my head back when I did. I hadn't seen that answer coming. "Very funny."

"Turns out what I hate, more than being cooped up, is bureaucrats. Executives talking in my ears all day. When will this be done? How about you do this instead? I stopped being able to produce. Truth is, I'd be a much better physician than an engineer researching and developing medicine. They need me to do this. I do this."

He was really beautiful to look at. Facing forward to drive, he wasn't avoiding my eye contact or staring at the floor. I liked to see him so animated. "I love everyone's stories of how you got out here. How you came to be here together."

"It really comes down to a conversation I had with Damian. Drunk. Who makes plans drunk? I guess we do. He wanted to know how we could be productive, helpful, and serve Evander without the whole world breathing down our necks. I shrugged at him and finally said we could try to fix the Infected problem at the end of the universe. Next thing I know, he's making plans, and I'm signing on. That's Damian. Give him a problem. He fixes it. He thought of Judge and Sterling right off. Cash surprised us. Seemed such a golden boy. And there we all were." His eyes widened. "I've been talking too long."

"No." I shook my head. "Not long enough. Keep going. I love the sound of your low voice."

He smiled like I'd given him the biggest compliment on the planet. "Thank you."

There was white everywhere. I'd told Cash I thought the landscape looked like it needed to be colored. I was wrong. This was perfection as it was. Next time—if there was one—I'd change my opinion and let Cash know I'd altered my thoughts. Sometimes it was okay to leave things untouched.

A ringing sounded, and Lewis rolled his eyes. He pressed a large black button on the steering wheel. "Yes?"

Damian voice bounced around the vehicle. "You took out a vehicle without even telling me? Forget asking me if it's okay? You went ahead and just took it?"

He rolled his eyes. "Yep."

"Yes. Yep. That's all you're going to say. You're missing. The car's gone. I had a small heart attack."

I took his hand in mine and squeezed it. He smiled at me before he answered Damian. "Because you thought what? That I was overcome by a Zombie and then took the car out to take a drive?"

"Aren't you having your date with Diana today? When do you plan to get back? What should I tell her?"

Lewis shifted in his seat. "She can hear you. She's sitting right next to me."

"Diana?" Damian's voice rose. "Well, hello. Good morning."

"Good morning, Damian." We hit a small bump, and Lewis adjusted the gear in the truck.

"You took her out of the enclosure, and you didn't even think to let me know? I realize we are doing things differently these days. I get it. I'm adjusting. I think you have to admit I am. But there are reasons for protocols."

Lewis must have had enough. "Talk to you later, Damian."

He disconnected the call by pushing the button. "Sorry about that."

"Look at you. I had no idea you were a rebel. Taking out the truck without telling him. Why didn't you?"

He drummed his fingers on the steering wheel. "Although I have learned how to obey rules and do as I'm told by Evander, and sometimes Damian as their representative, I am not, by nature, a rule follower. Sometimes I've got to steal the car and take the pretty girl out on an adventure without telling a soul what I'm doing."

"We are having an adventure." I grinned at him. "We're going to find out what's hot in that cave."

"Yes we are." He nodded vigorously. "Then we'll go home, and I'll hear from all four of them about all the reasons I should not have risked you doing this. What's the point in life if we never have any risks? This one was calculated. No Infected. Just a warm cave."

We arrived at the cave about an hour later. By then, I knew Lewis wasn't afraid to be quiet. I'd never felt the need to fill the silence, and neither had he.

The caves on his map were huge. Lewis grabbed a flashlight, and we stepped outside. The cold hit me hard, but the clothes protected me from the onslaught. Lewis gripped my gloved hand in his. He had a bag slung over his other shoulder, and I had no idea what was in it.

When we got inside the caves, Lewis pushed a button on the flashlight. It brightened the entire area in front of us. Before the light went on, I knew there was something quite different going on. The caves were warm, almost stiflingly so.

The outdoor wear we had on made me sweat.

"What the hell?" Lewis pulled his hat and headpiece off. I followed suit.

I pointed at the water in the center of the cave. "Heat's coming from there."

A pond of blue water filled the center of the cave, and hot air shot up from it, making the whole cave feel like an enclosure from the cold outside. I wandered to the sides of the space.

Old-looking pots and discarded clothing were all over the place. They were all old.

"Lewis." I caught his attention. "I think people stayed in here. For a while. Look at this old stuff."

He came over my shoulder to look down. "You're right. There's no life signs here now. I wonder if some of the populace took shelter here after the bombs."

Lewis backed up until he was over the pond, looking down. He pulled the backpack off his shoulder and took out some equipment. I almost asked him what he was doing. Then I remembered how many times I'd had to stop to explain a plan I had to those around me when it would've been faster, more efficient, and easier if they'd simply let me do what I did.

He put on a different set of gloves and grabbed then dipped a vial into the water. After applying a lid to the vial, he started to shake it really fast. He stood back and watched it for a second. "If there was anything toxic in the water, this would turn purple."

I stepped toward him. "Are you planning on getting in it? Is it too hot? Are there creatures living in it?"

"No life signs whatsoever. I checked on them before we came. Maybe I will get in." He grinned before he looked down at the ground. "Want to swim?"

He took off his outdoor suit and threw it to the side. He only had on a pair of boxer shorts. "It's safe. It'll be like a hot tub."

"I've been to a sauna. Once. You have to be really rich to go on Mars Station. My parents don't like to show off money. It doesn't look good for the politics of it all. I ... Lewis, I don't know how to swim. There's a pool, but no one ever taught me."

He let the water run through his fingertips. "Want to know the good news about the amount of salt in this thing?"

That seemed like a completely wrong response to what I'd said. "What?"

"We're both going to float. I could teach you to swim. If we had a pool anywhere. We don't. You'll have to come off Orion with me to learn."

If we were going to float, I could get in. I pulled my clothes off. My underwear covered as much, I guessed, as a bathing suit—not that I'd ever had one on. I hadn't.

"If my skin peels off because of this pool of heat, I'm never going to forgive you."

He smirked. "We can melt together. Seriously? I bring you all the way out here; I plan this date where at any time you could run shrieking to the truck ... I must be out of my mind."

"I'm not the kind of person who shrieks. Oh, don't get me wrong. I'm plenty afraid of everything. I'm more likely to go silent."

His face fell. "I hope those days are behind you. Diana, I'm sorry; I know you hate being told what I'm about to say, but you are so ... lovely. I've never seen anyone as beautiful as you. I could look at you all day long."

"Thank you, Lewis." I let him see me admire his physique. "You're pretty spectacular yourself."

He offered me his hand, and we both got into the steaming hot water together. I laughed as I immediately bobbed up to the top, floating flat on my back. The sensation was odd but restful. Lewis held my hand tightly.

"This is odd, right?" Lewis laughed. "I mean, we're in hot water in the middle of Orion, floating, in the middle of a cave."

"I was just thinking if you'd asked me a little over a year ago if I could ever imagine such a thing as this happening to me, I would have scoffed. This is real. You're real. I'm here. This is happening."

He was silent for a minute. "If you'd asked me if there would ever come a time when the most beautiful girl I've ever seen—who also happens to know how to work tech and engineering and lived by herself in a ship while she was flung around the universe—would want to come to a cave and float with me, I'd never have believed it."

"Why not? You're smart. You're gorgeous. You have a wicked sense of humor you keep hidden. You say really incredible things. She'd be crazy not to want to." I closed my eyes.

"Because at best, I got lost and my family never found me. At worst, they didn't want to."

I didn't expect his response. I opened my lids. I couldn't roll to look at him. We were both kind of stuck where and how we floated. I didn't need to see him to hear his pain. "The thing about this side of the galaxy is you're all really preoccupied with where you came from. Your background. Like it has some kind of weight on who you should be. Where I'm from ... the head of the council my mother sits on, he was born on a cargo ship and abandoned by the door of a military institution that raised him under hellish conditions not suitable for an animal. No one would ever suggest he couldn't be whatever he wanted. There's political power and financial power. Anyone can rise to it. Anyone can fall. I don't care where you came from. I'm sorry it happened to you; it caused you pain. It would never change how I feel about you. Not for a minute."

"I want to be in your world. With you." He squeezed my fingers tighter. "Tell me about Earth."

"I hardly remember it, but what I do is that it's green. Blue. Alive. It's always in turmoil. My grandfather is important there. He recently suggested if my parents couldn't marry me off properly on Mars Station, I could come to earth and he'd do the job."

Lewis laughed softly. "Nope. You had to come to us. That's all there was to it."

"I maintain if there was another female even anywhere nearby, you'd be less enthusiastic about me."

"I'll prove it to you someday. I'm not crazy. I know how incredible you are."

Chapter Fourteen

Lewis Hurst

We got out of the pool and sat on the side together, holding hands. Somewhere in the distance, water dripped. It wasn't cold inside the cave, and I'd gotten enough of floating around. Salt made my skin tingle. My muscles were relaxed, maybe more so than they'd ever been.

Lewis leaned over and kissed my shoulder. "I don't know what you're doing with everyone else. We've made a pact not to discuss it with each other. You get to have a separate relationship with each of us. Cash read through research in the system saying that's the way it works best."

"That's pretty much how my parents and uncles manage it. There's some crossover. They all love each other's kids. They all take care of us. If my mom has a fight with Nolan, my dad stays out of it unless he absolutely has to get involved. We're a family."

He nodded, looking down at the pool. I wondered if there would ever come a time when he would hold my eye contact or if this was how it was always going to be. I didn't mind either way.

"Right. So, I'm wondering if you would be okay with us not rushing through the beginning of this. I'm hearing a lot from the guys. They're ... anxious to be physical. They want the drugs out of their system. I get it. They have to report their physical symptoms to me. It was decided I'd manage better than Cash knowing which of us can get hard, which ones can't, and when the change starts to happen. Please believe me, I want that, too. But do we need to rush? Can we enjoy the beginning? I never expected to have one. I'd like to kiss you many, many times. Share you bed because I want to hold you. Hold hands. I don't want to rush through that. Is that okay with you?"

He was so sweet my heart swelled and I couldn't hide my sigh from him. "You're incredible. I want whatever you want. I never thought ... that is, I'd hoped ... I didn't believe this would be my life. I expected eventually I'd have no choice but to get married to someone. I thought maybe I could manage one person. He wouldn't want to talk much. He wouldn't expect much of me in terms of ... emotions. I'm sure I'm bumbling this, making you all unhappy ..."

Lewis interrupted me, fast. "No, just the opposite.

"Okay," I put my hand on his arm. "Let me finish. I'm so grateful to have this time with you. I want to have our relationship however you want to have it."

He took my hand and kissed my knuckles. "Awesome, Doll. Thank you."

"Doll?" I asked him while he brought my palm to his mouth to plant a kiss there, too.

"Don't like it?" His dark eyes met my gaze.

"I do."

He pulled me against him into a hug. I closed my eyes. He didn't want to rush the physical. That was fine. I'd dream about him just the same.

"We should go back." He kissed both my cheeks. "You can't know how much today means to me. When you were first on my table, I never thought I'd keep you alive."

I breathed him in. "You did. Then you shined the light in my eye and called for Cash."

"I was scared out of my mind about you. You made me ... hope, again. That's a dangerous thing."

We dressed each other, which was awkward and funny at the same time. Eventually he zipped me into his black coat, and we walked back out into the cold Orion wind. Lewis stopped and grabbed some of the artifacts from inside. He was pretty sure Cash would want to see them.

I hopped into the truck, glad to be out of the wind. It seemed kind of dark outside, much more so than I would have expected.

"How long do you think we were in there? An hour?" Lewis stared at the clock in the truck. "This thing says it's eight o'clock at night."

"What?" No way had we been in the cave for any length of time. I couldn't see it being more than two hours at most.

He shook his head. "Let's get back quickly. Something is weird."

The leisurely drive from the compound was different than the ride back there. We made it in about half the time. A muscle ticked in Lewis' cheek. Tension radiated off him. He clicked the black button and got only static. "I think you're going to have to fix this thing. Sometimes it won't call out. Only in. We missed dinner for sure."

I wasn't hungry. It still felt like I'd only eaten breakfast a few hours earlier. Were the others going to yell at us?

I didn't have to wait long to find out. No sooner had Lewis swung open the door than the whole group descended upon us.

"Are you okay?" Judge shook while he hugged me and then passed me to Cash who touched my face before Sterling picked me up in a bear hug.

I didn't, however, touch Damian who stared down Lewis like he wanted to ring his neck. "Do you have any idea how terrified we have been? Where the hell did you go? You don't call. You don't let us know you're wherever. You take her out there and don't think we might all be worried about both of you."

My date for the day held up his hands in surrender. "Took her to the caves. We were in there for an hour. Not more. Came out; it's dark. I don't know what the fuck happened. I would never have kept her out there that long without touching base."

"Oh." Judge jumped back on his feet. "There must be a time differential in the cave. Anything else weird in there?"

"Hot springs," I answered, which brought Damian's gaze to my own. "You float."

"Sounds fucking fantastic. I thought you were both dead." He stormed from the room, slamming the door behind him when he did.

Lewis let out a long breath. "Shit. I really didn't have any idea. We were in there, and it felt like an hour."

Sterling patted his back. "Give Damian the night. You're only going to get fear tonight. You know that ..." His voice trailed off.

"I do know."

I didn't. But it couldn't be good. Judge knocked into Lewis and grinned. The others weren't angry, but Damian really, really was.

There was no game night that evening. With Damian pissed off, the others seemed to retreat to their rooms. Lewis came back with me to Artemis. We both showered, and when I came out, it was to a message from Judge beeping on my computer. I played it quickly.

"Goodnight. So glad you're okay. Hot springs and time differentials. How cool. Night, Di."

I smiled. Tomorrow I would send him a message back. My clothes were folded nicely on my dresser, and five new sets of panties and bras were with them. Sterling had taken care of things.

I lay back on my bed in my too big pajamas. They'd all been afraid, and it sounded like Damian the most so. I felt terrible about the time they must have had. Still, I couldn't regret the day. It had been utterly fantastic.

Lewis crawled into bed next to me, and I told Artemis to dim the lights. He pulled me up against him. "Feels like the middle of the day. I can't believe it's night. Yet I'm also exhausted."

"The way we could float in there. Must play with gravity, which in turn must push on the differential."

He snickered in my ear. "Talk to Judge about time stuff. Makes my head hurt."

"Are you okay?"

Lewis nodded. "This would not be the first time Damian has been really angry at me. We've known each other the longest out of anyone in here. We actually understand each other quite well. He feels responsible for all of us since he put this group together. He worries. Obsesses. I go along at a pretty good pace of listening, and then suddenly I don't. We yell at each other. Then we both get over it. This case, I can see why he'd worry. Nothing I can do. I'm not going to apologize for having the day—or morning—I wanted with you."

"I had a great time."

His fingers stroked down my arm gently. Lewis gently drifted off to sleep over the next few minutes. I was wide awake, and I couldn't sleep worrying about Damian. It might break some kind of rule, but I had to see for myself that he was okay.

I got out the bed as quietly as I could manage. When I finally put feet on the floor, Lewis let out a loud snore. I smiled. He wasn't going to wake up simply from my leaving for a few minutes. I slipped on my shoes.

As quietly as I could manage, I made my way to where the others slept. Lewis' room was first on the left. I knew where he was, so I passed on by. Sterling was next. His door was cracked open, and I saw him flat on his stomach, sleeping. I wasn't going to bother him. Judge's door was open; he had headphones on, and he waved when I walked by. I waved back but hurried to Damian's door, which was across from Cash's, currently closed. Damian wasn't in his room.

I could never find him. Where did he go?

Judge was awake. I was going to ask him to point me to Damian.

He took off his headphones when I approached. "Hi, Di. Everything okay?"

"Lewis is out cold. I feel bad leaving him, but I can't sleep until I know Damian's okay."

Judge waved his hand. "I'm sure by now he's fine. He's probably stewing in the barn, where he always is, by his office.'

I put my hands on my hips. "No one told me to look there for him. I never see him."

"Oh." He rocked back laughing. "Sorry, you had a defunct tour guide." He winked at me. "In addition to monitoring all the workings here, he takes care of the animals. Boy is busier than any of us combined."

I didn't think any of them were ever going to be accused of being lazy. "I'm sorry if I scared you today. We didn't mean to."

He lifted his eyebrows. "I don't think I've ever known worry like that. The two of you ... just gone. We couldn't find any life signs anywhere."

"I really am sorry."

He smiled. "Not your fault. It's okay. Just don't do it again."

I laughed. "Thanks. I won't."

"Welcome." He put his headphones back on, although his eyes never left me until I exited the room.

I made my way to the agricultural center. I'd not been back since Judge showed it to me. Walking in, I realized he'd only let me see a small portion of it. The barn and growing areas were huge. They probably took up the majority of the enclosure. Fake lights, which were now dimmed, must light up the area for the animals and the crops. I walked for a while, encountering horses and pigs in their enclosures. I still hadn't seen Damian.

And then, there he was. He sat on a fence, staring down at the cows beneath. He'd either not heard me or wasn't acknowledging me.

"Hey," I called out, and he jolted, nearly falling off the fence. I gasped, but he righted himself and didn't fall.

"Diana?" He jumped down and strode to me. "What's wrong?"

Damian was intense, even when he wasn't yelling. I took a deep breath. I wondered if he was ever easy, other than sleeping. "I came to say I was sorry. You must have been terribly worried. We didn't mean to be so late. Still, being afraid is awful, and I couldn't sleep thinking of you being upset."

He stopped right in front of me. "You came here because you were worried I was upset?"

"Yes." Lewis had left Damian alone, and I wondered if I'd made a terrible mistake not doing the same. Was he going to turn his temper on me now? Yell?

He raised his hand and put it on the side of my face. "No one has ever done that for me. Not even my parents. Thank you. I'm okay now. Well, sort of. I might never be okay again. I'm good for the night."

"We missed dinner." I walked past him. "So this is where you hang out. I never see you during the day."

"Ah ... yes. This is what I'm good at. I'm a farmer. I was raised on a farm. This was all I knew how to do before Evander. They made me a manager. I guess my heart is still in this. I love the animals. And seeing things grow."

I touched the fence he'd sat on. "Must run in your family."

He stood next to me. "My uncle does this, too?"

"He does. Well, not the animals. We don't have any on Mars Station. All food, except the vegetables we grow in the hydroponics bay, is shipped in. Big problem. Lots of money. Trade. Pirating. Can be a big mess."

"Wow." He rubbed his chin. "Really amazing you came here. But I have to ask, what did Lewis say when you said you were going to come here on his night? We have this set of rules, and I don't want him getting pissed off. He stews."

They'd made additional rules. I probably needed to learn them. I really might not be cut out for this. "I left him asleep. He doesn't know I'm here."

Damian snorted. "Ah, that's why you can't sleep. The snoring, huh?"

"What do you mean?" I really didn't follow.

"The guy snores bad. Give it an hour. When he's really out, it starts. We had to share a room a couple of times on previous assignments." He walked toward the back of the agricultural area. "Come with me."

Damian brought me into his office where there were video screens showing the outside of the enclosure and the rooms where the Zombies were. I guessed this was how he kept track of things. The room was small but efficient and even had a cot in the back. Did he sleep here sometimes?

He opened a drawer and handed me two small devices. "Stick them in your ears."

I'd never seen anything like the devices. "What are they?"

"Electronic ear plugs. They'll calculate the noise in the room and give you just enough blockage. You aren't going to be sleeping otherwise."

"Um, thanks." It was a little weird to be discussing Lewis' sleeping habits with Damian. "I'll see you tomorrow then?"

"Yes. Oh, there's one thing. See that beautiful horse over there? The white one? We keep horses because we're actually doing a small secondary experiment on how horses do in enclosures like this one. The answer is: well—at least if I give them room to run. Anyway, that one is pregnant. Very. I may have to come back a few times to check on her tomorrow. I know it's a day off but ..."

I touched his arm. "Can I come, too?"

"You would want to?"

"I love it in here. I've never seen anything like it. Please?"

He grinned. "Sure. I'd love that."

"Great. Goodnight, Damian."

His eyebrows rose. "Are you hungry? Do you want me to make something before you go back?"

"I'm not. Thanks, though." I'd answered my own question. He could be calm when he was awake. I simply had to face him on his own turf.

"Goodnight, Diana."

"'Night, Damian."

I hurried back to my ship. Lewis was sprawled out on my bed, and he wasn't snoring. I slipped into the covers next to him, and he rolled over, flinging his arm over me. "Assuming Damian's okay?"

"You're awake? I'm sorry. I had to make sure he was okay. He is."

Lewis kissed the back of my neck. "I woke up, and you weren't here. I took a guess. If you hadn't come back soon, I'd have come looking. You have a big heart. We all need you, Diana. Thank you."

I didn't know what to say, so I didn't answer. "Goodnight, Lewis."

An hour later, I was really glad Damian had given me the earplugs. Lewis was so sweet, and he held me like I was a lifeline in a world that made no sense. But he did snore. With the earplugs, I didn't notice at all.

I woke up when Lewis rolled over. I opened my eyes a bit. The light was bright in the hall. It must be getting up time. Lewis groaned, which woke me up more.

"Are you okay?" I took the earplugs out of my ears, set them aside, and then I touched his back.

"I feel like I've been hit by a spaceship. Sorry. I knew the exhaustion would be coming. I didn't realize how much it would hurt."

I hated that he was in pain because of me. "I'm sorry. I ..."

He patted my leg. "Whatever you're about to say, don't. I need to go through this to be with you properly. I'll do it. End of story. Don't fuss. That'll just ... piss me off."

"Okay." So he was really grumpy. I stood from the bed and made my way to the bathroom. He needed space. I would ... Lewis grabbed my arm.

"Aggression and aggravation. We might all be more negative than we would normally be. It'll pass, and then we'll get our full faculties back." He tugged me against him, and I gave him a big hug. He was hurting. I'd give him a break for his bad mood. "See? I feel better already. Thanks for last night. Did you have any, ah, trouble sleeping with me?"

I shook my head. "I have earplugs."

"Oh." He grinned. "That's good. I've been checked. There's nothing wrong with me. I just ... snore."

I kissed his cheek lightly. "There are worse things."

His dark eyes watered for a second, and then the wetness vanished. "You're so beautiful."

I hit him lightly on the shoulder. "Knock it off."

His tablet dinged, and he jumped, running toward it. "Shit on toast."

"What is it?"

He hissed his breath while he tugged on his pants. "Judge fell. Out of the rafters in the pod room. Damian has him making more space in there for storage. He's hurt."

My heart stopped. "Badly?"

"Sterling doesn't think so. They need me. Fast."

He dressed fast, and I did the same. I ran after him, and he didn't complain or tell me not to. When we got to his lab, Judge moaned on the bed, holding his knee. A bone in the bottom half of his leg stuck out. I covered my mouth to keep from screaming. Not hurt badly?

I rushed to Judge's side. "Oh, Judge. What happened?"

Sweat broke out on his forehead. "Oh, don't worry, Di. It's nothing. I fell. No big deal."

Sterling snorted. "I heard it in the gym."

"Doll, keep him calm for me, okay? Resetting a bone and helping it stitch sucks." Lewis walked over to Judge. "It just does."

"Put me in the machine." His voice shook, and I stroked my hand through his hair. "Please. Not the shot first. Nothing hurts more than the shot."

Lewis shook his head. "I'm sorry, buddy. This protects your vitals. I can put you in the machine without it but this makes it work better. I'm also going to knock you out. You'll be sour as hell when you wake. In two days." Lewis turned his attention to me. "Judge doesn't like needles. Or the machine. Put him in awake, and he screams."

Judge's eyes darkened. "No need to absolutely humiliate me in front of my girlfriend."

Lewis stuck the needle in Judge's arm, and Judge cried out but didn't otherwise react. I could see a muscle in his jaw tick. "I see I should have Diana here whenever I treat you."

Judge started to sway, and I grabbed his head. "It's working fast. I'm going to be out in a minute. That's fast. Faster than usual ..."

He slurred the last few words. Lewis and Sterling took him by his arms and carried him together to the machine. I hated being in it, too. His eyes drooped while he looked at me. "It'll be our date night when I wake up."

"I'll feed you soup."

He grinned, and then his eyes closed. Lewis closed the machine around him and turned it on. He stood over the machine watching it as it showed Judge's vitals. Lewis made some adjustments and then stood there staring at it. After a minute, he nodded his head. "He'll be fine."

Sterling exhaled loudly. "No way should Judge have been doing that alone. Crazy man."

"You know danger sometimes escapes him." Lewis turned around and grinned at me. "Thanks for your help."

I held my hands up. "I did nothing."

"He would have been so much worse without you here to show off for. Screaming. Cursing. Fighting. I'd have had to knock him out much less gently. Sterling would have held him down. Big mess."

I walked to the side and sank down in a chair. "When I got concussed on Artemis, I just got in the machine. I didn't think to set anything. I crawled inside. Shut myself in and laid there."

Lewis stormed over to me, and a second later he had the light in my eyes he'd used the first day. "When were you concussed?"

"Months and months ago." I swatted at his hand, pushing away the light. "I imagine whatever damage was done is done now."

He turned off the light. "I'm sure your medical machine did fine. It'll work in an emergency like that. In most situations. It won't solve a bite from an Infected. That's an injection protocol."

"I hope never to find out."

Sterling walked over and kissed me on top of the head. "See you tonight for dinner, and then tomorrow is our day. Don't fuss over her too much, Lewis. Diana's made of strong stuff. She's a steel backboned rose. See you later."

Lewis met my steady gaze. "Am I over fussing?"

"No." He kissed my hand. "I like your level of fuss."

I must have said the right thing because his intense gaze softened. I helped him clean up the mess of where Judge had bled, and when we were finished, he backed me into a corner. He kissed me, square on the lips, not saying another word. We stood there for minutes, not talking except where our mouths met over and over again. I melted into him. Eventually, he had to hold me up because my knees gave out. Lewis made no other moves to touch me anywhere or advance from the light kissing in the corner.

Eventually, he pulled back, breathing hard. "I kept you alive. It still amazes me. You were so close to death. Not moving in my arms when Damian passed you over to me. I put you in the machine, your pulse was thready, your breath sounds barely there. Here you are now. Kissing me. Giving something to my life I never had or expected to have. I want to know where you are all the time. I want to take your hand and rub my finger over your pulse to feel it. I do that. You don't notice. But I have to tell you. I'm checking on you. All the time."

I took his hand in mine and ran my hand over his wrist until I could feel his. "We'll check on each other."

His voice shook. "Great answer."

Chapter Fifteen

Best laid plans

It was well after nine when I left Judge asleep in Lewis' care. Although Lewis assured me Judge would sleep for a day and wouldn't know if I was there or not, I insisted on coming back whenever I could. I knew he'd do the same for me.

I hoped Damian would understand.

I rushed to Artemis, expecting him to be waiting for me but found no sign of him anywhere. Had he come and gone? Was he going to yell again?

Not knowing where else to start looking, I ran so fast to the agricultural section I was out of breath when I got there. Damian sat on the ground outside of the horse enclosure, staring into space. I didn't think it looked like he'd changed from the night before. The same black stain that had been on his left pant leg was still there.

I approached him slowly, kneeling down. "Hi."

He jumped an inch off the ground and blinked rapidly. "Diana. Hi. Oh, hell. It's morning isn't it? I missed our date. Or is it later? I've been ... I'm sorry."

I placed my hand on his arm. "Damian, what happened? Are you okay?"

At least I'd not stood him up. More concerning, however, was how out of it he seemed. His pupils were huge. Had he slept at all?

"Um." He ran his hand through his hair. "Last night that horse I was showing you? The white one? She died giving birth. There wasn't a thing I could do. One of my degrees is in veterinary medicine. Not a thing. She died all of a sudden and without any warning. So did the baby. Looks like ... she had a blood vessel burst. I've never seen it before. Could be an Orion thing. The pressure here. Two others have given birth without a problem, but that's why you need a large sample."

He stopped talking. My heart broke into a million pieces for him. It was clear he loved the animals. I pulled him against me, hugging him tightly. "I'm so sorry."

I ran my fingers up and down the wide expanse of his back. He sighed, not moving otherwise. What a night he'd had. I'm not sure how long we stayed like that, breathing together and not doing anything else.

He eventually lifted his head. "Thank you. I don't remember the last time anyone held me."

"Don't thank me for caring. That's something we can expect from each other, okay?"

His sad smile made my heart pang again. "Okay." He rubbed his eyes. "I had this whole day planned. Do you like cooking? I thought maybe we could do a whole meal together. From picking the vegetables to preparing the meal."

"I would have loved that. I have an idea instead. Why don't you let me do the cooking tonight for you? Take the night off. And you can get some sleep."

He shook his head, his brown hair falling into his eyes. He really was so gorgeous. I never stopped to admire the long angles of his face. With just the two of us sitting together, I could really see how strikingly handsome he was.

"I'm not going to sleep through our date day. No way. No how." He stood slowly, stretching his arms over his head. "I shouldn't get so attached to the animals. Every time I have to end one to make dinner it puts me in a horrible mood. I guess I thought I wouldn't have to lose the horses. Stupid."

I put my arm around his waist. "I wondered whose job that was."

"I could automate it. Let the robots Judge invented do their job. I figure I owe it to them. Left to my own devices, I'd be a vegetarian. Evander wants us eating meat. If I have to eat them, I do them the courtesy of doing it myself."

I didn't envy his role although I loved all kinds of meats. "Thank you for doing what you do for all of us. Damian, listen, I see how it is for you. Being in charge of everyone and all of their safety. Don't feel like you have to add me to that list. You didn't ask for my arrival. The last thing you need is another person to worry over."

He kissed the top of my head, and I shuddered from the warmth travelling my spine. "Too late."

I determined right there I would go out of my way to not be another burden on him. "I'm cooking dinner. You can sit and talk to me. How's that?"

"Sounds like a plan."

We held hands and strolled slowly. I wasn't going to rush anywhere with him today. He needed rest, and if he wouldn't take it, I could at least see to it he didn't do anything taxing.

"Do you mind if we stop and check on Judge?"

His eyebrows shot up. "What happened to Judge? Why does he need checking? He's doing storage inventory today."

He didn't know. I unlinked our hands, rubbing his back gently. "He took a bad fall this morning. He has to have a bone put back together. Lewis has already gotten him in the machine."

Damian abruptly stopped moving. "Shit." He rubbed his face. "I didn't even go to my tablet this morning. What the hell is wrong with me? Judge is hurt, and I'm sitting around and ..."

"Stop." I grabbed his arm. "It's done. He's in the machine. For two days. I'm being all crazy wanting to check on him. You can't do anything and couldn't have then either."

"We'll go check on him together."

Nothing had changed since I left Lewis' medical bay earlier. In fact, Lewis was nowhere to be found. He'd probably gone to help Cash. The machine ran, making a slow hum. Damian walked to it slowly. "He's out cold, right?"

"Yes."

He placed a hand on the medical machine. "Good. He hates this thing. How did he get hurt?"

"He took a fall from the storage area in the Pod room."

Damian scowled. "I'll have a talk with him when he wakes up." He narrowed his eyes and then touched a button on the machine.

"Should you be messing with that?"

"See this indicator here?" Damian showed me a bunch of squiggly lines moving up and down rapidly on the display. "That's his dream state. Judge's shows nightmares. Bad ones. I'm not surprised. He has terrible dreams. We had to make the gas they gave him during cryogenic sleep more happy, if you will. Judge gets more pleasant dreams than the rest of us in hyperspace. I just fixed it for him for a bit."

Did the others know the measures he took to keep them happy and safe?

"Do we have to start cooking right now? Could we do something with noodles that doesn't take as much time?"

He turned to look at me. "Sure. Did you want to do something else?"

"Well, I was thinking I could use a nap."

Damian smirked at me. "You could, huh?"

"Please?"

"Sure. How could I say no to you?" He took my hand again, and we walked into the hallway just in time to hear a large roar. A large pipe flew across the room, slamming into the wall a short distance from us.

Damian shoved me behind him. "Sterling? Diana, stay behind me. You losing it, brother?"

Sterling breathed loudly, his hands on his hips. His nostrils flared. "You think I would hurt her? I'd cut out my own liver first. I don't need you to stick yourself in front of Diana."

"You threw a pipe kind of close to her head. Wanna tell me what's going on?" He inched toward Sterling. "Want to talk to Lewis? We're all getting more aggressive. It's to be expected. Do I need to worry about you?"

Sterling put his hands on his knees and stuck his head between his legs. "I dropped the pipe on my foot, and it hurt. I took it out on the pipe. I'm sorry it came anywhere near you two. I'll get this under control. I always did before the US, and I will again."

Damian patted him on the back. "I know you will again. Don't throw anything else."

"Deal." Sterling raised his head and winked at me. The cool, funny Sterling returned to his eyes. "Sorry."

I crossed my arms. "Are you okay?"

"Don't be afraid of me and I'll be fine." He extended his hand. I hesitated for a second before walking toward him. I'd seen violence. Lots of it. My Uncle Nolan had been clear that the best thing I could do when it came to men who had lost their minds was to give them a wide berth. There was plenty of pain in the universe. Still, Sterling said he'd cut out his liver before he hurt me. I took his hand. "Thanks. You're not afraid of me are you?" He'd said it a number of times. It must have been really bothering him.

"I don't like that you threw a pipe. I don't believe you threw it at me. So, no. But if you start tossing things around ..."

He nodded. "Won't happen. I promise."

"Then we're good."

Sterling stood straight up and then nodded to Damian and me. Without another word he left, picking up the pipe when he went.

I wasn't sure how I felt about what had happened. I'd rushed into this with them. What did I really know about any of them? Maybe they were all tossing large objects all the time. Except I didn't think that was the case, and I didn't even believe it of Sterling. I sighed.

"Don't hold that against him. He's the most controlled person I know. That's a weird reaction from him, not the normal."

Damian's eyes pleaded with me to listen to him, and I did. "Okay. I believe you. And him, for that matter."

"Awesome." His smile was one of relief. "Hey, instead of sleep, up for something else?"

I nodded. "Are you sure you don't want to go somewhere and close the door and rest?"

"That's just what I want. Only difference is, I want my eyes open to do it." He ran a finger down the side of my cheek.

"Let's do it." He led me down the hall toward the game room.

I didn't spend any time there except after dinner. What did he have in mind? There were a number of choices. Maybe a movie?

"Okay with you if I lock the door? This is a public space. They can all come in whenever they want. I'd kind of like to be alone. Is that okay? I'll leave it unlocked if you prefer."

Damian made me want to wrap him up and hold him close all the time. "I want to be alone with you, too."

"Great." He walked to the corner and pulled out what looked like two pair of binoculars. They had a strap on the back to hold them on the head. "Have you used these yet?"

I shook my head. "Binoculars?"

"No." He handed me one. "Although I can see how you could think they were binoculars. This is a hologram device. Makes us feel like we've gone somewhere else. Programs are only ten minutes at a time. We can share an adventure. I find it really ... fun."

He'd searched for that last word, and I didn't miss the stumble. Did Damian have a lot of fun? "What should we do?"

"Put them on."

I did as he told me to. The device sucked onto my face, and at first I wanted to pull it off. Then the next thing I knew, I wasn't standing in the game room with Damian anymore. I was sitting on a beach—which I recognized from movies, I'd never been to one—and the sun was setting. Damian was right next to me.

He took my hand in his. "I think this is what it used to look like on Ochoa. At the beach. Before you were born. I like the way it feels to be here."

"Damian." I turned around looking right or left. "I can really feel this. The sun. The salt. The sand."

He pulled me against him, laying me down on his lap. "The program only works ten minutes at a time. We can only use it three times in a row. The idea is not to get addicted to being elsewhere. I don't let myself do it more than once a month. It didn't dawn on me to bring you here. Then you said relax ... and this is pretty much how I do that."

"You come here alone?"

He shrugged. "Which one of the guys do you think would want to hang out on this beach with me? We're only in here ten minutes. It'll feel like an hour or so."

"Tell me about your farm. The one you grew up on."

His eyes brightened up. "Oh, it was small as far as farms went. My father really needed to hide. The Jacksons were not welcome in many places. He'd married my mother. She was a maid in the Jackson home before the destruction. Marrying her was really not the thing, I guess. He didn't care. They found a small homestead and made a go at it. Some years it flourished.

Some years it didn't. I never knew the difference when I was little. Later, when I helped, we really did well."

"You made things grow." I could picture it—Damian as a young man discovering he had a green thumb.

"I did. The house was white with yellow shutters. My mother used to let the chickens run here, there, and everywhere. She couldn't stand to pen them up." His face fell as he spoke. "She died from the flu. The one Cash would eventually cure. My father thought it was better if I had a different future. Evander was it."

I sat until I straddled him. "I wanted to make you happy. I think I just made you sad instead."

"You didn't. We don't talk about our pasts anymore. We know each other's stories, and it's easier to simply be. I like telling it to you."

His gaze was on my lips, and I knew he was going to kiss me a second before he did. His breath was sweet, and his lips gentle. He didn't push, he didn't force, just gave me the kindest affection. Eventually his hand found the back of my head, and he drew me closer. I wrapped my arms around his neck and held on.

"Diana." my name was so soft I barely heard it, yet it moved through me like a warm bath. I rocked against him, knowing what I needed even though I'd never had it, not like this anyway.

Damian moaned against my lips and drew me tighter. His hips jolted against me. That was when I felt it.

I pulled back and stared at him. Damian was hard. His gaze was lazy while he regarded me.

"Damian?" I didn't know how to ask him what I needed to know.

He sucked in a breath. "I don't know if it's only in here or if I'm hard out there in the real world too. Come here, Diana."

I was soon back in the same position I'd been in before. He kissed me, hard, possessing me, and I really wanted him to.

He laid me back on the sand, coming over me. We were both still fully dressed. His hands travelled my body while he kissed me, sometimes gently, sometimes not. Every so often his hard cock would push against my core, and I'd moan at the same time he would sigh. Or vice versa. We weren't in the real world, yet it felt pretty damn accurate to me.

Pressure built inside of me. I knew what was going to happen from the other times. This time I hadn't even taken off my clothes. I squirmed, wanting him to be inside me when it happened. Damian made no moves to take off either of our clothes. I could see the muscles in his neck were strained.

"Damian, I'm going to ..." I never got the words out while I shattered beneath him. Damian cried out my name, coming hard. He said my name over and over again until he finished.

He pulled me against him, rolling us both until he was flat on his back on the sand with me sprawled over him.

Tears were in my eyes, and he wiped them away. "What's the matter? Are you okay?"

"I wish it was real." I kissed his neck where I could reach. "I wish we could be like this in real life."

He held me closer. "Me too."

The program exited, and I nearly fell over coming back into the real world. Damian grabbed me, shoving the glasses off both of us and onto the floor. He tugged me to him. Flat against him, I could feel the unbelievable. He was still hard. And we weren't in the program anymore.

"Damian?" I ran my hand down his chest and abdomen until I cupped him on the outside of his pants. "Is this okay?"

His eyes were huge, and he touched his forehead to my own. "I ... yes. There's no obligation though. Just because I can doesn't mean you have to."

I unzipped his pants, letting them fall to the floor. Through his boxer shorts, I found his hard cock. It was thick and throbbing in my hand. He moaned, loudly. Unlike in the holo state, he sounded almost pained.

"This okay?"

His hands shook on my back, and his eyes closed. He didn't answer me. I was nearly overwhelmed with wanting him. Only this moment wasn't about me. It was about him. I was hot, and my insides pooled. This was giving me pleasure, too.

I helped him get to the couch. With a long stroke, I embraced him, balls to tip. He sucked in a long gasp of air.

"Diana." His hands tangled in my hair. I hurried. Up and down, up and down. Finally, I covered his tip, using my other hand to continue the pace. I don't know how I knew what to do. His moans and jerks told me all I needed to know about what felt good and what didn't.

With a long groan, he emptied himself against my hand. His head was thrown back, and my name was on his lips. I didn't move and neither did he. I was in no hurry. Eventually he softened, and a few seconds later, his eyes opened.

I thought he might say something, only he didn't. He grabbed me and kissed me over and over again. There were tears on his cheeks and soon on my own as well.

He laid me back on the couch, holding me tightly.

"Diana." My name sounded strange on his lips. I raised my head to see that his eyes were mostly closed. "Wow. I ... Give me a minute. I know how ..."

I covered his eyes with my hand, closing his lids. "Sleep. That's all I want from you right now."

He didn't fight it. It took only a minute at most, and then Damian was out cold. I didn't dare move. I wasn't tired and, much as I loved giving him pleasure, I had been left wanting with nothing to do for release.

Damian whispered my name, only he wasn't awake. He was dreaming of me. I smiled. Well, I had just brought him his first release outside of a US machine in years. I didn't mind thinking it earned me a little dreamtime.

Finally, I had to move. I got off him as gently as I could and wandered over to the door. I quietly unlocked it. He wasn't in any condition to make dinner. I'd have to do it for him. My culinary expertise was slim to none. Still, I could do scrambled eggs and hope none of them minded breakfast for dinner. Toast I could also manage and some juice.

Although it took me a few minutes to find everything I needed, I soon had everything set up. I hummed to myself. This wasn't a perfect situation, but it was close. I couldn't focus on the future. My family would come. I'd have to figure out what to do about things then. For now, I'd been to the beach and made Damian really, really happy on a day when he'd started out so upset he'd lost track of time.

Strong arms came around me, pulling me against his chest. Damian kissed my neck. "Good call on the eggs."

"Thanks." I giggled. He kissed me over and over. My cheek. My neck. The top of my shoulder. "How are you doing?"

"Nearly perfect—except I woke up without you. There aren't words, Diana. You're mine, okay? I know I have to share you. I'm good with it. But you belong to me and vice versa. Whatever happens with them, it happens. I'll always be here." He flipped me around, turning off the stove. "Okay?"

I kissed his lips. "More than okay."

"Tonight. I am going to make you feel so good. I promise."

"I'm not worried."

Damian took the spoon from my hand. "Move. My stove."

I scooted over and watched him make the eggs much more complicated than I would have. Spices went into the eggs. He quickly chopped vegetables and then added them, too. The meal became the most sophisticated scrambled eggs I'd ever seen.

We were only five that evening. Judge's absence at the table seemed acute to me. Every so often, one of my guys would look at Judge's empty space. Damian was the most animated I'd ever seen him. He told jokes and smiled at Sterling's story about locking himself out of the weapon locker temporarily.

Cash set down his fork. "Are you okay? Are you on something?"

"I'm on Diana. I had my date today. Big high." He winked at me.

Lewis raised his eyebrows. "I can attest to the high."

"I'm not disagreeing." Cash nodded. "Only you seem really ... different."

Sterling shrugged. "We should all be so lucky to be happy like that."

My cheeks must have been a tomato. I excused myself after dinner and made my way in to see Judge. His dream bars weren't good again. I hit the button to fix them and relaxed when I saw them move into the positive direction.

After a bit, Lewis stood next to me. "I can't permanently fix the dreams. It's too much happy juice, and it messes with the healing. But a few taps during the day is fine. Thanks for doing that." He paused and then finished. "Anything you want to tell me?"

It wasn't my story to tell. "No."

He nodded. "All right then."

If Damian wanted to share, then it was his right to do so, I guessed. It was weird to think Lewis was going to have a running tab of who was back to fully functioning and when. Hopefully that would be the last time we ever had to discuss who did what with me.

The activity that night was a movie. A drama Damian chose that had to do with a boy, his dog, and losing his father before finding him again. I leaned against Damian, and he stroked my arm gently with the tips of his fingertips. He was warm. I closed my eyes. The movie and the room faded away.

"Diana?" Damian's soft voice woke me. I blinked, trying to make sense of where we were. The others had left. We were alone in the game room. "I guess boy adventure movies knock you out."

I nestled my face into his chest. "Sorry."

"Don't be." Damian scooped me up. "I get to be all hero-like and carry you back to Artemis."

Why had I thought he was dangerous? He was ... soft inside.

Chapter Sixteen

Damian Osborne

Damian set me on my bed on Artemis then covered me with his body. I loved the weight of him on top of me. "Tired?"

I shook my head. "I had a nap."

"We're keeping you up all night. That's why you're conking out during game night. I'm not about to change that. Just pointing it out."

I wrapped my arms around his neck. "I'm not complaining."

"Diana." His voice was low. "Can I make you feel good? Please?"

I stroked my hand down his face. "You never have to ask me that. But I'd like to make you feel good, too. Now that you, ah, get hard, we can do all sorts of things, right?"

He raised his dark eyebrows. "We can. Anything you want. That's what I want. More than anything. To give you what you want. To make you feel amazing, to show you in every way I can what being here with you like this means to me."

His words moved through me, bringing tears to my eyes. Damian was so sweet. "You do already."

He shook his head. "No, not enough. I scared you. Twice. First, I busted into your ship and yelled at you. Second, I didn't tell you I hadn't contacted Evander about you. I get caught up in things. I don't think about feelings. I ..."

I placed my hand over his mouth. "The first time, you thought I was a spy here to steal what Cash was doing. That was your job. Second, I don't think any of us could have anticipated we'd end up like this. You didn't know me. It wasn't your job to let me know your plans."

"You're wrong." He scooted up a bit and pulled my shirt over my head. "I did imagine this. Well, maybe not the sharing bit. That's fine, though. I like the thought of the others protecting you with the same fervor I would. The moment I stopped thinking of you as an enemy, maybe three minutes after I saw you, I knew I would want to be here. I knew you. Instantly. I knew your heart."

I leaned over to kiss his neck. He shuddered. "Damian, you stormed out of the dining room. You were really pissed that I grew up in a family with Cooper. Don't romanticize how you felt about me. It's okay."

"Diana," he whispered my name. "You scared the shit out of me. How would I ever keep such a tiny bundle of perfection safe? Easier to be mad at you. You don't remember our ride from your ship here. That's a good thing. You were in so much pain. I held you up against me. And I knew if I'd been responsible for killing you, I'd never be okay."

He kissed me then. Slowly. With his body right over mine, I could feel his hardening length against my stomach. Damian made no move to speed up what we were doing. We kissed, his body on top of mine. I lost any sense of time. There was only Damian and the heat he generated. Eventually, he moaned against my mouth, his hips jerking.

His eyes were slits when he pulled back. He didn't stop kissing me, just changed where he did it. My neck, my cheeks, eventually moving down to take my breast in his mouth. I gasped, my hips pushing against him. Damian moaned and bit down on my nipple.

My whole body was on fire. His hand reached out, massaging the other breast while he feverishly sucked on my nipple. My heart raced. I couldn't get enough. I grabbed onto the back of his neck.

Our bodies rubbed against each other, and it was different than when we'd been in the holo machine. I gripped his shirt, and he pulled it over his head. Under his clothes, I had no sense of how built Damian was. His chest was a wall of muscles. I stroked his chest, and he moaned, this time louder. His hip movements were faster, and I moved to try to match him when I could. I was so wet, so hot, and I wanted ... .something.

Damian slipped my pants down my body. He ran his hands from the top of thighs to my calves, his eyes following where his hands went. "I know you hate to be called beautiful. Can you see how I feel about you? Can you tell?"

My breathing kicked up. His eyes caressed me in a way his words never could. I reached out, touching the tip of his cock through his pants. He closed his eyes, his nostrils flaring. "I have little control yet. You touch me, and I want to instantly explode. I'm not ready to be inside of you yet. Not until I'm sure I can make it good for you."

I didn't care about how good it was or wasn't. If he wanted the connection, I'd be happy to do with him what I'd never done before. "I ..."

He shook his head, interrupting me. "I need that. I have to know I can make it good for you. I can't yet. Not like that. Doesn't mean I don't have other ... things I can do."

Damian pulled off my panties, removing the rest of his clothes after. I had no idea what he meant to do if we weren't going to be actually having sex. He must have seen the confusion on my face. "I want us skin to skin. I crave it. Please."

I lifted my head until I could kiss right above his heart. "You never have to say please with me. Ever."

He kissed me fast before he moved down to my pussy. I had no idea if he'd even heard me. He was focused, and he needed me. That much I could tell. I felt the same way, too, although Damian seemed a man possessed.

Right before his tongue found my clit, he breathed me in, moaning when he did so. I closed my eyes and tried to just feel. I had to get out of my own head. Soon, I had no choice. His intensity made him thorough. My hands gripped the bed when he found the perfect rhythm, making my clit throb.

"Damian," I cried out his name. "Yes. Like that. Don't stop. Please."

He groaned, his hands digging into my hips. As I'd asked, he stayed right where he was, not stopping the rhythm he'd found that really did it for me. I was going to explode. Shatter. I might never be put back together again.

I opened my eyes, and the sight of him so completely taken with pleasuring me set me off. I came. Hard. Again and again. I couldn't breathe. Couldn't think. Damian cried out my name, his seed covering the bottom of the bed. He panted, moving back to where he'd been before when he'd covered me. He kissed my cheeks, over and over.

He sighed against my mouth. "Your pleasure is my pleasure. Okay?"

I held him against me. Damian had gotten into his position in life because he was good at taking care of people. Being who he was, he always did it without fanfare or expecting anyone to notice. He needed me to *know*.

I stroked his back softly. "More than okay. Thank you."

He sucked in his breath. "Sweet, sweet Diana."

Neither of us was asleep; even as time passed we stayed awake, not moving. "Can I ask you a question?"

"Always." He leaned up on his elbow.

I stroked his forehead. "When I watched you from the ship, before you came, you always carried two guns. Why two when Sterling only had one?"

"Truth is, Sterling only carries a gun at all because I insist. There isn't an enemy out there that Sterling couldn't disarm with his hands. Scary as that is, please don't be afraid of him. Today's incident aside, you'll never find a less violent person that Sterling. I carry two guns because I believe in an abundance of caution. What if one jammed? How would I keep everyone safe from the Infected?"

I pushed away the image of Sterling taking down the Infected with his hands. What if he got bitten? By contrast, I understood Damian. I'd want two guns, too.

"My turn." He didn't say please, which I liked. I wondered if I'd only see him in that state when he was really turned on. I by no means minded giving him whatever he needed, whenever he needed it. However, I really hoped he didn't walk around feeling like he should have to ask for what he should simply expect to have all the time.

I kissed his shoulder. "Absolutely."

"How long did you watch us?"

"Every morning."

His eyes widened. "I never knew that. Or if I did, I forgot. You were going to stay there alone and never come over? If your fire alarm hadn't triggered our alert computer, I would never have known you. You'd still be there by yourself, and I'd be all alone without my Diana."

"I'm glad with how things turned out. I'll always be grateful you broke down my door."

He sighed and rolled off me. We readjusted until he spooned behind me. "Tell me something about you I don't know."

"Wow. Suddenly I can't come up with a single thing about myself."

My brain had gone completely blank. I'd never been good at discussing myself, but this was ridiculous.

"Did you go to school with other kids? When you were young?"

"Oh, that's an easy one. I did. On the station. There was a school. For a while, Uncle Cooper actually taught the class. Then a teacher moved to the station, and he went back to doing what he preferred. It depended on how many kids lived on the station at a time. There were regulars, like my one friend, Paloma. Others came and went. I think we had several hundred kids at one time."

His eyes were closed, and he breathed on my shoulder. He wasn't asleep, unless he'd suddenly fallen asleep with a smile on his mouth. "You?"

"Just me. My mother taught me. Until I went to Evander. Then we went to school based on aptitude and future abilities."

That sounded dull to me. I'd enjoyed hearing what the others were interested in, even if all I did was listen. "So then we wouldn't have been in class together. No one would ever have me manage people."

"I think you did a great job at it when we decided to all give this a go. Tell me something else."

I stroked his arm hair. "Ask me a question. I don't know what to say."

"Tell me about your family."

"That's a lot of stuff to talk about. Could go on all night."

He kissed my shoulder again. "Okay."

"Damian, I think you need to sleep."

His fingers held my own. "I do. Only I want to fall asleep hearing you talk. Is that okay? Please."

"Yes, of course." I already knew there would never be a time when he said please and I didn't give him whatever he wanted.

So I talked. I told him about my mother, how she was the center of the universe. Or at least I'd always thought so. Damian made a sound in his throat when I said that but didn't otherwise comment. I talked about my father and the way he quietly held us all together. I talked about Dane and how he hadn't smiled a lot when I was young because he was so guilt-ridden over things he had done when he worked for the Nobles. These days he did. He wasn't *not* haunted; he managed it better. By the time I got to C.J., Damian breathed steadily against my back, out cold.

It was just as well. That was a lot of speaking all at once for me. I closed my eyes.

A loud alarm woke me from a deep sleep. I jolted upwards, and Damian cursed. He grabbed my arm. "Don't be afraid. It's the drone alarm. They don't care. Day or night. Evander sent supplies."

My heart raced, and Damian jumped out of bed, pulling on his pants. "I've got to meet him. The machine will want my current report, and it'll take a picture of all of us, showing Evander we're still alive. I'm going to have to account for Judge. Shit. Shit. Shit." His eyes widened. "Diana, you stay in this ship. Don't move. Don't come out. If the robot sees you, I won't be able to stop them from wanting to come back for you."

"Am I safe in the ship?"

He nodded. "Yes. Even if the robot wants to see this room—and I doubt it will—they won't know you're in here. If they take a picture of the ship, I'll tell them I found it and brought it in to examine it. Stay here. This could go on a long time. Sometimes it does. If I can't come back, I'll send someone with food."

"Then I'll go back to sleep. I won't go anywhere."

His eyes lightened up. "Perfection, love. Perfection."

Damian took off running. A few minutes later, the alarm stopped. Presumably my five were handling the drone and the new supplies. I rolled over. The bed smelled like Damian. It would until I changed the sheets in the morning. I breathed him in. My body tingled. I wanted him. Hell, I wanted all of them. So far, only Damian could actually preform, and he wasn't ready. That was fine.

I'd dream about it.

I made myself fall asleep.

In my dream, I walked through a city I'd never seen before. Buildings that touched the sky were all around me. I felt even smaller than I usually did. I was in a hurry, although I didn't know where I was going.

My mother appeared before me. She crooked her finger and ran around the corner. I ran to keep up, but by the time I got there, she was gone. Instead of the unknown city, all I could see was a field of grass. A gravestone appeared in the center of the field, and a cold wind blew around me. I shivered and approached to read the inscription.

Diana Mallory—died alone on Orion.

I gasped and covered my mouth. No, I wasn't going to die alone on this place. Judge walked up next to me. He shook his head. "You didn't think we could stay here forever, did you?"

I rounded on him. How dare he be so flippant when I was dead in that grave? He was older than he was now. A small beard covered his face, and lines were next to his eyes. A wedding ring donned his left hand. "I had to go home to Evander. You were right. I didn't choose you. When Cash solved the Infected problem, we were all heroes. I've got a wife and kids now. I'm sorry you ended up here alone."

"Judge," I cried, but he was gone. In his place was Sterling. He wore a military uniform. His eyes were distant.

"Death isn't so bad. I did it long before you. Shot right in the head. I never saw it coming. I am sorry you were left alone. I had no choice. I always planned to come back. But then there were wars to fight and battles to win. I'm sorry, Diana."

I wiped at the tears coming down my eyes. I didn't want to see anymore. I didn't ...

Sterling morphed into Cash. He had the most beautiful woman I'd ever seen holding his arms. "Celebrities don't travel to Orion. I really thought one of the others would."

Lewis walked up next to me. "I meant to come back. I just ... didn't. Life moves on, right? And you thought your family was coming. I assumed they would. You died here? What a mess. Sorry."

There was just one person left to break my heart. Damian stood next to my right shoulder. The others were gone. It was just the two of us staring at my grave.

He was dressed to perfection, an expensive suit. Like the others, he was older. His eyes were cold. "Truth of the matter is, Evander doesn't make mistakes. I'm royalty. Unlike Cooper, I have no plans of not being man enough to lead. They need me. I'm there. No one ever cared about you, Diana. Your family left you here, and while you were a great diversion during the time we were stuck on Orion, when real life called, I had better things to do."

I cried out, sitting up in the bed, sobs wracking me.

"Hey, hey." Damian's arms came around me. He was still dressed and sitting on the edge of the bed like he was going to take off his shoes and get back in. "What's the matter?"

I sobbed, and I couldn't stop it. I hadn't been dreaming much since I'd come to stay with them. This nightmare must have been a long time coming. Abandonment had always been an issue for me. The first time I'd quit talking had been after my mother got back from being abducted by the psycho queen's army. She'd gotten back, and I'd quit speaking.

My voice was still working. "I had a terrible dream. Lots of issues showing themselves for the first time in a while."

He lay down. "The drone is gone. Sorry it took a couple of hours. Still night though. What was the dream?"

"I was standing over my grave. I'd died here alone. You all went back to your real lives. Had some choice things to say to me about why. My family never came. I died here alone."

Damian's eyes were serious, and a tic showed in his jaw. "The only way I'd leave you here alone would be if I died. You and me, Diana. The others would say exactly the same thing." He touched where his heart was and then did the same where mine pounded.

"You were running Evander. Or something. You told me no one cared about me, not really. That's why everyone left."

"Ouch." He pulled me to him, sticking my head against his chest. "That's my heart. It beats for you. I know it's too fast for me to be so attached. I can't help it. When I commit, that's what I do. You're mine. Close your eyes and sleep knowing that. Okay? Please?"

I would never deny the "please."

When I woke up later, I was alone. Had I dreamed Damian coming back? I didn't think so. A knock on the door caught my attention, and Sterling walked in slowly. "Hey, sleepyhead. It's finally my day. It's almost nine, and I want to ..."

"No." Damian rushed through the door. "8:58. You said nine. I get two more minutes. Sorry I left. I ran to get you breakfast." He handed me a protein bar. "Eat this." Damian leaned down and kissed me. "Remember what I told you."

Sterling rolled his eyes. "I swear I would have fed her. Diana will never starve when she's with me."

Damian patted him on the arm. "I know." He pulled out another bar. "Brought you one, too."

Sterling nodded at Damian and sat down on the side of my bed while Damian left. He took a bite of the protein bar, and I did the same. This was weird. I'd never woken up to any of them before. I was really groggy.

He kissed my forehead. "You okay? Did you get back to sleep after the alarm?"

"I did. I just had a bad dream, and it shook me. I'm not usually this out of it in the morning. Sorry. I'll get up. Give me ten minutes. I'll shower."

His eyebrows furrowed. "Absolutely. Take all the time you need."

I quickly got into the hot water and let it soothe away the memory of the dream. I'd had such a great time with Damian.

Why had the monsters of my psyche chosen then to raise their ugly tentacles and strike at me?

"Hey, sweet baby." Sterling called into the bathroom. He must be by the door. I was totally covered; he couldn't see me. Still, the nickname made me blush. I really liked it. "What was the nightmare about?"

The separation from being in the shower made me feel brave. Telling Damian had been one thing—we'd been naked together. Sterling and I had made out once and the result had been the relationships I was in now. We'd not been together since.

I touched the shower door and told him. Everything. Including what he had said and how he died.

I heard him walk into the bathroom. He touched the door with a thump. "The only battles I fight anymore are personal ones. For myself and for those I love. I'd kill for anyone here. You'll never be alone on Orion, not as long as there is breath in my body. And no one shoots me in the head."

"Hand me a towel."

He passed it over the top, and I wrapped it around myself after I turned off the water. "Thanks."

"You're welcome."

I stepped out of the shower, and he backed up to let me. "You couldn't stop a bullet. Not from a sniper rifle. They could shoot you in the head. You're not bullet proof."

He bent forward, pressing his forehead to mine. "When they made me, in the lab, they gave me skills. Spliced genes until they had the perfect soldier. I've been shot at many, many times. Even from snipers." He tugged on his ear. "I know this makes no sense to others. I can hear the bullet. I can see it. I move. They could kill me. It would have to be a decision I made to sacrifice myself for others. That's in my DNA too. The need to save someone before myself. That's why I make damn sure I'm only around those I'd be okay dying for. You are in there. The guys here, they are too. I'm not alone in that. You've spent enough time with the others now. They've got the gene too. Even if they weren't created to have it."

I don't know why I put my arms around his neck. I only knew that what he said made me sad. I didn't want him hearing bullets because I preferred he never see one again. He lifted me up. "Come on. Let's get you dressed. I want my day with you. Unless you need to sleep. I get that. I'll stay here and not bother you."

"I'm feeling much better."

He lightly spanked my rear end, and I squealed. "Good. Because it's a happy day."

I quickly dressed and met him outside the ship. We walked hand in hand to Lewis' lab without my even having to suggest it. Lewis looked up when we entered and nodded. Cash stood next to him, frowning at something on a screen.

"Hey, Boo." He grinned at me and blew me a kiss.

"Doll, Sterling." Lewis acknowledged us both and then yawned. "Like our wakeup call? Those drones have no sense of things. At least wait to enter the atmosphere until morning."

I walked to Judge's machine. His brain waves showed happy dreams. That was good. I raised an eyebrow. "Lewis? Did you fix him?"

"No, Cash did. When he came in."

They took care of each other. They'd done it before I arrived, and they'd do it if I ever left. I wasn't certain my family was coming for me anymore. The likelihood was small. I didn't know why I was finally willing to accept that fact, but I was.

Sterling kissed my cheek. "Happy day, remember?"

"Happy day." It would be.

Chapter Sixteen

His Special Glitch

To say I was surprised when I ended up holding a rifle and pointing it at a target would be an understatement.

"This isn't our date, but I'll feel better when I know you can defend yourself. In the ten seconds it takes me to get to you, I want to be sure you can put down some motherfucker who would do you harm."

I blushed at his words. When Sterling said them, they didn't sound like swearing. He meant them. Whoever came after me was a person who would do harm to their own mother.

"Who's going to come here that I'll need to shoot?" I'd be glad to shoot anyone who came from Evander to cause my five harm. "Something come with the drone that concerned you?"

He shook his head. "No. News was fairly routine. They took one of Damian's horses to see if what he said was true. Photographed us, the robot did. Took readings on Judge. Damian doesn't think they'll make a fuss. Judge broke his leg doing work. It happens. The computer will show he's healing. Even if his hormone levels are off—and they are indicated as such on the medical machine—they'll assume that Lewis will stick him in the US when he gets out. The one surprise was good old Archie—the man technically responsible for my existence since he authorized the program—stepped down and was replaced by a guy called Franco Maxwell. I know the man. Not a fan. It doesn't matter. We make no issues out here, and we have the potential to make him a lot of money." He pointed at the target. "You're all lined up." He'd showed me how earlier. "Point and shoot."

I rolled my eyes. In ten seconds I'd hit the target twice in the center. "That's easy. Move it back or get it shifting around so I don't know where it's going. Otherwise don't bore me with baby steps."

His mouth hung open. I'd quoted my father. That was what he said when someone drove him crazy. I wasn't really annoyed. It was fun to play with Sterling, though. I suspected that few did.

"How did you do that? You know how to shoot?"

I leaned against the barrier separating us from the target. "I'm the daughter of a bomb maker. My uncle Nolan is in charge of station security, and my mom calls my uncle C.J. the spymaster. He's the one who shot Olivia Jackson in the head, by the way. I don't know if that fact made it through history. You think I don't know how to wield a weapon? I was nine when they taught me how."

Sterling walked up next to me, standing shoulder-to-shoulder. He pushed a button, and the targets changed. They moved and jumped, much harder to shoot. "Go."

We spent forty-five minutes shooting the moving targets and avoiding hitting the civilians. He was better than me—I'd known he would be—but I didn't stink, and at the end of the circuit, he grinned like he'd had a great time.

"Not bad, Diana. I had no idea. I won't worry about you defending yourself. I'll be more concerned about you taking me down."

I unloaded the weapon and brought it back to the weapons locker. Sterling did the same.

"You know, I once spent days hiding from the Sanders Cartel with my brothers who were six, four, and two. They never found us."

He frowned. "That's impressive. I'm sorry you had to go through that. Happy you made it through. Sanders Cartel is the group that drove you into the black hole, right? They're bad news."

"Exactly. They want Mars Station. I've never really understood why. I don't think anyone knows except Brent Sanders himself. It's endless." I took a deep breath. Had they managed to take it this time? Had they killed my family? I shook my head. I might never know. Better not to obsess, which was of course, easier said than done. "Think you could find me? If I hid?"

He grinned, which quickly became a smirk. "Absolutely. No question. Right away."

Sterling was filled with talent, had been bred to be the best soldier. I didn't even begin to know all the things he could do. Damian had said Sterling could take out enemies with his bare hands. He didn't, however, know what a damn good hider I was.

"If you were going to take this place, how long would it take you to get in? From detection to through the door?"

"Hmm." He rubbed his chin. "I've run this scenario in my head. I'm fairly certain that a trained person like me wouldn't be detected until seconds before the door came down. Let's say, for the sake of time, it took a minute to get through. I'd be to Lewis' office in two. Three if I had to stop to get rid of someone in the meantime."

"Fair enough." I'd hoped for five but three would do. "Give me three minutes. Come and find me."

His voice was low. "Are we playing hide and seek today?"

"Nervous?"

He brought my hand to his lips. "Not in the least. Three minutes. Okay. I'll have you captured in five. Are you going to scream when I find you?"

"Are you going to tickle me?" I'd never flirted exactly this way before. It was different than the others. The more I challenged him, the more Sterling's color heightened. He liked it.

"Done. Then I'll take you to start our real date. Shooting the gun doesn't count."

I put my lips on his arm, feeling his muscles beneath them. "You looked really hot doing it."

He jolted, and I grinned. "Go stand by the entrance where Lewis takes out the garbage. Five minutes. I'll expect you."

"All right. I'll start the five minute countdown in thirty seconds, when I reach the front."

He turned his back, and I checked the time on the wall. Thirty seconds. I moved—fast. I wasn't sure where I was going. This was meant to be fun. I had no doubt he'd find me. Quickly, I slipped into the pod room and climbed inside one of them. I knew Judge's, not the others. I had no idea which one had been Sterling's. It didn't matter. I closed it and shut the lid. I was sure he could hear people breathing. With his super-hearing, he made out flying bullets. My heartbeat would offer no trouble. Although the pod was titanium, it flew through space. It might offer some shielding.

I supposed I should be lucky we'd never had to face Sterling's brand of super-soldiers when we'd been hiding.

The pod was small, but then the guys were not awake during any of the time they'd spent in it. In the event of an Infected problem, they'd be sent home in this thing while it travelled through space. They wouldn't be awake then, either. Gassed and kept asleep until they landed in Evander Corporation headquarters. There wasn't a thing inside of it to look at. I saw where it would monitor their vitals, where it would even collect urine and other bodily functions.

This would keep them alive.

Five minutes came and went. Sterling didn't come. I'd stumped him for that long at least. I grinned and then quit when Sterling entered the room. He stopped and listened, obviously searching for a sound, a breath, a heartbeat which would tell him I was there. I kept still. I might scream when he found me because it would be fun.

He turned and left the room. Huh. I hadn't expected that.

I'd really not anticipated still being in the damn thing an hour later when he hadn't located me.

A voice came over the loudspeaker, the first time I'd heard the speakers used. They communicated using their tablets and face-to-face. I didn't have a tablet, so he couldn't reach me that way.

"Diana, this is Cash." He sounded put out, not afraid or angry. "Sterling is in a panic. You've won. Can you come out and show him you haven't been abducted or died? He's simply not infallible, and he misjudged how well-trained in stealthy hiding you actually are."

I pushed a button and released the lid off the pod. I'd no sooner walked into the center of the room than a pale Sterling appeared. "Oh, thank the universe you have a pulse. I've been listening everywhere for it." He gripped my arms tightly but not so much they hurt. "Where have you been?"

I pointed at the pod, and his eyes got wide. "I can't hear in there? Shit. I didn't know."

He tugged me upward, and I wrapped my arms around his body. "I thought you'd find me right away. I was just playing. I didn't mean for you to get scared."

"It's always important to know where we're weak. I'll know that the pods are a point I need to pay close attention to in the event of an invasion. You're okay. That's what matters."

He closed his eyes. Okay, this had gotten way out of hand. I didn't want to frighten him, not even a little bit. "I've been away from you too long. It's been a whole hour."

"Sixty-two minutes." He didn't open his lids.

I wondered what he was doing. "What are you doing?"

"Bringing my heartrate back to normal. Helps me to control my adrenaline. I'm in charge, most of the time, of what my body does."

I kissed his cheek. "Want to do something else?"

"Yes." Not putting me down, he opened his eyes and walked with me in his arms toward his bedroom. We passed Cash, who waved at us while he sipped coffee in the hall.

"Glad you found her. This boy has been up in arms. He was going to lose his mind. I went ahead and paged you." Cash touched my leg while he passed. "I get it. I'd have been a wreck too. Don't be so excellent at disappearing."

A few minutes later, I plopped down on Sterling's bed. The room smelled like soap—he must have just cleaned it—and his bed was perfectly made, hotel corners and all. He had nothing on the wall except a mirror, and his bookshelf was filled with art supplies. His desk had folders filled with paper. Other than that, Sterling's room was bare.

"Can you sit still?"

His question startled me. "Maybe. What did you have in mind?"

"I had a different date in mind. I was going to use the holo machine and take you skiing. But I think I've had enough adrenaline for now. Painting, sketching, they calm me. I've been trying to get you down on paper since you got here. It's been a disaster. I can't do you justice. You're too beautiful."

I sat forward. "You're an artist?"

"Not supposed to be. But I enjoy it. They don't give us artistic tendencies when they make us in the lab. I'm ..." He raised his gaze to mine. "Glitchy."

I reached forward, and he took my hand. "Can I see?"

"Sure." He took out one of the folders. It took me a minute to realize that the person who stared back at me was myself. Not because Sterling didn't do a good job in his rendering but because I'd never looked so good in my whole life. The picture on top had me wearing a sweater that was too big on me. It was a charcoal drawing. My hair was long and down around my shoulders in waves. The sweater looked warm. He hadn't shown me from the bottom down, so only face in profile and the sweater showed. I had one arm raised, like I was about to touch my face when he caught me in the pose.

"See?" He sighed. "It's not right. I can't get it. You're much more beautiful than this."

It took me a second to respond. "Sterling, I've never been this lovely. You have made me way too pretty."

He kissed my cheek. "You can't see yourself. I figured that out really quickly about you. You don't know. I do."

I flipped the page. This time I was in a long dress. The picture was also in charcoal. I was laughing, my head thrown back, looking at someone outside the picture. The dress was sleeveless with an intricate design around the bottom. I had a necklace with five rings on it around my neck. My lips looked darker and my hair less long than in the picture before it.

"What color is the dress in this one?"

He stayed silent, and I wasn't sure he was going to answer. Finally, he did. "If I were to do this one in watercolor, you'd be wearing white."

I held his gaze. "A wedding dress?"

"It's stupid. I know. A long way off but ..." I touched his arm, and he stopped.

"I think it's beautiful. I never thought to get married unless it was political. You. And the others. You've made me feel like life is possible for me."

He tugged my mouth to his. "You do the same for me. You make me feel ... .like there might be a reason I exist beyond being someone's killing force. You make me feel like *life* is possible, too."

I kissed him, hard. "Of course there is a reason for you to be here other than killing. You are smart, sensitive, kind, funny, gorgeous, strong, protective ..."

His mouth pressed to mine, taking back control of the kiss and stopping me from continuing. He laid me back on the bed, coming on top of me. His hand travelled my body, and he found my breast. He squeezed it through my shirt, and I moaned.

Sterling didn't stop kissing me, and I could barely come up for air. I didn't mind. Who needed to breathe? There was such power in Sterling. I could feel it in the way he restrained himself.

His hips moved, and I felt his erection. He moaned against my mouth. "Don't worry about it. Started the night after our first encounter where nothing happened the way I wanted it to. I've got it under control. No pressure from me."

I ran my hand down his body, finding his cock and squeezing it. He groaned, his neck jerking backwards at the contact. "You've been able that long?"

"Five or six days. Not sure at what point that night I got the ability back. But yes."

I stroked him through his pants, watching as his pupils dilated. Yeah, Sterling liked this. The strongest man I'd ever known was under my control for the moment. I'd never thought I wanted sex before I'd come to Orion. I felt strong and sexy, not a combo I was all that familiar with.

"You didn't tell anyone."

He shook his head and panted once before he spoke. "Not in the mood to hear all the ways I'm different than the others. Seriously, none of their business. And no pressure from me. What you're doing is amazing. I'm not going to lie. I didn't know it would be that good. My own hand and picturing you hasn't been this intense, and we're not skin-to-skin yet."

I dropped his penis and pressed down on my elbows to sit up a bit. "You want to paint me, Sterling?"

"I do." He looked confused. That was exactly what I wanted. He'd either like it, or he wouldn't. I got off the bed and took two steps back. I dropped my clothes.

Sterling gasped and nearly reared off the bed. I was in my underpants. "This okay?" I moved toward his desk. "Or maybe I can do better."

With his eyes fixated on me, I slipped both my bra and panties off until they hit the ground. "Better?"

Sterling's pants tented outwards. He made a growling sound in the back of his throat. He ripped off his shirt and his pants. I thought for sure he'd come for me then. His boxers showed the peak of his cock where it slightly slipped through the slit in the fabric.

Instead, he grabbed his charcoal and paper. With his eyes so intense I wondered if they'd burn a hole through me, he started to draw on the paper. I should be embarrassed. Only I wasn't. The longer he drew, the hotter I got. Every so often, he'd moan deep in his throat and stroke himself outside of his boxers. He was really hard, and that couldn't be comfortable.

Hours passed. He'd told me to stay very still, and apparently I could when I was pinned in place by Sterling's attention.

I was like a giant nerve ending. I didn't know if he needed release, but I really did. I finally got up. Sterling moaned. I hadn't touched him yet, but he had to know I was going to. He chucked the picture to the side when I approached.

"Diana ...?"

I answered his unanswered question. With just the top of my pointer finger I pushed at his chest and he fell backwards on the bed. "You've been hard for hours." I brushed my nose over his. "I'm so turned on it hurts. You must be, too."

He nodded once. "It's okay. I can manage it. Don't worry."

"But I am worried. I'm so worried that you think I don't want you inside of me. I do. Badly. Would you be willing? I don't want to force it."

His eyes widened, and he nodded again. Sterling was losing the ability to form words. That was okay. We didn't need any.

I took his boxers off, admiring the sheer size of him before I stroked him once, long and hard. His eyes closed, and his breathing picked up.

I had to speak. "I've never done this before. If I do something you don't like, tell me."

His lids lifted. "Are you kidding? You couldn't. I've never done this before either. I ... I ..."

I was hot, wet, ready, and I wanted Sterling inside of me. Badly. I climbed on top of him. I could try to direct him I supposed, but this was easier. He needed me this time. I had to be in charge.

He was so hard, and while I pressed down on him, sticking his cock inside of me, he jerked before he moaned. Sterling held on by a thin cord. I could see it in the way all the muscles in his body tensed. He was big, and he quickly reached the tissue I knew was there. I'd heard about how painful it could be to do this the first time. It wasn't. I was too wanting to even notice the discomfort for long. Finally, inch-by-inch, my body welcomed his into mine. He was fully sheathed inside of me, and we both panted.

"Diana, hold on." His voice was strikingly low. "I'm inside of you. I just want a second to feel this. You and me. As close as we're ever going to be."

I wanted it, too. Eventually his hands came to my hips, and I could see in his face he was ready. I moved upwards over his cock, almost coming off him exactly before I pushed back down. His hips met my own, shoving himself deeper into me.

Pretty quickly we found a rhythm. With each pass up and down, I got hotter. Seconds later, he flipped me over. Sterling's eyes were gentle while he kissed me, taking over the joining. Insecure Sterling was nowhere to be seen. He might be new at this, but his body quickly caught on. He pushed forward, balls deep inside of me. I cried out, and he smiled. His finger pressed between us, stroking my clit while we moved.

Soon I was coming, hard. His nostrils flared as he jackhammered inside of me, following me into oblivion. I was done. Spent. I didn't know which way was up or down. I didn't care. Why did anything matter? My mind went blank.

I came back to myself some time later to the strangest sound. Sterling hummed lightly to himself, and the sound of charcoal hitting paper accompanied the music. I opened my eyes to watch him. He was really interested in what he drew, and it took him a second to notice I was awake.

He set down the work. "Hey, sweet baby."

That was the second time he'd called me that, and I loved it. "Hey, yourself."

He leaned into me, kissing me gently on the lips before he tongued my bottom lip. I gasped, my body waking back up immediately. He smiled, his gaze lazy.

"I didn't expect that. I would never have imagined you'd give that to me. I'll never, ever ... that is to say, I know it's too soon, but I love you. I know your soul. I felt it move through me when we first found you."

I kissed the tip of his nose, the sides of his cheeks. Everywhere. "You're mine, Sterling."

It must have been the right thing to say. He pulled me against him, tucking me into his side. He sighed, a contented sound. "That's all I want to be."

At dinner, Sterling leaned against the chair and yawned. Lewis stopped talking to Cash about the Infected they'd worked on earlier. "You okay?"

"Huh?" Sterling rubbed his eyes. "Sure. Yes. I'm always okay."

"You yawned."

Damian snickered and took a sip of his drink. "He's fine. Leave him alone."

Cash looked between them and raised his eyebrows. "His color is good. He looks fine."

Lewis shrugged. "I've never seen Sterling yawn before. Seems like he has endless energy." He turned his gaze to me. "I'm going to wake Judge in the morning. He'll be out of it most of the day. Maybe the whole day. But he'll be awake."

"That's good," Cash responded. "I miss him. It's too quiet."

"Agreed." Damian raised his glass. "We work best when it's all six of us together."

He'd included me. I tried to contain the surge of emotion moving through me, but Sterling must have noticed. He rubbed my knee under the table. I smiled at him, loving the contact. We'd been together in the most intimate way possible. It had changed something between us. I could still feel him as though he remained somewhere deep inside of me.

He'd never let me down. I believed it.

We all watched a movie about a spaceship adrift in space. The couple on board had been on their way to divorce and changed their minds as they repaired the ship. I was bored, and I kind of thought the others were, too. Sterling held me in his arms and snored lightly in my ear.

Cash looked up from where he sat on my other side. "He is out. I've never seen him conk out during a movie."

"That's what I was saying earlier." Lewis shook his head. "I need to check him out."

Damian waved his hand. "He's fine. He's happy. He's relaxed. Trust me, he's never been better."

"You got your medical degree when?" Lewis threw a book at Damian, who ducked and grinned.

"Lewis, you're a doctor. For God's sake, use your brain. He's out of it. He's happy. So am I. Leave it be. Okay?"

I turned bright red and sunk down further under Sterling's arm to hide. He readjusted and didn't wake up.

"Oh." Cash grinned. "I get it. Good for you two. Okay. All is well. It's probably a total adjustment to the system. Hope to know soon."

"Aha." Lewis nodded, turning his attention back to the television. "You're all supposed to tell me for this reason. Your health is my concern. It would have been a two second conversation we could have had without making Diana cower in embarrassment. Sorry, Doll. All is well."

I hoped so.

Chapter Seventeen

Sterling Whitworth

About three quarters of the way through the movie, it got more interesting. The wife had conducted an affair. How were they going to get through that kind of betrayal? But the husband loved her. The actor gave a great performance and I was riveted to the screen. Sterling adjusted his position slightly beneath me, and I felt his erection.

He'd gotten hard. I turned to look at his face, which remained passive in sleep. He breathed evenly. I turned back to the television. He adjusted again, this time making the smallest noise in the back of his throat. He was clearly getting harder. It must be a hell of a dream. But I didn't want him to have it in the room with all the guys around.

I touched the side of his face. He remained asleep. Gently, I eased up to his ear to whisper. "Sterling."

His lids fluttered and after a second he regarded me with half-asleep, lazy eyes. "Hey, sweet baby."

"Think you might be dreaming."

Cash shushed me. He must have really liked the movie too. I ignored him, my attention on my current situation with Sterling. Confusion covered his face, and then his eyes widened as he realized of what I spoke. "You're right." He bit his bottom lip. "Never had that happen before."

"What would you like to do?"

He sat up slightly and grimaced. "Put your arms around me and block me. I'm going to carry you out of here." In a louder voice, he continued. "Night guys. I'm snoring, and she wants to go to bed."

"Uh-huh." Damian waved his hand. "Have a good night."

Cash smiled. "Are you sure? You seemed like you were really liking the movie."

"She's sure. You can give her a catch up later." Sterling hauled me up against him. "You're going to cover me with your body, okay? From here to my room and then to Artemis. I have something I want to get."

I did as he asked, and as we left the room, Lewis called after us. "Let our girl get some sleep, please. I don't want to have to start treating her for exhaustion."

"Yeah. Yeah. Yeah," Sterling answered rounding the corner already on the way to his quarters. What did he want to get? I asked him, and he grinned. "My dream created this little ... predicament ... and gave me plenty of ideas."

I snorted, which was so not ladylike, but he smiled even brighter. "Is that so?"

"Yes." He kissed my cheek, setting me down. "Thank the universe you woke me up before I started to embarrass myself in my sleep with all of them there. I'd never hear the end of it."

He rummaged through his drawers, eventually coming up with a box that he stuck in his bag. "Let's go."

"We can stay here. I don't have to be in Artemis every night."

He smirked in the way that made me want to kiss him. "Sweet baby, I don't want them hearing us. I plan to make a lot of noise."

I needed to give him some truth, even though it was uncomfortable to say. "I'm a little bit sore. From before."

His face fell. "Did I hurt you? Too rough? I would never want to cause you pain. Ever."

"I think it's just one of those lose-your-virginity things. Muscles stretching that hadn't before. You were ... perfect."

His eyes darted around in their sockets. "Okay, change of plans. We're still going to have a great time. I'm going to make you feel better."

I jumped back into his arms and let him carry me all the way to Artemis. Sterling dropped me down on the bed. He walked into my bathroom and came back grinning. "Your shower will be perfect."

"For what?"

He tugged off his shirt, and my mouth watered. Sterling had muscles on top of muscles. Maybe I wasn't that sore.

"Take off your clothes. Meet me in there." Sterling dropped his pants and underwear before he maneuvered into my bathroom. I stood up, following his directions. I'd stood naked while he drew pictures of me. But I'd been so invested in the moment, feeling flirtatious and sexy. Right now, I was insecure.

My bathroom wasn't huge, and Sterling took up most of the shower stall. Still, I was tiny, and for once it would work for my benefit.

On the sink he had his paint supplies laid out. "What are we doing in here?"

"I'm going to paint you. Your body. These are watercolors. They'll wash off as soon as I put the water on, which I will do. I want to paint your body. That's what I dreamed about. My brush on your body. Can I play, sweet baby?"

I'd never imagined being painted. "I'm up for whatever, Sterling."

"Now that is a dangerous proposition."

He turned on the water, letting the warmth beat down on us. I closed my eyes. It felt amazing. Sterling touched me gently with the tip of his brush. Red. He gently caressed my breasts with the color. I hadn't known how much I would like it, but the intensity of his gaze on me made it all worth it. He saw something in the colors as they travelled down my body, and his erection, which lengthened in front of my eyes, told me how much he enjoyed the show.

Soon I was covered in all kinds of colors. Purple. Pink. Green. White. They mixed together in a mess at our feet before running down the drain. His breathing quickened, and hearing it made my insides mush.

"Sterling." I sucked in my breath. "This is ... wow."

He dropped his brush. "You're magical. The most beautiful canvas I could imagine. And you're mine. If I could capture this for all time, I would. I'm going to make you feel so good, sweet baby."

"I want to. But I really do hurt a little bit."

Sterling whispered in my ear. "Trust me a little bit more. You already gave your trust to me in a huge way. Just a small extra step."

"With my life." He took the soap from the shelf and started to lather my body, getting the rest of the paint off. His hands on my body were light and gentle. He stopped right over my core, pressing two fingers inside of me. He wasn't rough, wasn't hurried. It was like he massaged me from the inside out.

His erection pushed into my belly. I leaned forward a bit, and he groaned. "Do that again."

"I can do better." I stroked him, long and hard. His eyes closed, but he didn't stop the beautiful stroking he did on my bundle of nerves. Sterling had strong, capable hands. His fingers played with my core, and after a few moments I came, hard, seeing lights pass before my eyes. My knees buckled, and Sterling caught me, tugging me against him.

His own explosion came fast; he cried out my name on a long groan. I held his throbbing cock until the moment ended.

We breathed together in the shower, the hot water tapping on the ground like a rainfall—or at least what I imagined one would be like.

After a minute, Sterling scooped me up in his arms. My muscles were languid. He dried us both off and carried me out to bed.

I spoke to the computer. "Artemis, lights off."

The lights dimmed on the ship while he covered us up together. "Love you."

I think I replied. I didn't know. My body had quit functioning. I needed sleep. He threw his arm around me, rolling onto his stomach, his face flat down on the pillow. I held his hand tightly in mine. We must have both fallen asleep.

Sterling sat up straight, gasping for air. I jolted upright, my hand coming to his back. "Are you okay?"

"I ..." He panted. "Sorry. Bad memory chased me from sleep. Doesn't happen often. Just sometimes. Sorry, I'll leave."

I shook my head. "No. Don't go. You don't have to always be strong."

Sterling groaned. "Don't I?"

"No." I kissed his shoulder, the arch of his back, his neck. "You don't."

"Then what do I have to be?" His voice didn't sound annoyed, merely curious, and it broke my heart.

"You. Mine."

He slid over, pressing himself on top of me. I thought he'd want to make out, to bring on intimacy again, only he didn't. He kissed me lightly and made no other moves. "Thank you for that. I was on a battlefield. My partner died. Could have been any number of places. I don't know which. I wanted to get home to you. I couldn't. Bad dream combined with memories. No fun."

"You could be so different based on what I imagine you've been through. You're not. You're hopeful. I love you."

"In my whole life"—he choked on his words—"no one has ever said that to me before you. Please don't ever take it back."

I buried my face into his arm, drawing him down until we held each other again. "I won't. Not ever." He was quiet for a bit, but I knew he hadn't fallen back to sleep. When Sterling slept, he did it hard. His breathing was too light, too even.

"Tell me something, sweet baby. What do you want? What could I give you that you crave the most in the world?"

I groaned. "That's a hard question."

"You have an answer." He kissed my shoulder. "Tell me so I can make it happen."

Stroking his back calmed me as much as it did him. "I'm not sure you can."

"Try me. If I can't make it happen, Damian can. He's amazing at making things happen."

I let the silence and the darkness make me brave. "The happiest I've ever been was when I took care of my brothers and sisters. I would love children. I've never seen that happening, not really. I couldn't marry politically and bring babies into that mess."

Sterling rolled onto his side. "And with us? You wouldn't want kids?"

"How could you do it? Evander could come any time. I had to hide when the drone came. What would we do with a baby?"

Sterling kissed my head. "Here's how it'll work. Six months before our contract ends—which is five years from now—Damian will declare me dead to Evander. We have five years to come up with a plausible reason. The other four will return to Evander and be debriefed. Meantime, you and I take Artemis, and we go somewhere safe. We wait for the others. They'll retire and join us. We'll have a baby. Live our lives together. I'm not sure what kind of father I'll be, but you'll help me."

"Just like that, you planned something that might work. How did you do that?" He amazed me.

"I'm designed to be a strategist."

I kissed his chest. "What do you want? What can I give you?"

"You. For the rest of our lives." He held me tightly. "Let me make your dream happen for you. I'd love a baby running around. Little boy. He won't be mine. I can't imagine actually fathering a kid. He'll be Cash's. Or Damian's. I'll teach him to shoot."

I drifted, halfway between sleep and alertness. "He might be a she."

"There aren't enough bullets."

I woke up because the light in the room had changed. Sterling slept deeply in the dead-weight way he did. I suspected I wouldn't get out without waking him up. I got out of the bed and cleaned off in the bathroom before Sterling opened his lids. He yawned.

"Damn. I slept hard."

I leaned down to kiss him. "Love you."

"Good. Love you, too."

I changed quickly and made my way to Lewis' lab. Today was my first day no longer having all-day dates. I'd have one tonight, if Judge was up for it, but I needed to work. Since Judge was only just being roused from his medical ordeal, the best thing I could do was to see to it that whatever he needed to do got done.

I arrived in the lab just as Lewis got Judge out of the medical machine. He remained asleep, not moving, while Lewis checked his leg. The bone had been reset, and the skin had closed up. Judge made small noises in the back of his throat that sounded like breathy moans.

Lewis nodded as he checked Judge's leg. "Looks good, Judge. Can you hear me yet? Your leg is better."

I walked up next to him. "Do you have to shout at him?"

"Judge is hard to put under and hard to wake up. He'll come to. I'm trying to wake him a bit."

I pushed Judge's hair off his forehead. "He's had an ordeal. If he wants to sleep a bit more, let him."

Lewis kissed my shoulder. "You're the nicest person on the planet. I want him up so I can discharge him. He hates being in here. Feels like the best favor I can give him."

"Di ..." Judge didn't open his eyes but called out my name. "Don't leave."

"I won't." I kissed his cheek. "Does he have to wake up here?"

"His vitals are good. The leg has good reflexes. No, I suppose he can go anywhere. Should I put him in his bed?"

I thought about it for a moment. "Put him in mine."

When Judge was set up and sleeping in my bed, I went to work. The first thing I did was leave him a voice recording on our private line. I let him know where I'd gone and told him I couldn't wait to see him later.

They'd gotten a big delivery from Evander, and I was sure the whole thing waited for Judge to wake up and deal with it. The best thing I could do for him was to get the project started. Judge had a system I didn't find hard to follow. He had labels for his labels. I quickly figured out that, in fact, he'd divided things up based on what room they'd eventually have to be stored in. I tried to discern, based on former labels, what would go where. If I did it wrong, it would take twice the time, but I suspected he wouldn't yell at me.

I worked most of the day, skipping lunch, and got everything put into transport boxes. I stood and examined what I'd done. Pride in a job well done filled me, yet I was nowhere near finished if I wanted to be sure Judge had less to do when he felt better.

Pushing the box that would go to Cash's lab, I made my way down to where Cash worked with the Infected.

He looked up when I came in, rushing to help me when he saw what I did. "Hi, Boo."

I smiled, wiping my brow. "Hey, Champ."

"How goes it?"

I pointed to the box. "Does Judge put it away for you?"

"He does, but I'm more than capable of it. Thanks."

"You're welcome." I watched the Infected in the tank walking around in a circle. "What's going on with him?"

Cash put his hand on the glass. "This is patient XXY. He's actually doing really well. The first one whose hand I've been able to regenerate human tissue on. His vitals hold steady. He is the most successful patient I've had since I started this."

XXY growled at the glass, and Cash sighed. "He hates me. Well, I don't know. There's no indication they have human emotions. He finds me distressful at the very least."

"Are you personifying him?"

He looked at me out of the side of his eye. "If I don't ... I assume he can't have those emotions ... then what am I doing? I'm trying to save him."

"Why do you lose so many? Are you experimenting on them?"

"No, we do everything in labs and holo before I ever try it on the real thing. We lose them to death before we've ever touched them. It hurts Lewis a lot. They live with us a lot longer than they do out there. Still, they die."

"Then how do they still have so many? Do they have baby Zom-Infected?"

Cash shook his head. "They regrow. They die. They fall apart. Lost a limb, the limb regenerates into a new person. That's why Lewis burns them. Stops the regeneration. Puts them to rest."

I wanted to say *eeww*. But I wouldn't. This was science. I needed to not be queasy.

"Looking forward to tomorrow. I miss you."

I put my arm around his waist. "I started with your equipment so I could see you."

We stood there for a while. Eventually, he leaned over and kissed me, slowly. Heat travelled from my feet to my head in seconds. "Hello, by the way."

"Hi." I breathed out. "Going to be hard to concentrate now."

He grinned, a self-satisfied smile. "For me, too."

That was when I saw it: Cash had clearly gotten over the US machine. His pants pressed out in front of him. "How long?"

"Two nights." He kissed my temple. "Hard to wait my turn. Not when I want what's mine when I want it."

Cash was so seriously hot. I leaned against him. "Tomorrow night I'm all yours."

XXY pounded on the door, spoiling the moment. Cash exhaled loudly. "See how his hand is human colored again? I just need to figure out how to move it through the rest of his body."

"How long has he been like that? I mean, if you had to guess. He dies, he regenerates or something—how long has he been doing it? How long has he been that way?"

Cash shook his head. "Hard to know. The bloodwork doesn't give me that information nor does the degeneration in the spinal fluid, muscles, or bones. My best guess? He changed when they all started to. About thirty years ago. I know what you're thinking; I've given it a lot of thought myself: maybe there is no coming back. Maybe this is how they are now, a changed creature, and I should leave them be."

He'd pretty much read my mind. "Cash, I'm not placing judgment."

"I know you're not, Boo. But I do. I think it all the time. Lewis can obsess about it. Here's the problem. It's spreading. Say someone gets bitten from an outer planet, from a less affluent corporation than ours. If they come to a town square somewhere populated, then there's a problem. If the people get the shot protocol Lewis invented, which requires someone to administer a series of intense shots within eight minutes of being bitten, the people bit can be saved. Otherwise, that's it. Done. I have to believe I can bring the Infected back. I have to. It can't be over that fast."

I kissed his arm. "Hey, Champ. You keep saving the world, don't you? How many things did you cure before you were twenty?"

He snorted. "A whole bunch of things."

"You're amazing. I want you to know I see how much you care about all of them. They're your patients. You want to make them better."

He leaned his head on top of mine. "I want babies, too. Sterling told me it was something you wanted. He has a plan. His plans tend to work. He needed to know if any of us were going to put a wrench in it."

I put my hands on his hips. "An hour ago he was still practically passed out in my bed. What did he do? Jump up and run here?"

"He started his rounds here. Maybe he thought I was the one who'd say no. I'll probably be a lousy dad. I had a terrible one. Can you help me with that?"

I gave in to the urge to crawl up his body. Wrapping my arms around his neck, I circled my legs around his waist. His eyes got huge before he swung me around and pressed me against the wall. He kissed me, hard, and I closed my eyes, drowning in Cash.

"What did I do to earn this kiss?" He smoothed the hair off my forehead. "Not that I am complaining."

"Sometimes I don't have the words for what I want to say. I spent a lot of my life in a fog, existing in a state I didn't realize was unhappiness. No one was cruel to me or anything. I didn't fit in. I get you, I think. And for that, I just want to kiss you all the time."

He cupped my chin. "I think you have the words. Some of the best I've ever heard."

The Infected banged on the glass. Two of them joined XXY, and they were all making a racket now. Cash shook his head. "This is so not romantic. Tomorrow night. You and me. Okay? I want to talk about ... everything. Every single thing you ever think and want. And I want to be with you so badly; I'm burning from the desire."

I left his lab and went back to delivering the supplies out to where they needed to be. Sterling found me half-way through the job and helped me get the rest of it out. I'd have to carefully go through the stuff and figure out where Judge stored things room-to-room.

When we were done with putting things away, I stopped to stare at Sterling. His handsome face stared out in the distance through one of the few windows in the enclosure. I wondered what he thought about when he stared in the distance.

I put my hands on my hips. "Did you run to Cash when you left my room to ask about the babies?"

He turned toward me and winked his left eye. "Things go easier when Cash thinks he's been consulted first. He's my brother. I get him. No control in his whole life. You and I made plans last night. I wanted him to want it, too. It didn't even take convincing. Turns out he loves kids. Learn something new every day, right? I haven't spoken to the others."

I wrapped my arms around his waist. "More strategy, huh?"

"It's how I'm built. How they designed me. Are you mad? Was it something you wanted to stay between us? I didn't discuss what we did together or anything that I thought was truly private."

I kissed him. "I'm not mad. I hardly ever get mad. I forgive really easily, too. I've never understood the point of anger. To steal your line, it's not how I'm built. I don't want you to change. Be who you are."

He nodded, kissing the top of my head. "Wish I could keep you with me all day. But you're actually understanding Judge's organizational plan and I completely do not. This would take a week if Judge were doing it because he hates it. I think I need to let you get back to work."

"Okay." For a person who'd had so little affection over the years, I'd really taken to it. "We're all programmed right? Nature versus nurture. The roles our genes play in who and what we are. Maybe you just got the really good ones. Did you ever think about that? Maybe you're the best parts of humanity. I look at you, and all I can see is ... your beautiful heart."

He blinked away tears. "I don't cry." He cleared his throat. "Ever. You make it worth it. You're my reward for all the hellish years and the lonely nights. It's like the universe said, 'Okay Sterling, now it'll be okay. Here is this perfect person for you. Take care of her.'"

Sterling kissed me once, hard on the mouth, and then took off to work. I went back to work. By the end of the day, the job was done. Everything had been stored where it should go. At least I'd found something I could be good at doing for all of them.

Chapter Eighteen

Feeling the Heat

When I came in, Judge rolled over and sat up in bed. His eyes were clear, and he was awake. I grinned at him. "How are you feeling?"

"My leg feels much better. I walked to the bathroom on it and barely a twinge. Amazing what that machine can do with Lewis' direction. How did I end up here?" He rubbed his nose. "Not that I'm complaining. If I had my way, I'd be in your bed with my head on your pillow every morning. I just don't remember."

I lay down next to him. My muscles were stiff from all the shoving and carrying I'd done. I needed to get back to my workout routine if I wanted to stay strong enough to be of use. "You were really out of it, which was normal, and I asked Lewis if you could be here instead of the lab since you hate it there so much. He agreed. My guess would be that he got Sterling and they carried you here. You missed a supply delivery from the drone. Damian explained to the robot that you were hurt, so it should be fine. I spent today putting away all the new stuff and categorizing it for you. Nothing much different. They sent more pots and pans, which I thought was funny. Otherwise, more of what it looks like you get every time."

He frowned. "You did all of it? Today?"

"Sterling helped me deliver some of it, but yes, it was mostly me. I heard you hated doing it. It seemed to make the most sense to keep me busy today. I'll fill in where I can."

Judge wasn't moving as fast as he usually did. He managed to slide over to me. "Thank you."

His kiss was gentle. I melted into him. It had been two days since we'd gotten to speak, and it was too long as far as I was concerned. He pulled me tighter up against him, and yet his hands remained easygoing when he rubbed my back. We kissed without stopping, and eventually the simple affection changed. I felt the second he realized he was getting hard. His body jolted against my own, and I clung to him, not letting him pull back.

He stopped kissing me only long enough for him to open his wide eyes and stare at me for a second. Then his mouth was on mine again, harder, faster; he moaned against me. I wanted him inside of me, which meant we had to slow down.

"Judge," I whispered against his cheek. "Do you want to be inside of me?"

His eyebrows rose. "Is that actually a question?"

"Just because you can doesn't mean you want to." I really couldn't be pressuring him to complete something he might not be ready for.

He nodded, fast. "There's no question, Di. I've never wanted anything as much as I want you."

"Then let's take a breath. If we rush into this, it'll be over before either of us is satisfied."

Judge kissed the edge of my nose. "Okay."

I tugged at his shirt and then my own until we were both naked from the top up. He reached out to stroke my breasts. I closed my eyes and let him. He explored me, softly. Each caress sent shivers down my spine. I was so happy to be this way with Judge. He made me feel connected to him each time we looked at each other.

After a while, I opened my lids to place kisses on his hard chest. I could hear his heart beating fast. He'd slowed down for me, but it must have been an effort.

Reaching down, I cupped his cock through his pants, and it jumped at my embrace.

"Di," he whispered. "I'm not sure ..."

"It's okay." There would be plenty of time for long, drawn out lovemaking. Like everything else he did, Judge would become an expert at pleasing me, and I hoped I could do the same for him. I pushed down his pants and quickly followed with my own.

When we were both naked, I ran my hand over his length once to feel his thickness. He was big, completely erect, and throbbing in my fingers. I kissed his mouth gently, easing him onto his back. I didn't want him to do anything, just to enjoy our being together. His lids were half closed and his nostrils flared when I finally climbed on top of him and pressed him inside of me.

He cried out, his neck arching and his hands digging into my sides. "So beautiful." His voice was still not more than a whisper.

I moved slowly up his erection. It wasn't like I had all that much experience with this either. Judge inside of me felt so ... right, like we'd always been meant to feel this way.

Up and down I slid. Surprisingly, we were both able to hold off completion a lot longer than I expected. His eyes followed my movements like he was lost in me.

"Good?" I asked him.

He bit down on his lower lip. "I never knew. I didn't understand it could be like this between two people. I think it might just be you. You're the only woman in the universe who could make me feel like this."

Judge was so sweet. I kissed him on the mouth, and his hips rose to meet mine. He moaned against me. Maybe he'd gotten out of his own head. His body wanted completion, and so did mine. He came hard and all of a sudden. The jerk of his erection against my clit set me off, and I followed him quickly down the rabbit hole of pleasure.

His stomach rumbling sometime later woke me up. Judge had my fingers in his hand, and he drew circles on my palm. I opened one eye and then finally the other.

"Hungry?"

He grinned, kissing my hand. "Like I've never had food before. It's almost dinner. I was going to wake you in a minute. I ... I just liked lying here with you, admiring how gorgeous you are, and feeling this way."

I rolled over and kissed his chest. "Then let's go get some food. You must need it. You didn't eat for two days in the machine, even though it keeps your nutrients up and your hydration okay. Then I went and ravished you."

Judge tickled me, and I laughed before I scooted out of the bed so he couldn't do it again. "Feel free to ravish me anytime."

Dinner was a vegetarian meal. Spaghetti, squash, cheese, and a red sauce that tasted like garlic and onions. Damian had also made a salad. He winked at me when he set down the plate. I hadn't seen him when I'd dropped off and put away his agricultural supplies. Even though I thought I'd figured out where he hung out during the day, he still had the ability to surprise me. Where had he been all day?

Judge cleared his throat. "Hey, Damian. I woke up thinking about that cave Lewis and Di got lost in."

"Oh yeah?" Damian sat back in his chair. "What about it?"

"I need to know why it's on a time differential, and I'd bet dessert you are bothered by it, too."

Was he? Damian hadn't uttered a word to indicate any interest in the cave at all. "I have been thinking about it a lot. Want to take a trip?"

"I figure it's a good time for you and me to go. Cash and Lewis are up next for date nights. If we take a long time and miss a day, we're not missing our time with her. Sterling can hold down security here. The drone just came and went. You won't be missed by Evander. Let's go. See if I can figure it out."

Lewis drummed his fingers on the table. "I'd kind of love it if you did that. I want to go back there, and I want to know why I came out to nighttime when we'd been gone an hour. Seems a strange time differential. Usually you lose or gain years. Not minutes or hours."

The talk about the time differential made my stomach hurt. Was my family okay? Had they been killed? Were they coming? Were they not? Was I going to see them in a month, but they'd all be eighty? Or would they show up looking the same when I was at the end of my life? Would they come, and I'd already be dead?

Judge leaned over and kissed my temple. "What put that look on your face?"

"Time differential equals worry about her family," Cash supplied. "Use your heads. Diana should be forty-something years old. She's not. Time differential. Her family is either on the other side of the black hole or on their way here. It's hard on her."

I played with my spaghetti. "Don't forget dead. They might be dead. Sandler could have killed them all. I'll never know. Even if I pointed Artemis at the hole—presuming she was space-worthy enough to do that—I could arrive a hundred years from now. Turning around, I'd never get back to you guys. Anyway, you can talk about time differentials. It just threw me. I'm good now. Please continue."

Only they didn't. Cash immediately launched into a story about his frustration with XXY. The Infected had started running from him, and he needed Judge's robot to help tomorrow. They talked about the logistics of that while Lewis caught my eye contact. He smiled sadly at me, and I gave him my best impression of a smile in return. Was it okay to be so happy and also not, at the same time? True emotions were so new to me.

Judge tried to wake up three times that night, and three times I soothed him back down. I thought it might have to do with the movie we'd all watched together. A boy lost his parents and only had his dog on the spaceship to guide him to the planet where his grandparents lived. I imagined that struck pretty close to home for Judge. Maybe next week we'd play cards more. The movies did strange things to my five, and the wrong one could really set me off, too.

I ran my hands through his hair and watched him sleep. He settled back down with a smile and proceeded to roll over onto his stomach.

I kissed his shoulder, hoping it would be the last time for the night. It was.

The next morning we got up together. He smiled at me, a sleepy expression on his face. "I sleep great with you. Are you going to tell me sometime how you make that happen?"

"No." I kissed him lightly. If I did, he'd make me stop doing it. I liked knowing that when he was in my bed, he didn't suffer through the nightmares that plagued him otherwise.

Dressed in my too-big clothes, I got to work helping Judge out on the projects he never had time for. He left with Damian shortly after we exited Artemis. His list, which he'd reluctantly given me, included things like replacing circuits and checking on the workings of all the vehicles they never used. Evander had given them the means to get around. So far, I'd only seen the trucks used to get me and to go to the cave.

Where else would they take vehicles?

I was glad to have busy work to do, despite Judge's preference I sit around. What did the women in this part of the universe do all day?

I checked all the trucks. They had full batteries, and they turned on just fine. It was then I noticed how completely dirty the bay where they stored the trucks had become. Had anyone ever cleaned it? I got to the job. I liked making things shine, adored the way a place would become after I got finished with it.

Before I knew it, Cash tapped me on the shoulder, catching me totally by surprise. I gasped and then cracked up at the way he jumped backwards.

"It's dinnertime. I looked for you everywhere. Have you been in here all day?"

I wiped my forehead, which was covered in sweat. "Do you not spend all day in the lab sometimes?"

"Good point." He looked around. "Did you scrub this whole bay area?"

"Sure did." I squeezed the remaining water from my mop into the bucket and poured the whole thing into the dirty water depository, which would get it recycled and cleaned in the system. "Should I make dinner?"

"No." He laughed. "I did that. It's almost done cooking in the oven."

"Guess they're not back. I hope they're not gone weeks. Do I have time for a shower?"

He nodded. "Absolutely. Lewis and Sterling are both finishing up some work. Sterling doesn't like the way some of the security beacons are offline. More than usual. He's working on it. And Lewis is trying to get XXY to let him inject him again. So far it's not happening. I had enough. I cooked dinner."

I took his hand. "I'm a sweaty mess, Cash. Want to have a shower with me?"

His eyes widened. "Yes."

By the time we made it to Artemis' shower, we were undressed. I had clothes strewn all over the ship from the entrance to the hallway and the doorway of my room. Cash pressed against me in the shower, the hot water beating down on us. He raised my hands over my head, holding them steady against the wall. I breathed against him. Cash would take care of everything. I loved knowing with him I'd simply have to be.

He palmed by breast, tweaking my nipple between his fingers. I cried out in pleasure. "I told you I want to know your body, Boo. All of it. So you're going to tell me. With your moans and your cries and the way that you squirm. I'm a quick study. Don't hold back. If you like something, and you even think it's odd, you still tell me."

He was erect. His cock appeared thick and heavily veined. My mouth watered. "Can I take you in my mouth? I'd like that."

His breathing sped up immediately. "Yes. But I'm coming inside of you. Not your mouth. Your pussy."

"Yes." I dropped to my knees, the water messaging my back while I took his hard length in my lips. He was big. I was never going to get all of him inside of me at once. So I concentrated on the head. I swirled my tongue around it, which Cash seemed to like. He leaned back against the side of the shower and closed his eyes.

With my hands, I stroked the part of his cock I couldn't get into my mouth. His moans were my reward. He wanted to know my body, and I loved that, but I also really wanted the chance to explore his. Eventually he sucked in a long breath.

"Stop, Boo. I won't make it if you go anymore." He was hot and throbbing. I could feel it in my mouth how he'd grown since I started. I gave him one more lick and pulled back. He yanked me to my feet and turned us until I had my legs around his waist and my back against the shower where he'd been.

I closed my eyes, knowing what was going to happen, wanting it, craving it. He pushed inside of me. I cried out his name, and he bit down on my shoulder, lightly. I moaned, my insides pulsating with need. I hadn't known I wanted to be bit. But oh yes, I really did. By Cash. As often as he wanted.

Whenever he wanted.

He surged inside of me, pushing in and pulling out. Over and over. My back hit the wall. It didn't hurt, and even if it had, I doubt I would have cared. This was what I needed. I came around him like an explosion. I said his name over and over and over.

When Cash came, it was quieter. He sighed his release inside of me, mumbling something when he did. I didn't catch all of it, but something sounded like *home*. If that was what he said, I understood his sentiment. He felt like home to me, too.

Dinner was somewhat subdued. Damian and Judge weren't back. We'd all known that could happen; it didn't make worrying about them any less troubling. What if the time differential moved and they were gone for years?

Still, Cash's stew tasted delicious, and I ate it all down like a starving woman. When Sterling suggested skipping game night, since none of us were concentrating well on anything, we all agreed. I fell asleep in Cash's arms in my bed. I knew his strong arms would get me through the night of worrying.

A ding on his tablet woke me before it did him. I kissed him awake, and he checked the message. Damian and Judge were back. They'd felt like they'd been gone for about twelve hours. As the sun setting made its way through my door, I knew it had been much more than that.

"It's a device." Judge pointed at it, a grin on his face over the breakfast table. "Don't worry. It has an on-and-off setting. I turned it off. Honestly, I've never seen anything like it before. This is not tech from this world. Do you have it, Di?"

I shook my head. "No way. Never seen it. If it's over there, then someone is hiding it."

"Then we're dealing with something quite new. Well, old. See how it's all started to rust a little bit. Honestly? It looks like tech that's fifty years old. Yet it's beyond my understanding. I think it should be hooked up to a ship. Like it has to do with time somehow. I'm going to have to study it without turning it back on. I think it would take the whole enclosure and mess our time up. When I turned it off, the hot springs stopped, too. I'm sorry guys. I think this controlled the heat over there too."

Lewis met my eye contact and raised his eyebrows. We'd had such a good time there. I guess it really didn't matter, when it came down to it. We'd always have the memories.

I walked up next to it and stared down at the small device. "Where did you find it?"

"Hidden behind a rock. I did a real thorough exam of the whole cave, or I'd have missed it."

Damian sighed loudly. "Once again, I'm going to hide something from Evander. I don't want them interested in this and coming here to investigate with a team more appropriate for managing this strange event. I don't want them finding Diana."

"Another thing that'll weigh on you." I touched his arm. "If we can get Artemis fixed, I can come on and off the planet at will. Evander comes; I leave. They leave; I come back."

"No." All five of them said at the same time.

Damian touched my arm. "Too risky. Not going to happen. Something could happen to you up there."

I wanted to argue and didn't. Truth was, I had no interest, really, in bopping around in space either. If not for Damian's stress, I wouldn't worry about it at all.

The device really did have an on-and-off button. It was even labeled as such. I ran my finger over the words.

"What is it?" Cash caught my attention. "Something wrong?"

"I feel like I know the handwriting. Weird. I can't possibly." Still, the eerie sensation of an impossibility suddenly becoming plausible didn't leave me. Where did I know that writing from?

Lewis brought a card game and taught me how to play it. We sat together on my bed while he instructed me.

He'd made no overtures of doing more than kissing me, despite the fact I could see he'd gotten as excited as the others did when his lips met mine. He wanted slow, and that was what we were going to do.

"Do you suppose I could be going crazy?" I asked him when he beat me for the third time.

"No, I'd notice." He winked at me. "I have the anti-crazy drugs. Anxious about something? Paranoid? Depressed? What's going on, Doll?"

I scooted toward him and held his hand while I talked. "I think I've seen that handwriting. I know I said it earlier and dismissed it. Still, I've got this crazy sense ... I don't know."

"Maybe you have seen it. Maybe you saw it in the cave and didn't realize it. When you full on read it today, the experience brought on déjà vu."

That would be a good, logical explanation. I set down my cards while we started a new round. I wasn't going to figure anything out tonight; that much I was sure about.

I must have eventually dozed off playing cards because the next thing I remembered was Lewis taking me in his arms and shutting off the light. I was really, ridiculously tired. I hadn't had a very busy day. It didn't make a lot of sense. Still, I slept like a baby. If he snored, I never heard it.

The next morning, Lewis kissed me awake. "Are you okay?"

"Sure." I felt a little bit sore. The gym was a must-do. I couldn't be in this much pain from a basic day of working. I'd clearly been sitting around too much and for too long. "I think I'm going to take up running again. I'm lazy."

"I wouldn't use that word to describe you. Did I keep you up last night?"

I shook my head. "Out like a light."

"If I ever do, kick me or something."

He leaned down to kiss me, and I let him. "Not going to happen. I love you, Lewis."

I hadn't said it before, and my heart fell into my stomach. He wanted slow, and I'd thrown myself right over the cliff into too much, too soon. His smile stunned me. He kissed me rapidly, my mouth, my nose, my eyes.

"I love you, too. Thanks for being brave when I'm not."

My day dragged. I managed to change most of the circuit breakers and started on the tires in the truck we kept using, when it was finally time to change for dinner. Damian had made spinach and beef wraps. Nothing tasted right. I couldn't stomach any of it.

"Not your favorite, huh?" Damian knocked his shoulder into me playfully when I helped him clean up.

"Sorry." I grinned at him. A slight headache formed behind my eyes. I didn't get them all that often, but it could happen. I'd been so out of sorts all day; maybe that was why.

I curled up next to Damian for the movie he'd chosen. It was an action flick about taking over a building that had been infested with monsters. Two minutes in, I was out cold.

"Diana." Damian's voice was loud. I felt his hand on my face and then another set of hands. Why was everyone touching me? I groaned and tried to push them off. They needed to let me sleep.

"She's hot." Lewis shook my arm gently. "Can you hear me?"

"Yes." I tried to shove him away, but my arms were too heavy. "Hot. Need to sleep." And my throat hurt. My joints. My headache had gotten worse. They needed to leave me alone.

"Diana." Cash's voice tried to command my attention. "What hurts?"

"Everything." I closed my eyes as someone—Sterling, I could feel the muscles in his chest when I laid my head down on him—lifted me.

Judge sounded frantic. "What's wrong with her?"

I was too hot to care.

Chapter Nineteen

F12902

The medical table in Lewis' lab was cold. Too cold. I shivered on it. The lights were bright, and the noises from the machines all around zapped at my consciousness, making me want to scream. If I'd had the energy to do so.

"Do I have the infection? Am I becoming a Zombie?" I managed to croak out.

"No." Lewis looked down at me. He looked funny. It took me a second to realize he wore a mask over his mouth and nose. "You have a virus. The flu actually. A bad one. But you're not going to be an Infected like the ones behind the glass."

I vaguely remembered him taking blood and putting it into a machine. A readout caught my attention. It flashed a letter and some numbers: *F12902.*

Cash came into my viewpoint. "How you doing, Boo? Thirsty?"

I could have laughed if I'd had the energy. I was very, very thirsty, but that wasn't what amused me. When I'd first woken up in their enclosure, Lewis had sent for Cash, saying he had a better bedside manner. I'd not believed it at the time. Cash had seemed sort of hostile. But now I could see what he meant. Lewis was all business when it came to lifesaving, and Cash offered things like water. Or maybe I was simply delirious.

"Tell me it's not the one that killed my mother." Damian spoke from a distance away. Where was he? Why couldn't I see him? And why wasn't I in the machine if I was so sick? He sounded ... frantic. His voice hitched when he spoke. "Please, tell me that."

There was the *please*. I would do anything for the *please* ...

"It's not the one that killed your mother." Phew, I hated to let Damian down. "It's from the same family. The F family flu is what killed your mom. That was a different strand. I cured that one. If that was what she had, it would already be on its way out. This is F as well. It's not been cured. It has to be endured."

Damian said something I couldn't make out, and then it was Sterling's voice I heard. Low, clear and direct. "Fatal?"

"It can be."

"Hey," Judge answered. "Maybe we should talk about this somewhere else. We don't need to terrify her."

"In this case, she's the patient," Lewis responded. "Technically, she's the only one I should be speaking to. You're all here because I think she would want you to know. Doll, this is going to be rough. You have the flu. It's a bad one. You can survive it. The medical machine, it's not going to be much use to us except in treating symptoms. If your fever gets too high, I'll put you in. If you are having trouble breathing, I'll put you in."

His voice was soothing. I believed him. He knew what he was doing. I could sleep. Maybe. I was hot and the table was so cold ...

"I'd rather keep you out of the machine. I can watch you more closely. Your face tells us a lot more than the readings do. If you're suddenly in horrible pain, I need to know. I've given you an anti-viral injection. It should help shorten the time and maybe lessen the symptoms. As for the rest of us ... checking your immune readouts, Sterling is, no surprise, not going to catch this. Judge and Damian, you might. You've both been exposed to Fs as children, which should give you some immunity to all of them. You might get a low impact case. There's always a dose of F in the flu shots; unfortunately not this one specifically. Cash and I are in the same situation. We'll wear masks, and the best thing would be if you two would stay away."

Damian made a sound akin to a growl. "Like hell. I know what happens. I've seen it." His voice choked again. "I'm not leaving her. She needs me."

"We all need you to not come down with this too," Cash responded. "Although you might have it. We'll know in three to five days. We've all been intimate with her. Slept with her. I'm going to go figure out where the virus came from. It shouldn't be here at all."

Whatever else they said, I didn't hear. Sleep was my best friend.

"Doll." Lewis sat me up, which is what made me wake up a bit. "I need to cool you down a bit in the machine, okay?'

Whatever he wanted. The walls bled. I pointed that out to him, and he made a non-committal sound. "Fever is rough. I've given you something for it, but it's not working. The machine will get it down." The unspoken *I hope* hung off his words.

I passed out before I ever saw the medical machine close.

"Oh, Diana. Love." My mother helped me sit up. "How hard did you hit your head? You've been in this thing for so long."

I was so confused. I'd just been in the medical machine in Lewis' bay, and suddenly I'm with my mom on Artemis?

"You must have concussed yourself when the ship went into the black hole. Took us two days to tug you out. I'm so sorry, baby." She kissed my cheek. She sounded like my mom. Smelled like her strawberry shampoo. But, no, this wasn't right. I hadn't been out cold for two days on Artemis. I lived in an enclosure on Orion with my five.

"Mom, where are they? My guys? The five? Where are they?"

Her eyes were kind. "I heard you muttering about five guys. You were dreaming. Is that what you want? A multiple marriage? We can get looking into that. She's going to be okay; isn't she Dane?"

The walls bled around me, and I backed up. "No. This isn't real."

Fever is hard.

I was dreaming. I was in the machine. I loved my family. They'd never be a nightmare to me. But my mother telling me my five weren't real constituted something else entirely. They were real.

"Diana ..." My mother reached for me, and I sat up straight, grabbing onto ... Cash. Yes, I could see his dark eyes over the mask on his face.

"Sshh." He held me against his shoulder. "You must have been having some fever dream in there. It's down a bit. Lewis said to let you out if it dropped below danger threshold, so that's what I'm doing. He's in charge in here. Probably not surprising to you. He does people better. I manage the Infected."

Cash rambled. So unlike him. I took a better look at his eyes and fear stared back at me. "Am I going to die?"

"No," he answered, and behind him someone made a sound of pain. I lifted my head a little. It was Damian. He sat on the floor by the door. His eyes were red-rimmed, and he had hair growth on his face like I'd never seen before.

Sterling was in a chair to the left, unmasked. Judge stood, leaning against the wall near Damian. None of them had shaved. If I took off Cash's mask—which I wouldn't do—would I find that he had whiskers as well? I closed my eyes.

I woke up to raised voices. Cash and Lewis. I looked left and right; the other three were gone. That was good. I hoped they slept.

"I found it. It must have come in alive on the shipment Evander sent. It was alive on one of the battery packs she stored away in the pod room," Cash shouted, his hand on the wall.

"So we, what? Can't even expect them to clean the stuff they send here anymore?"

Lewis made a growling sound. "Fuck them. If she dies, I'm done. I can't—won't—live here without her. Hell, I don't know how I'll live anywhere without her but damned if I'm doing it here. Damian can pack me in the pod and send me back. I'll buy out my contract or go to jail. I don't give a shit."

"She isn't going to die." Cash's voice was low.

"She might. Is she getting better to you? She doesn't seem better to me. Her blood work isn't improving. The fever is up more than it's down. A side infection will come any time now. You know it. I know it. Damian for sure knows it. If Judge and Sterling don't, then I wish them well in their ignorance."

Cash grabbed Lewis' shirt. "You saved her from radiation poisoning. You can do the flu. I am not leaving. I will be right here. You're a better doctor than me. I'm lab; you're patient care. Let's save her. What do I need to do? Tell me."

"There's nothing to do," Lewis yelled back, louder and angrier than I'd ever heard him. "I am not in charge of the universe. And neither are you. We might have pretended for five years there was a hot chance in hell we'd ..."

I reached out my hand. "Don't fight."

They both jerked around and rushed to my side. Cash spoke first, through his teeth. "Fever is still up. Damn it. Want some water, Boo?"

"Don't mind us yelling. We sometimes do that. You should see us really go at it over who gets the last piece of pie."

I coughed; my throat was dry. "Listen, I need to tell you something. And I want you to tell the other three, too. If I don't make it through this ..."

"Stop that." Cash used his in charge voice, and I almost did. This was too important.

"This was the best time of my life. I never imagined moments like the ones we had. I love all of you. I don't want to die. But if this is it, I don't want you to be sad when you think about me. I want you to remember me happy with all of you. Brief, but the best."

I saw the tears running down Lewis' face come out the side of his mask. He pushed them away. "I love you, too. We all do."

"You're not dying." Cash must be speaking through clenched teeth. "We love you. Lewis is not giving up. He's just fatalistic. Always has been. I see the future. I see the place away from here. I see the babies. It's all happening. You're going to be our wife. It's not just dating. It's not 'trying it out.' You are our forever. We all see it. I'm not letting go, and neither are you. Go to sleep and get better."

When I woke up, I couldn't breathe. I gasped for air. Like I was under water. My back hurt. My ears rang. I couldn't hear what Lewis said to Cash, but he gave directions for something. Sterling was suddenly there, his hand on my back. He pressed hard on it, and they were sticking something over my face.

"Oxygen." Sterling said it loudly enough I could hear it. Damian was there; Sterling shoved him away, yelling something at him, and then Judge came into my sight but just for a second before Sterling knocked him back too. I didn't want them sick. I couldn't breathe. There was no air. Cutting off the air ...

"Please, Diana. Please," Damian shouted into the room. "Don't do this. Not like this. Can't lose you. Please."

The machine closed around me. Darkness.

I woke up again to the sound of beeping. It was the medical machine moving off my body. Lewis had his mask off, and he smiled down at me.

"Hey, Doll. Sit up." He helped me.

I'd never felt so weak. I'd been sick with childhood illnesses, but I'd never felt anything like this. "What's happening now?"

"You." He tugged me against him. "You lived through it. Vitals are good. Breathing is good. Fever is gone. Twenty-four hours I waited to be sure. You're still here. It was close. Pneumonia. Scared the crap out of me. Longest two weeks of my life. But you're here."

The room spun, so I didn't let go of Lewis. "Two weeks?"

"Yes." He kissed my cheeks, my hair, my nose. "I've done something kind of bad. I didn't tell them I was waking you. Wanted a minute. Sterling's across the enclosure. He's probably already heard you're awake, so he'll be here any second. I don't know if he'll tell the others. We don't have long." Lewis kissed my lips, biting down on the bottom. I must have been a sweaty mess, but he didn't seem to care. "I don't want slow. Okay? I don't want it. I need you. I love you. I can't have regrets. I want the babies too. The whole dream. I told myself if you lived, I'd believe like Cash does. No more holding back. If you want that, too?"

I touched the side of his face. "Is that what you were doing? I thought you didn't want to rush the beginning."

"I lied." He pressed his forehead to mine. "No more. I love you."

Sterling appeared next to him. "I didn't tell the others, but I think Judge saw me run by, so he'll be here momentarily. I can hear him jumping out of the top of the pod room." Sterling tugged me into his arms. "I love you, too. Sweet baby, if you ever get sick like that again, it'll kill me. I'll drop dead."

"I'm sorry."

"Were you seriously not going to tell us?" Judge sped toward me, knocking into Sterling. "You haven't let me near her in two weeks. Not even when she was in the machine. Scoot over."

Sterling kissed me once more before he moved over to give Judge room. Judge took my cheeks in his hands and gently caressed my lips with his own. "I love you."

"I love you, too ... Listen, I am ..."

"If you say you're sorry, I'm going to spank your pretty ass." Cash appeared out of nowhere, wrapping his arms around me.

"Welcome back to the land of the living. You scared me, and I deal with the Infected all day long. Cut off a hand, drop it on the ground, it grows a whole new body around the hand. That's scary stuff. Nope. Nothing as bad as you nearly quitting breathing."

I wasn't sure what to say, and then I saw him—Damian. He stood by the door. He'd lost weight. His face was haggard, and his eyes clouded. I took a better look at all of them. Not one of them had slept much, and the weight loss seemed true for each of them in turn. I opened my arms, and Damian fell into them. Stumbled forward like he couldn't walk. His head found my shoulder.

He exhaled his words. "Thank you."

Soon they were all wrapped around me and each other. A big, giant hug in the med bay. I must be disgusting. They didn't seem to care.

"I fixed Artemis." Judge spoke low. "She's all fixed. Just like I promised she would be."

I squeezed his hand. This was the best hug ever.

After I showered, ate, and was once again declared fit by Lewis, I met them in the game room. No one wanted to work. A movie seemed the best idea.

"It's still Damian's night," Cash let me know. "We're going to start over with the movie. Try again. Tomorrow you can ease into work slowly. One thing. Then a rest. Build back up to a full-on schedule over the next two weeks. You're going to feel better quickly thanks to the machine, but make no mistake, you are going to be weak."

I nodded. "I won't push it. I'll do as you tell me to."

"Good." He seemed satisfied with my answer. I plopped down next to Damian, who pulled me into his arms just like he'd done before I passed out on him two weeks earlier. I ran my hands over his chest to feel his heartbeat.

"I'm sorry I got sick like that. I know that's how you lost your mom. I'm so sorry."

He nuzzled my hair. "You didn't make yourself ill on purpose. Don't apologize. I got a different ending than the one I thought was coming. You're here. I'm ... I don't have the proper adjective."

The movie started again. Presumably they'd not finished it the night I got sick. It was exciting. The heroes had to beat back monsters, and then there was this secondary love story that ...

The snore alerted me to someone being asleep. I looked over at Lewis, but he sat with his eyes closed, quiet. He was out, but not deeply asleep yet. With my head raised, I could see Damian's lids closed, his dark lashes a contrast to his pale skin. His hand was limp on my side. The snores turned out to be from Sterling, who never snored as far as I knew. He sat in his chair, his head leaning to the side. For good measure, I checked. Judge and Cash were both out cold too. All of my five, in the middle of the day, passed out on the couches.

I picked up the remote and shut off the television. If we were all having a nap, then we were all having a nap.

I closed my eyes and sleep came. Deep, untroubled, healthy sleep.

None of us roused until the next morning. Dinner was forgotten; the whole evening through the deep of the night, no one moved. I only woke up the next morning because Judge tripped over Sterling while getting up to use the bathroom. They both stumbled forward, which made a huge racket— enough to wake everyone else at once.

"Shit." Damian rubbed his eyes. "I'm sorry. What time is it? I have to make dinner."

"Breakfast, brother." Sterling laughed. "We missed dinner. You okay, sweet baby?"

I nodded. "I'm good." I hadn't lifted my head off Damian. He was comfortable.

Lewis walked over to us and looked down. "Your eyes are clear. That's good."

Cash held his hands over his head. "She's going to be fine now."

"I missed my night." Damian groaned. "Sterling, can I have till dinner?"

"Yep." Sterling patted me on the head and then twice on Damian's cheek. "Have at it."

I ended up shaving Damian's face for him. He was awake but by no means looked rested. He didn't speak much while he sat in my bathroom and let me shave the whiskers of the last two weeks—which were practically a full on beard—from his cheeks. His eyes followed my movements. I'd only just finished cleaning him off when his hand grabbed my wrist.

I stopped moving. "Damian?"

"You know I love you, right? Please tell me you do. I wondered for two weeks if I hadn't really made you understand."

I climbed onto his lap, straddling him in the chair. "I do. I can feel it in my own heart. Deep inside. Your love for me is there. Do you feel mine for you?"

He kissed my lips gently, raising his hips when he did. "I do. But you're only just better. I can't show you the way I'd like to what your love means to me."

I pushed down on him. "Could you show me gently? Slowly? Just this one time? Because I think I could handle that."

"I can."

He kissed me lovingly before he picked me up to bring me to the bed. "You don't move. You let me love you. That's what I need. Please."

"Sounds like heaven."

He grinned his half smile that went crooked up one side of his face. "It will be for me."

I lay on the bed while he undressed me piece by piece before slipping off his own clothing. I'd not been wrong about the weight loss. He was still strong, gorgeous. Still, his pain was evident in the way I could now make out some of his ribs.

I leaned up to kiss where his heart beat. He smiled down at me. "Don't go without taking me with you. Anywhere."

"Damian ..."

"Shh. I'm ... I'm sorry. No sadness right now."

He kissed down my body; parts that weren't usually a turn on suddenly were with him. The back of my knee. The crook of my elbow. There was nowhere Damian didn't want to make love to me. I closed my eyes and let him. His breath was warm, his heart beat, and he loved me.

After a time he found my pussy and ravaged affection on my clit. He moaned when he did so. I opened my eyes to see him. Damian—who asked for so little—made me hot in the way that he adored my body. He pulled back, his breath fast, his eyes wide.

I nodded, knowing what he asked me, and he moved until he could push inside of me. Slowly. We didn't rush. Slow movements eventually hurried but never got frantic. I came the same way. My body needed the release, needed Damian, and it was a blissful joining when he followed me into oblivion.

He was out cold a few minutes later. I ran my hands over his back lightly, watching every breath he took in and out.

A few hours later, I rolled him onto his stomach, waking him gently with a kiss when I did so. He breathed in through his nose. "Sorry, I guess I ..."

I put a piece of a protein bar between his lips. "I only woke you to feed you. Then you can go back to sleep if you want."

His eyes widened, but he chewed what I placed in his mouth. I broke him off another piece. "Open." He did as I said, and I gave him another bite to chew. Damian ate the whole protein bar from my fingers. When I was finished feeding him, he grinned at me, true happiness as some of the weight of the world seemed to leave his gaze.

"Thank you, Diana. That was kind of awesome."

I sat back. "I know."

"I want the babies, too. Sterling told us all when you were sick. That's what you want? I do too. Your babies. I'll love them all, even if none of them are mine. Let's be parents. It'll be so ... normal. No more Infected. No more time differentials. No more you getting sick. The five of us. You. Our babies. I'll quit today, if you want."

"Sterling said five years. I think that'll give us the least amount of attention."

He agreed. And made love to me slowly again to show me how much.

When Sterling joined me that evening, after I'd bathed, shaved, and changed all of my sheets, he plopped down on the bed, saying something about needing game night soon but not that night. I'd no sooner turned around than he was out cold, flat on his stomach.

My five were going to need as much rest as I did. Maybe more.

When I was finally up to par, I went back to my full time duties, which tended to be helping wherever I was needed. If they didn't have something specific they wanted from me, I found plenty to keep me busy.

XXY lost his hand. It fell off while I cleaned the filters on the other side of Cash's lab.

"Damn it. Damn it. Damn it." He stormed over to the glass. "I'm going to have to send the robot in before he grows another Infected."

I put my hand on his arm. "I'm sorry. I know you were hoping he'd keep the hand you managed to fix."

"You'd think I'd be used to it by now."

Cash would never be that way. Those he didn't save would always weigh on him like he failed. Each and every time.

Chapter Twenty

Forever

Lewis didn't waste any time. I walked into Artemis on his night on the schedule, and there were candles lit everywhere. I stopped in my tracks. He'd poured a red substance into two glasses and handed me one.

I sniffed at the drink. "Lewis Hurst. Did you find wine? Alcohol?"

"I have my secret stash. I don't drink alone. So I haven't in five years because I think Damian would flip out over this. His father had a bit of a problem with booze. I thought it was safe enough for you and me to enjoy one bottle together."

I sat across from him. "I can have one glass. Two puts me on my rear end. And I think you might have plans for tonight that don't include watching me sleep with my mouth hanging open, wondering if I'm going to throw up."

"Good call. So one glass for you. Two for me."

I let him pour me some. Mars Station had a ton of bars around. Alcohol wasn't forbidden, and for the most part people let off steam pretty well. My Uncle Nolan ran a tight station, and there was always security on the main strip when the bars were open. When I had turned eighteen, Uncle C.J. brought me for a drink. My father had been furious. He had wanted to take me for a drink. We'd done it the next night, which had made my mom mad. Why hadn't anyone told her? She'd wanted to come. Night three. By the end of the week, I'd had a drink with everyone but Cooper. He didn't consume alcohol—with the way his family sometimes turned out, he liked to keep his head totally clear. He'd given me my first water wrench instead.

Funny memories. Paloma had been shipped off to the Sisters of the Universe right after that. I'd never known why, and since I hadn't had others to drink with, I'd pretty much stopped except for birthdays or special occasions.

I sat on my knees. "Tell you something I haven't told anyone?"

"Yes," he scooted over and handed me my drink, which I sipped. The aroma-filled liquid slipped down my throat with ease. Just the smell itself was enough to make me feel relaxed.

"Today is Asher's birthday. My brother."

"Cooper Jackson's kid. The one whom you saved from Sandler."

Lewis had an amazing memory. "Yes, that's the one. When I think about any of it, and honestly, I hold back a lot of family recollection, it does me no good. Maybe there will come a time I can really think about all of them without pain, but not yet." They hadn't shown up. I'd turned off the countdown clock. Why make myself crazy? "Anyway, when I think on it? Worrying if he got away or if they caught him or if he died, that's what gets me. That's always there. Today my tongue got thick in the way it does before I can't communicate for long periods of time. I almost quit talking in the pod room."

His brow furrowed. "What stopped it?"

"Not what. Who. You did. You came in, and you asked me if I wanted to come see the newborn calves and say hi to Damian with you. I've never been able to pull it back before. But I did. For you. Thank you."

He took the glass from my hand and set it aside. Then he was on me faster than I'd ever seen him move. His mouth drank from my lips like I was air itself. I clung to his body. I don't know who stripped whom, only we were soon naked. My breasts were sensitive, and when he sucked on my nipples I cried out from the pleasure. His hands were everywhere, and I tried to keep up, finally giving up to let him run the show.

He'd held back for so long. His hand felt inside of me, finding my clit and stroking it. He hummed while he pleasured me, as though he'd never been so happy in the world. I cried out, coming all over his fingers. He grinned down at me, his smile proprietary. I was his, and he knew it.

"Feeling a little full of yourself there, doctor?"

"A man likes to know when his woman is getting what she needs." He pressed his knee against my core, and I ground against it, loving the fullness, loving the pain that came with the pleasure of feeling that part of his body right there. With a quick shift of his body, he moved around behind me. "Hold onto the headboard, Doll."

He wanted it from behind? This was new for me. Sometimes they wanted to be on top or me on the bottom, but from behind? Okay. I was game.

Lewis's swift fingers found my clit and played with it again, getting me close before he slipped inside of me. From this angle, he could drive in deep. I cried out from the penetration. He was big, but I was ready.

His right hand cupped my breast, the other covering my hand on the headboard while he pressed in and out of me. I pushed back with my hips, meeting his surge, and he cried out, too. Lewis wanted it a little rough, and I wanted him to have it. The harder I made it for him, the more it seemed to turn him on.

He was a man who liked a challenge.

Our joining wasn't easy or sweet, but it was ours. He reached between us, finding my clit and pressing on the nerves. I came hard and fast, over and over again. I couldn't catch my breath, and he held me up while he came deep inside of me.

We both collapsed down onto the bed. He lay on top of me, and I gasped for air. The candles in the room danced shadows on the wall.

I could see our movements reflected in the shadows and I knew I'd never forget the sight.

"I love you." He kissed my shoulder blade. "Love me?"

"Forever."

Time had a way of moving forward. I jumped down from the rafters several months later to find Judge waiting for me, his arms crossed. "Well?"

I looked left and right. "Think I'm missing something."

"Everyone here has told you they want a baby. A family. Except me. Don't you want to know if I do?"

He looked so despondent I couldn't laugh at him. "That's not for me to ask. It's for you to tell me. I've been waiting on you."

"I do. I want a baby. I'd be a terrible father. You're going to have to teach me how to do it. But, yes. Okay? When we leave here, I'm game."

They'd all told me how bad they were going to be at parenting. We had five years before we could consider the subject. I wasn't worried. I'd never known a more protective group than the five here. When it came down to it, I suspected they'd be holding my hand and not the other way around.

Judge's statement had me thinking about it. I'd been away from my own part of the universe a long time. We were rounding on nine months together, day and night, with my five. They seemed happy, and I really was.

Our routine worked well. Time healed a lot of wounds, made the flu feel far away, and the worry of discovery leave quickly. Cash still hadn't cured the Infected. XXY died shortly after losing his hand. Lewis had burned both parts of the body, and now a female with what I could only describe as mean eyes had taken his place. She'd kept her hand thus far. They were using a drug regimen on her which seemed to be helping.

I hardly noticed the Infected when I came in the room anymore.

We were eating eggs for dinner. I could always tell when Damian had a long day. He cooked eggs. One of the cows had died. He wasn't sure why, and he hated doing the autopsies.

I cleared my throat. "You all love me, right?"

The room went silent. Cash looked between the others. "Absolutely. Everything okay?"

"Well, if you love me and you want forever and the babies"—I shot Judge a look, and he rolled his eyes at me—"then do you think you might like to marry me? Make this official? Be my husbands, not just my guys?"

Silence surrounded me, and I wondered if I'd made a terrible mistake. Should I have waited for them to propose? Was I misreading them? Did they not want this?

Noise followed almost instantly. Bursts of "Yes"es and "Of course"s filled the air, and then they were kissing me, one by one. I grinned into the affection. This was the last step I'd needed. I loved them. I would never want anyone but them. Ever.

For now and forever. Sterling dashed from the room and came back in holding rings. Damian grabbed his arm.

"Where did you get those?"

He grinned. "I made them. Borrowed Judge's tools. Didn't think he'd mind." He handed one to each of them. They were all the same except for letters on the front: LH, SW, JT, DO, CW He handed me five rings with the initials D.M. on them. "Give those to us. We'll give these to you."

"I can't wear five at once. Unless they fit all the fingers on my left hand."

"No, wait." He dug a necklace out of his pocket. "We'll each stick one on."

Lewis cleared his throat. "Take it you've given this lots of thought?"

"Pretty much from the moment I met her." He bent over to kiss my cheek. "Can't do the white dress. We'd need prep time for that. Too much taxing on the replicator. So I'll just keep that image in my mind."

I stood, walking first to Sterling since he'd planned the rings over so much time. I wished I'd known. I had these gorgeous silver rings to give them, but I'd not had anything to do with making them. I would make it up over the years.

"Thank you for the ring, Sterling. Will you take this one from me?" He held out his hand, and I slipped the ring onto his left ring finger. Sterling took the necklace from me and slipped his onto it.

"Will you take mine?"

I grinned at him. "I will."

He kissed me gently on the lips.

One by one, I asked the same question. I had no idea if this was traditional or if we were making it up as we went along. All I knew was when it was done, I had five husbands. And they loved me. I don't know how I got so lucky.

Six months later, I lay with Lewis in the bed. He snored pretty loudly for as late as it was in the morning. We'd been up kind of late. He'd been reading books that showed him new positions and couldn't get enough of me.

I crept from the bed, showered, and dressed. I wanted to go over the beacons and see if they were working. We were getting weird signals from them. The wind blew loudly. It was a change of seasons. I had to get used to the idea that four times a year I was going to be inundated with the noise. I'd almost slipped from the room when Lewis moaned and extended his hand.

"Don't leave without a kiss."

I bent over and kissed him as sweetly as I could. Damn, I loved this man. All of them. Every day since our spontaneous wedding had been better and better. I couldn't ever do without them. Thoughts of my family came and went. I missed them; I always would. But if I had to be sucked through a black hole, where I ended up was pretty spectacular.

The strike of lightning caught me by surprise. The lights flashed before they went out. I jerked around. Had we actually been hit?

It would take a few minutes, but the secondary devices would turn on. We were safe. Judge would need help, and he was probably cursing up a storm. This time of day he tended to be in Cash's lab with the Infected.

I rushed down the hallway and nearly collided with Damian, who had clearly had the same thought.

"Nothing to worry about," he assured me. "We'll get it fixed."

"I know." I kissed his cheek. "Morning."

"Yeah. What a way to start the day. Four years. We'll have a farm. A really normal farm. No lightning strikes."

We ran into Cash's lab together. "Can you control the weather, Damian?"

He nodded. "On our farm I can."

Judge typed furiously on the central computer while Cash tapped his feet. "I can't believe this morning. Lightning."

"What do you need?"

He tapped his cheek. "A kiss and then I need you to go to the pod room and hit the breaker. Can you?"

I ran over and kissed him once on the cheek, lingering for a second. Before I ran from the room, I gave Cash one, too. He grinned and gave me one back. "And I was right in the middle of reading last night's results."

"Poor baby. Having to wait ten minutes."

He pinched my rear end while I ran away, and I yelped. Judge had given me a task, and I would get it done. I passed Sterling in the hall. He'd pulled out his gun. I grabbed his arm, and he bent down to kiss me.

Sterling must have just come out of the shower. He smelled like soap. "Today is going to be that kind of day."

"Nah, we'll have it together by lunch."

He kissed me back. "I love your enthusiasm."

I made it into the pod room and started resetting the circuits when the second boom sounded. I was thrown backwards, my hands on the machine when it was overrun with electricity. My body buzzed, and I must have screamed. Seconds later I was okay. A bad jolt sucked, but it wasn't the first time I'd endured one. Working with electricity got me shocked often.

My head pounded. Lewis was going to freak out. A thought hit me hard. Judge had said something about the enclosures and lightning strikes. Two in a row. First one takes out the secondary systems. Second one breaks the glass.

I jumped to my feet, even through my dizziness. The Infected might be out.

I stumbled into the hallway where Sterling caught me. "Okay, Infected are out. I'm going to contain them. Damian's got the stuff. Judge says you need to stay in here and get the computers back on line. As long as the computer doesn't recognize the Infected as being out—which Judge doesn't think can happen while the secondary system is out—we'll be good."

I took a deep breath. "Okay. I'll get it done."

I worked hard on the computer. It was easy for me. I loved making things work again when they quit doing so. If I hadn't gotten blown through the black hoke, I would have gotten the beacons working. I was a fixer. And my five loved me for it.

The lights came back on, and I stepped back, grinning. I'd done it.

A second later, the rest of the machines went back online. I stared at the board. That had happened a lot faster than I'd expected.

The pods behind me buzzed to life. I swung around. Why were they on?

Judge roared in the hallway, and I jolted. What was going on? His pod opened, and he was flung into the room, off the ground as the metal chip in the back of his neck sucked him toward the pod. He grabbed onto the doorframe.

"Diana, get the system off. Shut it off. Cash's current test subject grabbed the computer bay. It read him. The system is sending us back." He roared in pain. It must be horrific to be yanked through the air by his neck. The others would be there soon.

"I have no idea how to turn it off." I hit the power down, and nothing happened. "The system's in a loop Judge. It won't shut."

His eyes met mine, and I saw his terror a second before the magnet ripped him off the wall and threw him into the pod.

"Diana, I love you. I'll come back. We'll all be back. Hear me. I ..." The pod closed on him and the gas started. One second he was awake; the next his head leaned forward. He was asleep, gassed into oblivion for his trip through space. I pounded on the machine. Why wouldn't it react to me? The pod launched Judge into space with a sonic boom that nearly deafened me.

Cash flew forward, swinging wildly to hold onto anything. The wall was gone from where Judge had hung onto it, and there was nothing for him to hold onto.

"Nine months, Boo. I'll be back. You stay safe. Live on Artemis. I don't care if this whole place folds. I only want you. Nine months. I love ..."

His pod closed. I went numb. This was happening. This was actually happening. I'd never given one thought to those pods. They'd been nothing, an afterthought. Like Judge before him, he knocked forward, asleep when the pod took off.

I dropped to my knees. Sterling was next, which shocked me. If he couldn't stop the pull then no one could.

Tears dripped down my eyes. "Sterling."

He gripped the computer. "Diana, this is ... nuts. The Infected are out but contained on the other side. Get in Artemis. Don't lose faith in us. We are coming back. Nothing will stop me."

He let out a yell I'd never heard from him before he fell into the pod. He pounded on the door and it did take him a few extra seconds to fall asleep. Once more, I watched as my husband went away. Damian and Lewis came in together. They must have been a distance away.

"No," they were both yelling.

I wiped at my eyes where I outright wept now. Evander was taking my husbands back. Maybe it was my complete desolation that kept me from hearing what I should have heard. An Infected stood behind me—and not just any Infected, the one Cash currently was trying to fix. I only realized it was there when Damian cried out.

The Infected bit down on my arm. I screamed out in pain. While he screamed in horror, the pod knocked him out cold.

"Eight minutes ..." Lewis' pod closed. I knew what he was telling me. I had eight minutes to get treatment. I kicked the Infected off, grabbing a broomstick and shoving it through her eye socket. I never saw Damian or Lewis take off. I didn't need to. I knew what it looked like.

I ran for the lab. The hallway was filled with Zombies. That's what I'd call them from now on. For the little bit of time I had left.

I'd never make it through the mob. I was dead.

I stumbled into Cash's lab; everything was smashed, but it was empty. I closed the door, blocking myself in. I was beyond pain, beyond sadness, beyond feeling anything at all. They were gone. They were knocked out by a computer I'd never bothered to learn. I crawled up Cash's ladder. I didn't even know why.

The view of Orion that Cash hoarded from the others but never me lay out before me. I lay down.

They were gone. Blood dripped down my arm. I was all alone, and I'd already missed the eight minute window. I wouldn't be living through this. I finally gave in and sobbed. Peace set in sometime after that. I didn't want to die. So maybe it was the Zombie infection taking over. I shouldn't feel okay about this.

I'd had love, and I'd never thought I would. My five had loved me. The sun set on Orion, and for the first time since Sterling and Damian had beat down my door, I was alone.

I knew they'd come back. They'd never lied to me. Not once. They would come back, and instead of finding me here to have a reunion, they would locate me up above the mess. Unless Zombies could climb ladders. Maybe I'd make my way downstairs. Who knew what I was going to do once I was dead?

They'd have to kill me. They'd promised I wouldn't have to be a Zombie. They wouldn't leave me one. How long did it take to change? I'd never asked them.

Two days later I shivered violently by the window, watching the white landscape. I couldn't sit up anymore. The place where I'd been bitten had quit burning. It was pale now, like dead skin. I sweat, but I was freezing. The flu had been worse, which was some kind of weirdness. I couldn't stop shaking, but I no longer had any pain.

A loud boom caught my ears, and then nothing happened. Maybe my mental facilities were leaving.

Time ticked. The last thing I would see with these eyes was Orion in the way Cash had shown it to me. I was lucky. Their faces flashed before me all the time.

"Dane, I've got her. She's up in this storage space." A voice I should not have heard called up. I tried to raise my head. C.J.? He couldn't be there. He was on the other side of the galaxy. "Shit. No. No. No."

My Uncle's face appeared before me. I loved C.J. He'd always been there to play with me when I was young. He'd been the first to find my mom and me when they'd come back for us.

"Hi." I tried to speak. It hurt.

"Baby." He kissed my forehead. "Don't worry. We've got this."

Dane looked down over C.J.'s shoulder. I could see his terror before he covered it. "Look at this mess you've gotten into. Tsk. Tsk. Always causing trouble. We saw the launch of the inhabitants from here. Were so relieved when I saw your vital signs. Now I wish you had been with them."

"I missed the eight minute window. They can stop it if you've been bitten in less than eight minutes."

Dane sniffed. "Is that so? All right, well then there is more hope than I thought. Diana, I am going to sedate you then stick in you a state of extended sleep for the ride back home. I'll fix this and then you."

My father and Cooper were next to arrive. Dad was pale. There was no other way to put it. He kneeled down next to me. "Baby, this is going to be okay. We found you. This will be okay."

Dane patted his back. "It actually will be. I'm going to fix it. I've got to get the records off their computer. Did you get the rooms cleared?"

Cooper nodded and then knelt down next to my father. "Diana, it took a little bit to get here. Wes had to hook up the

CRASHING INTO DESTINY 267

computer on the ship with this new tech so we could follow your specific time stream. We are so sorry."

"Guess I'm just a constant screw up."

His face scrunched up. "Don't say that. You're the most amazing woman ever. You saved Asher. He is alive. On the ship waiting for us to bring you. He's been a mess for a year to get to you. We love you. You never screw up. You survive."

My father took my hand and kissed it. "Mom wanted to come. She, Wes, and Nolan had to stay. The station—I don't know if it'll be there when we get back. They took the kids to protect them. You don't need to hear all this. You're going to be fine."

Dane came back and injected me with something. "That's good. Your heart rate is lowering. Phew."

C.J. touched my necklace. "What's that?"

"I got married. They're gone. Evander took them. I loved them. Five of them. They're gone."

My father touched my head. "When you wake up, I want to hear about all of them. I have to know the guys my daughter picked out of the whole universe."

I laughed. "Come on, Dad. I was kind of thrown at them."

"Trust me, baby. There's not a guy in the universe who would complain."

The world was fading. Dane's drugs were working. "Dane, I don't want endless sleep. I don't want to be revived when you're all gone and everyone I love is dead. There has to be a time limit. Two years. You end this."

My father gasped, and C.J. grabbed his shoulder. Only Cooper kept my eye contact. "You sure about that?"

"Yes." My husbands were gone. When I could feel again, I was going to weep.

"It won't take that long." Dane stood over me. "What should we do with Artemis?"

I fell asleep not knowing if I'd live or die.

Chapter Twenty-One

Because He Promised Her

Sterling Whitworth sat on the edge of the medical bed and watched the poor woman who took his vitals sing to herself. She had no idea he was awake or that she was about to not be. He'd never seen her before; she hadn't been involved in the program that created him or the abuse afterwards. It wasn't her fault she happened to be in here right at this moment.

But she was between him and Orion, where his girl remained waiting for him. From this moment on, anything that got between him and Diana would either be knocked out, killed, or destroyed. There wasn't much that Sterling wanted in life. His wife and his friends were it. They were his family. He'd promised her he wouldn't leave her, and he'd broken that promise. When he saw her, he would fall to his knees and beg her forgiveness. When he finally made her smile again, and the others had their turn, they'd move on to someplace warm where he could see her in the sunlight.

He stood. In two seconds, he'd grabbed her neck and cut off her oxygen. He choked her until she passed out but wasn't dead. He gently set her on the medical table and took her keys. He hurried through the hall. He was personally worth more money to Evander than any of the others. When he was discovered missing, it wouldn't be pretty.

So he needed to be out of there with his brothers before anyone realized it. Sterling locked the door behind him. He listened to the noises in the hallway. After five years, he knew the others by their heartbeats, even when they were asleep. It had been everything he could do to not listen to Diana's all the time when they were on Orion. Only a few times a day when he had to make sure she was safe.

Sterling couldn't believe all the ways he'd failed her. The universe gave him Diana, and he hadn't kept her from harm. She had to be terrified by now. It had taken him six months in the pod to get to Evander Corporation. The stolen ship he would get after he found his friends would make the trip back in three.

She'd been alone for six. His sweet baby.

Judge's heartbeat called to him first. He was in the room next door. The knob twisted open, and Judge lay on the table, perched up on his elbows, clearly groggy. Still, when Judge spoke, it was with a strong voice.

"What took you so long?"

Sterling snorted. "I woke up, and I came right here. How long have you been waiting?"

"Six months. We have to get back. Diana." Judge didn't have to say more.

Sterling pulled him off the table. "Can you walk?"

"Yeah." Judge steadied the longer they stood there. "Let's go. I can't stand to think of her there alone."

Judge was quiet, but Sterling could feel the other man's endless energy coming back online. "Weird dreams in the trip?"

"All about Diana. Getting to her. Reaching her. Not being shoved into the pod."

Those sounded pretty much exactly like Sterling's dreams, too. "It's rough. I'm never doing that again."

"Her dream. Do you remember her dream where we left her, and she was buried and ..."

Sterling put his hand on Judge's arm. He didn't need the trip down memory lane. He knew exactly of what Judge spoke. "I do."

Cash was next. The doctor was awake, sitting up, and he stumbled off the table when they came in. "Let's go. Our girl has been alone too long. She's going to be starting to doubt."

Sterling loved that they were all on the same page. He didn't question their love for her. But he'd have gone by himself if he had to.

When they got to Damian and Lewis, it was a different story. They were both still out cold. His brothers must have fought the gas hard. It tended to knock the person out longer if the body tried to fight off the gassing. He'd fought, and it had still been fine. How hard had Damian and Lewis tried not to go under?

"Can you?" Sterling pointed toward Lewis, and Judge and Cash took him under their arms to drag him. Sterling hauled Damian over his shoulder. They headed in silence toward the shuttles. He was going to steal the fastest one in the fleet, and they'd be on their way before they were even supposed to be conscious enough to be questioned.

Evander wasn't used to people trying to get out.

Everyone wanted in.

Ten feet from the shuttle, a face Sterling never expected to see again stepped out of the shuttle.

Canyon Baxter stared back at Sterling. For once, Sterling wished he had his gun. One of the few people in any universe who could kill Sterling, if he so chose, blocked their exit. And Sterling had Damian flung over his shoulder.

"Sterling." Canyon stood at exactly Sterling's height. They'd slept next to each other in cribs and toddler beds, each ignored when they called for attention and love. Out of their group, they'd been the two to survive. The individual baby groups only produced so many young ones who made it to adulthood.

They might even be related. Brothers. Cousins. They were both blond, although Canyon shaved his head regularly, so it was hard to tell. His nursery-mate had been given a cybernetic extension to make his eye sight even better than the already-better, lab-created Warriors around them.

He was cold as ice. Always had been.

"Canyon. I don't want an issue with you. I have to go. I'm taking that shuttle. There's no time for me to waste. You'll never see me again. I've got a girl. She needs me. Us. She's our wife."

Canyon cocked his head to the side. "You're in love?"

"That's right. Let's not make this a thing."

He'd set Damian down and then go for Canyon's throat. There was a sharp piece under the wing of the shuttle. He'd jam Canyon's head right into it and ...

Canyon raised his hand. "I can't let you have it because I'm stealing it myself. They've broken a promise to me, and I will not work for them anymore. I will, however, take you where you're going. Call it curiosity. I'd prefer not to know which one of us can reach that sharp edge first. You're ... in love. I find this surprising. I want to hear more."

That would do.

Time passed pretty quickly when they made great time. "What is this woman like who could love you and the others? You can't offer her anything."

"I offered her my heart. It's what she wanted."

"I see."

A shout from the back caught Sterling's attention, and he ran toward the back, leaving Canyon to pilot. Damian had woken up, and not well. He screamed and struggled. Sterling held him down. Lewis groaned and then started to cry, calling out Diana's name.

Cash leaned over them. "This is not just waking up badly. Something is wrong."

"What?" Sterling sat Damian up. "What's the matter?"

"She got bit." He cried out his answer, throwing his body out of Sterling's arms to pound on the floor. "The Infected got her."

Sterling's whole world shattered into a million pieces. Lewis had told her to get help, but he didn't think she could have with the hall all filled with Infected. She was dead.

Color drained around him. Sterling knew this feeling. He'd had it in every battle he'd ever fought. Black and white and nothing else. Diana took all the color with her.

Tears streamed down Judge's face, and he otherwise remained silent. Cash sunk to his knees, his head bowed. Damian pounded on the floor of the shuttle, over and over. Lewis sat in utter silence.

Finally, Sterling stood. "I made her promises. I broke them. I will not leave her there. I will end her. It's the least I can do for my wife, whom I failed so completely. I won't make any of you. I'll leave you ..."

"No," Lewis spoke through clenched teeth. "I'm going."

They all agreed.

Sterling didn't know if that was a good thing or a bad thing. He never needed an audience when he did the work he'd been created to manage.

It took three months and three days to reach Orion. The three days because Canyon insisted on stopping on a planet Sterling had never heard of to buy them all civilian clothing. They weren't working for Evander anymore; they needed to blend in better. Sterling really didn't give a shit. He'd given no thoughts to anything past Orion. He might not leave it. Spend his days there until his days were over. Stay where she died until he could someday follow her there.

Cash read all the time, like he could find some sort of answer he'd missed in his five years of study. Sterling didn't know what he'd do if Cash got in the way of Sterling fulfilling his promise to Diana. He wouldn't leave her Infected. Cash had made the same damn promise. Oh hell, Sterling knew what he'd do. He'd knock Cash out until the promise had been fulfilled.

Damian hadn't spoken but single words in weeks. *Yes. No.* He had dark circles under his eyes. Lewis had finally insisted Damian eat more before he wasted away. It wasn't easy to get Damian to do what he didn't want to do, never had been. They'd all been following his direction for so long they were used to doing what he said all the time. Only he'd checked out. He wasn't home.

Lewis and Judge tried to stay busy. Judge found things to do on the shuttle all the time, and Lewis tagged along, helping where he could.

Sterling sat in the co-pilot seat next to Canyon while they landed. His former nursery companion spoke rarely but this time he had something to say. "I always thought that I wanted love. Couldn't imagine anyone wanting me, but I wanted it. The US machine, it doesn't feel right."

Sterling looked at him sideways. "I didn't even think. You must have been withdrawing."

"Maybe for a day. I kept it to myself. You're in so much pain. Why would you choose this?"

Canyon would never understand. He hadn't been loved by Diana. If Damian hadn't brought him to Orion, Sterling would be Canyon.

"Thanks for the ride."

His—colleague, friend, family member ... Sterling didn't know how to categorize Canyon anymore—pressed a button releasing the main doors to the shuttle. "How will you leave?"

"I don't know about the rest of them. I'm not sure I will."

Canyon shook his head. "You were always a caretaker. More than the rest of us. I admired your instincts. You won't leave them. Better to acknowledge it now."

"I ..." Sterling shook his head. "There's no point to anything without her. But you're right. I won't disappear. Not until I know they're all okay."

Sterling stood, his non-uniform clothes tugging at him in ways he had to get used to. He'd never lived outside of Evander. The uniforms had been his entire existence. Now he wore dark jeans and a grey t-shirt. They were landing inside the enclosure. They didn't have to be sprayed down for the cold.

Damian stood when he entered. He was also in dark jeans, but Canyon had gotten him a black t-shirt and a hoodie, which he pulled up around his head. Judge followed them. He had on a pair of khakis with a long-sleeved red shirt. Cash had on a pair of black slacks and a white V-neck t-shirt. Lewis rolled the arms of a white suit shirt and wore a pair of blue jeans.

Canyon had picked all the clothes; they'd not chosen them themselves, yet they all suited them. Canyon saw more with his cybernetic eye than Sterling gave him credit for.

The quiet of the Enclosure struck him first. The sounds he'd taken for granted in their years there were gone. A hum sounded, stating the main electricity was on but not more than that. Damian walked past him, and Sterling grabbed his arm.

"Where are you going?" It dawned on him he should probably keep Damian from the weapons locker.

Damian stared at Sterling's hand on his arm. "I'm going to the agricultural section. I want to get the monitors and see her from the day we left. I want to watch the whole damn thing. From the bite until she died. She deserves that. I might also be able to tell where to look for her so we don't have to delay what has to be done."

Sterling dropped his hold on Damian. That was the most the other man had said in three months, and it made sense. "The animals are all going to be dead. It won't be pretty."

"Nothing is pretty. She took that with her. Death is death. What the hell is the difference anymore?"

Damian stormed off, leaving them behind. Sterling walked, Judge, Lewis and Cash with him. The Infected were nowhere to be found, which was weird. Canyon had also not taken off and left. Sterling would deal with him after he assessed everything else.

The place should be overrun, and yet there weren't any to be found. Judge left them to go to what had been the pod room. There wouldn't be any pods in there now.

Cash rounded on him. "Where are they?"

"I don't have a clue."

Eventually Sterling ended up in Lewis' lab with the two doctors. Lewis pounded on his computer. "Someone downloaded all of it. Everything I have has been copied and taken. Also, all my vaccines are gone."

"Corporate espionage?" Sterling didn't care anymore. Let them have whatever the fuck they wanted.

"Any indication Boo took it? The dosages? The protocol?"

"How would I know?" Lewis shook his head.

"We'll watch it." Damian slammed down the surveillance software and hooked it up to the video screen in the lab. "The barn is a mess, as predicted. No Infected anywhere."

They stood and waited while Damian set the devices up to show the day in question. It started when Judge was shoved into the pod. There was no sound, just pictures. Sound was possible, but Damian hadn't carried the whole system with him. Sterling winced as he flew past her too, unable to hold on to anything. He passed out in the pod. It took off. By then he'd been dreaming of her, trying to wake up, screaming silently in his own head. Over and over again.

And there it was. He wanted to scream, to break something. Why didn't she see it? Hear it? Anything? But she didn't. And the Infected bit her. She jolted, screaming, as the last two took off, leaving her.

"I'm sorry, Diana," Damian whispered.

Their girl took a broom and shoved it through the Infected's eyes. Sterling shook his head. She was strong. With her attacker subdued, she'd run for it. Damian pressed a button, following her from the cameras. She couldn't get through the hall. He saw it when it dawned on her face that she wasn't getting to Lewis' lab. She took a right and ran into Cash's.

His friend sighed. "She tried."

"Where is she climbing to?" He'd always assumed Cash used their upper space for storage.

His friend let out a sob. He had never heard Cash really cry. Big, ugly tears travelled down his face. "Our spot. It's a private refuge. I brought her. Do you think she's still up there?"

"No cameras up there. I have no idea." They all stared above their heads. Was his sweet baby wandering around up there, an Infected? Right above their heads?

Damian sped up the recording. "Hold on."

"What?" Sterling turned his attention to what Damian stared at.

Four men entered the room. He'd seen them before. On Diana's computer. They couldn't see what her father and uncles did above their heads, but eventually she came down, embraced in her father's arms, unconscious.

Lewis gasped. "Her Uncle Dane is taking all the stuff. He's got her and the computers. Maybe he fixed her."

Cash laughed, wiping at his eyes. "Do you think it's possible? If we couldn't, could he?"

"Maybe. He's really, really smart."

Judge ran through the door. "I think someone was here."

"We know. Diana's family. They came; they took her. They may have saved her."

If that was true, her family had taken her through the black hole. She was gone, taken from them to where they might not be able to reach her. Fifty years, they could be separated in time. He didn't care. He'd take a ship, any ship, and go.

Judge bounced as he spoke. "I ... I've been thinking about that device. The one we didn't understand. I've been thinking about it since we found out she was bitten. I ... I had to think about anything else. I think it moves time. Hooked to an engine, it might be the kind of thing I could use to trace their steps through the hole. We could come out sometime in her time stream. Not one hundred years but maybe-maybe a five to ten year window. I want to go. I'll go alone. I don't expect ..."

Sterling snorted. "Try and keep me away."

Damian's color changed. He had red to his cheeks. It was almost disconcerting to see his friend come back to life in that second. "We need a ship to hook it up to."

Canyon spoke up. Why was his friend still there? "I'd actually give you the shuttle if I thought it would work. I've seen your device. It's sitting in your engine room for anyone to take. If I still worked for Evander, I'd take it. My ship isn't compatible. The one you have sitting in storage—the old one—I searched it. It'll work."

Artemis. "Judge can you ..."

"Yes." He answered.

Cash crossed his arms over his chest. "Then what are we waiting for?"

Lewis nodded. "What do you need to get it done fast?"

Sterling held up his hand. "And if what we find when we're over there is that she's dead? Or in permanent stasis? What do we do then?"

Damian raised his eyebrows. "We say goodbye."

"We help her family in any way we can," Lewis finished.

Canyon saluted him. "I stayed so you could all leave. I think you've got this. Maybe I'll see you in another life. Say hello to Earth for me."

Sterling nodded his thanks to Canyon. They had work to do. They were going to get his girl. And he'd never break another promise to her. Ever.

Please enjoy a sneak peek from the fourth book in the *Wings of Artemis* series (the second and final in Diana's part) entitled *Reclaiming Their Love.*

Chapter One

Home Again

I did my hundredth sit up for the day as I listened to my mother make her morning announcement on Mars Station. I knew what she was going to tell the population. It was time to leave. Sandler had been attacking us for years. We weren't going to make it. The Council had decided to evacuate, to give Sandler the station.

My mother had disagreed with the vote.

I didn't care. One place was much the same as any other.

My necklace, holding my five wedding rings, bounced while I did my last sit up, hitting me hard on my sweaty skin.

I grabbed a towel and wiped off. We'd gone over everything the night before. The kids—my brothers and sisters—had been evacuated with Cooper and C.J. to a place they'd acquired years before on a planet far away from here. No one knew about it outside of our family. The rest of us were going to help with the evacuation and then board our own shuttles. My mom had wanted me to leave too, but I'd scoffed. I could be of more help here. I needed to be busy.

For the last two years, I'd kept myself endlessly moving. Time couldn't catch me, grief couldn't drown me, if I never let it catch up.

Two years and three weeks earlier my husbands, who lived on the other side of the universe, had been forcibly taken from me by Evander Corporation using a chip implanted in their necks that had pulled them, against their wills, into pods that launched into space, leaving me behind. I'd only been there because I'd been attacked and shoved through a black hole the year before. I loved them—Cash, Lewis, Damian, Sterling, and Judge—with the kind of abandon that comes with finally believing happiness was possible.

They'd loved me that way too.

I'd been bitten by an Infected—a Zombie—and would have died if my family hadn't shown up to save me. Six months in a medically induced coma while my Uncle Dane used my husbands' research to fix me.

Well, most of me.

I got into the shower, letting the sweat wash off my body. This was my last day in my room. I had no idea what the place my parents had picked out for us to move to would be like.

I had no stuff to bring except my clothes.

I dried off and took a good look at the scar on my arm. The place where the Zombie had bitten me had never healed. A large, ugly patch of dead skin. Once a week, my Uncle Dane injected me with a serum he'd made to stop the dead skin from spreading. I'd have to do it forever. Sometimes it took fifty shots to get it right. Every Monday. Nine in the morning. By the time he finished, I was usually silently crying. I couldn't help it. Pain was pain.

I never fussed. I never objected.

I just endured.

I dressed in a black skirt, black boots that made me look taller and fiercer, and a black turtleneck sweater to match. No one bothered the girl dressed in black. It matched my dark hair and eyes. I grabbed my backpack, swinging it over my shoulder. My clothes and the serum I needed were inside. Dane had given me three months' worth in case, for some reason, we were separated. Nothing could be taken for granted anymore, not even our getting on the same ship.

If I had to, I knew how to inject myself.

My communicator beeped, and I picked it up. My mother was on the other line. I didn't say hello. I knew what she wanted. "I'm on my way there now. I'll be on the shuttle in an hour."

"Just making sure you didn't oversleep."

I fingered one of my wedding rings around my neck. "I never sleep. Not possible to overdo it on two hours a night."

Her sigh made me feel bad for being surly. "I want to talk again when we get there. Wes will recreate the time device that moved you through the black hole, the device that didn't allow the black hole to hold back years. He'll do it. We'll take you. After we get set up."

"I don't know where they are, and every minute we're here, their timeline moves forward. Time moves faster there. The second I arrived here, they were probably ten years older. Or more. I'll see you on the shuttle. Be careful. Sandler wants you as much as the station. They want to break the Alexander reign."

I didn't tell her anything she didn't know. I worried; we all did. In the time I'd been away, my family discovered a lot of things, including the Sanders' objectives of universal domination. There were individual accomplishments that meant things to their leaders. Capturing my mother was one of them.

She refused to cower.

"Uncle Nolan and your father are flanking me. You be careful, too."

I wasn't on anyone's list, which didn't mean they wouldn't use me to get to her. I wasn't going to be taken. No one hid as well as I did.

I disconnected our call and walked quickly from my small apartment onto the main pathway, which would take me to the shuttle where my family waited. The only people left on the station were either leaving today or staying through the changeover. Sanders wanted the station, and some people didn't care who ran it. I hoped they weren't all beheaded by the end of the day.

Two people nodded at me. They wouldn't have before I'd gotten sucked through the black hole and come back having survived a Zombie bite. I'd gone from odd to exotic. I didn't care.

The only people whose opinions mattered to me were probably fifty or sixty years old on the other side of the universe. I hoped they had wives. I hoped they'd made lives. I knew they'd loved me. I could still feel them in my soul. I would always be married to them. But I didn't wish my loneliness on them. Just the opposite. I wanted them to be happy.

And to remember me well.

Even if what I really wanted was to claw out their wives' eyes.

I hurried up. The sooner I got on the ship, the better. Time moved forward; it always did. This would be another phase in my life.

Maybe they hadn't all remarried. Maybe some of them had missed me forever too. Okay, maybe all of them had. I groaned. *Diana Mallory, crazy and lonely* ...

The hallway was crowded, and I was soon part of a crowd moving slowly. I didn't have far to go. I forced myself to slow and put up with the inconvenience. There'd been a time when I wouldn't have cared, when I wasn't running from a human enemy and from time itself.

Anything that got in my way made me want to throw things.

On my left, something caught my attention. I didn't know what it was. A man stood, leaning against one of the closed bakeries. He pulled his hoodie up over his head and looked left and right. I stopped moving, and the person behind me oomphed into my behind. I said a quick sorry and ran ahead a bit to get a better look at the guy who'd caught my attention. I saw my husbands a hundred times a week in other people. It was never them.

Despite my own family's story about getting through the black hole, the likelihood my guys could pull it off while they were under the thumb of Evander was slim to none. It had taken my family eight years to reconnect. If the exact same thing were to happen for me, it would be six years at least.

Still, the guy to the side seemed so damned familiar. He stepped toward the crowd, his hoodie falling back again.

It was ... him. It ... was Damian.

How was he here? My heartrate kicked up until I could hear it in my ears. I took off running. I couldn't speak, couldn't call his name. I ran toward him, my boots clicking loudly on the floor. I slammed into someone, couldn't even apologize, and grabbed Damian's arm.

He whirled around, facing me. I saw the recognition hit him as he saw me. "Di ... Diana." His voice shook, and then his arms were around me.

"Diana," he said again, tugging me close, so tightly I could hardly breathe. "We thought ... when we pulled in today, everyone was leaving. We thought you were gone. Judge was coming up with plans ...but I told them I had to give it a last look. You're here. You're here."

I breathed him in. He smelled *right*. One of my guys. My love. Two years without him and we'd almost missed each other. "Damian. We—oh gosh—we have to get out of here now. It's not safe. Where are the others?"

He nodded, his eyes steeling into focus. "On Artemis. Come on."

I grabbed my communicator and sent my mom a message. It was brief, unclear, but I hoped she got the gist I had found one of my husbands and was getting on Artemis. I'd meet her on the planet.

Damian took my hand, and I felt his strong fingers in mine. "How did you get here?" I shouted to be heard over the crowd.

"Later," he yelled back. "I-I can't think. If you're not safe, I'll get you safe. Please."

I never could deny his please. We walked what felt like forever but eventually made it into the docking station where ships came and went. Artemis was three-quarters of the way down. I saw Sterling and Cash talking outside of the ship and could hardly believe the sight. There they were. They were *there*.

I ...

Sterling saw me first; he leapt into a run and had his arms around me in seconds. I hung on. What was he saying? *Sorry?* What was he sorry for? I pressed my forehead to his chest. And then I was being passed into Cash's waiting hug. He said some things too. *Love.* Yes, I loved him, too. But I couldn't think.

Was it possible to go into shock from finally having your dreams come true?

Lewis and Judge were suddenly there too. They were all hugging me, all touching me. There was so much noise.

I breathed out. "Hi."

"She's going to faint." Lewis' voice pushed through. "Let's give her some air." His arm was around my waist. "Come inside. Sit down. Someone go get her water."

I was soon on one of the couches from Orion. They must have brought it onto Artemis. A blanket was around me, water in my hand, and they were all snuggled near me, either on the couch or the floor next to it.

I held out my hand. "We have to get off this station. I need to think. I'm so *happy* you're here. You can't know." My voice shook. "I ..."

Sterling kissed my cheek. He sat to my left. I leaned on Cash, who stroked my arm. Damian was right in front of me, kneeling down. Lewis and Judge were each touching my knees. They were so beautiful.

"Where do you want to go?" Sterling kissed my cheek again. "I'll put in the coordinates."

I had them memorized. My mother had insisted. Sterling jumped up to go enter them and fly the ship out of the station. Lewis took his place.

He touched my arm over the dead skin. "How are you here? Please don't get me wrong, this is what I'd hoped for. But you should be dead. I want to know what he did and ... why your arm is the way it is."

"Please don't look at it. I mean, I guess you're going to have to look at it. One of you will have to give me my injections until we get to where we're going. Or I can do it. Don't look. It's gross."

Cash actually kissed the yucky part of my skin. "It's not gross. You're alive. Help us understand."

"You'll have to talk to Dane. He's the one who did it. All I know is he used your research, and he could manage all of it except right here. This has to be constantly managed, stopped from taking over again. Every Monday."

Lewis stroked the spot. They were really preoccupied. "We can wound care. That's no problem whatsoever."

"It's not gross." That was the first time Judge had spoken since we'd come on board. "It's a miracle. A battle wound."

The ship jerked, indicating it moved through space, and Sterling came back to us, having put the ship into auto pilot.

He grabbed me from the couch until I could look him straight in the eyes. "We failed you. We all promised you'd never be alone on Orion and you'd never get hurt by the Infected. Both things happened. Please forgive me."

"And me," Judge added.

Three other repeats of the same request were made over and over.

I put my arms around Sterling where he held me. "You didn't do it on purpose. None of you could have predicted what would happen. There's nothing to forgive. How are you here in two years?"

Judge rose. "Do you remember that weird device that made the time differential in the cave?"

"Actually, I've seen it's like many times since then. My Uncle Wes made it. It's his invention."

Judge made eye contact with Damian. "What?"

Damian added, "Explain."

I knew where it had been hooked into the engine. I'd seen it on C.J.'s ship when they rescued me. I walked to the engine room, all five of them on my tail, and bent down to look at the device. "He made one. As far as I know, there's only the one. It let him hook the ship up to follow my time stream." I touched the writing. "It can't be but ... this is his handwriting."

"It can be." Judge exhaled loudly. "Time travel makes my frickin' head hurt. Or at least it does today. Can we figure out this mystery another time?"

"Yes," Cash added. "We've had two years to imagine this moment. You look ... *incredible*. Alive. Beautiful. Bright-eyed now that the shock has worn off. And wearing clothes that aren't too big on you. Pretty, actually. Do you have a thing for black?"

"Black tells other people to leave me alone. Off limits."

Lewis smirked. "It isn't telling me to leave you alone."

Heat surged inside of me. They all had that look in their eyes, and we were all together. What did they have in mind?

"We figure," Lewis continued. "You can handle two of us at once. There are five. Someone really has to watch the helm. We all know how to do that now. We drew straws. Are you up for a little sharing? We've never done it, but we think we've worked it out."

"I think I've missed all five of you for two years. If you want to share me in the bed too, then let's give it a go."

Lewis grinned. "That's awesome." He picked me up and threw me over his shoulder. I squealed, and Sterling patted my rear end. "Her room has the biggest bed."

"See you in a bit." Cash winked at me. "If you fall asleep, we're going to wake you up."

Lewis dropped me on the bed while Sterling kicked the door closed. They both stood over me, and my mouth went dry. There were little things I'd forgotten about them, even though I wouldn't have thought it possible.

Sterling had a freckle on the left side of his neck. I didn't think I'd ever tongued it. I really wanted to. Lewis stood with one foot slightly in front of the other, as though he might be ready to run at any time. Or in this case, jump on me.

Lewis spoke first. "We considered figuring out how we could all be together, all five of us, with you. It might be a possibility someday. But not today. Too much too soon. Ease into that. And we still all want our alone times."

"I'm not sure how to start this ... I ..."

Lewis' mouth was on me. He kissed me, hard. "We've got it. I promise."

Sterling jumped on the bed, coming up behind me. His hand travelled up my spine over the shirt before he pulled my shirt over my head and tossed it aside. "Not wearing a bra?"

"They're tiny. Sometimes I don't need one."

Lewis groaned. "Now I'm going to be hard every day, all day thinking of you bra-less."

"Sweet baby." Sterling nipped at my ear. "Are you wearing panties?"

I shook my head, and they both made growly noises in their throats. I could have explained that the skirt went to my calves, but they didn't seem to want to discuss clothing, and neither did I. Lewis tugged my skirt down my legs; my shoes were thrown aside. I was naked, and they were completely dressed. That quickly changed.

And then, before I could think, they were both all over me. Lewis was at my mouth, kissing me over and over again while Sterling gripped my hips, kissing my neck, my shoulders. I moaned. Every nerve ending in my body had gone on high alert. This was what it was to be worshiped. Lewis' eyes were hot—steaming—and his cock stood strong and erect against my stomach. I wanted it in me, but I suspected we were just getting started.

I grabbed onto Lewis' neck to hold on while, with my other hand, I gripped Sterling's legs. They were both erect and unashamedly into me at the same time.

"Stop thinking," Sterling ordered. He pressed me up against him to grind his cock into my rear. I moaned. And then it was more like I floated. Pleasure mixed with relief, making me giddy. Lewis pressed a finger inside of me, finding my clit. He stroked it, and my muscles clenched around his hand.

Sterling patted my rear end. "Think you missed us as much as we did you, pretty baby. I'm going to come fast. I knew I'd be worked up; I didn't realize I'd have lost all control."

"Same thing." Lewis' voice was low. "Here's what we're going to do. Sterling is going to come inside of you, and assuming you are willing, you are going to take me in your mouth."

My mouth watered. "I'm willing."

"Good girl," Sterling crooned in my ear.

We repositioned until I could take Lewis in my mouth and Sterling could enter me at the same time. The whole thing might have been awkward if it hadn't been completely organic. I tasted Lewis in my mouth. He was hot, throbbing, and ready for me. I didn't care if he was too big for me. I wanted as much of him as I could get. Who needed to breathe?

I deep throated him. Lewis' hips jerked off the bed just as Sterling pressed inside of me. I moaned at the taste of Lewis— salty and all male. My two husbands were in the bed with me; both liked to be in control, neither one of them liked to be vulnerable, and yet they both gave in to this moment like they trusted me to always take care of them. I would.

My pussy throbbed. Our dance of sucking and pressing became a movement all our own. Lewis gripped the bed, his head thrown back. As Sterling fucked me, he made the best noises I'd ever heard. He sounded desperate. His hand found my clit, and with a grunt he pressed on it. I came hard and long.

As I moaned, Lewis came into my mouth. He groaned his release while Sterling sighed his. I throbbed everywhere. My ears rang.

"Fuck." Lewis scooted around, pulling me with him until I was between him and Sterling. He kissed my forehead. "Missed you, Doll. So much." His voice shook.

"Too much. Love you. Love you," Sterling whispered in my ear. "The way you let us love you, the way you love us back. I thought maybe I'd imagined how good it was. Some nights I convinced myself you weren't real, that you couldn't be. You are. You're here. You're ours."

I closed my eyes. "I love you two completely."

I fell asleep. Waking up, I heard Lewis snore deeply behind me. Sterling breathed evenly, his eyes closed. How long had I dozed off, and more importantly, what had woken me?

I was lifted from the bed, Cash's strong arms coming around me. "Told you I was going to wake you up," he whispered in my ear.

Sterling made a whining sigh but didn't otherwise move, and Lewis continued to snore the sleep of the truly out of it.

Cash took me down the hall to another bedroom. They'd made the ship their own, and I loved it. It felt right that Artemis should belong to them now. They'd travelled the universe in it, and now it was as though they'd breathed life back into her.

Judge sprawled out on the center of the bed.

"Hi." I grinned at him, and he smiled back.

"Have a nap, Di? Been waiting for you."

His eyes were proprietary, and my heartrate kicked up. "I'm up now."

Cash kissed my neck. "Good."

Don't miss out!

Click the button below and you can sign up to receive emails whenever Rebecca Royce publishes a new book. There's no charge and no obligation.

Also by Rebecca Royce

Dragon Wars
Forever
Eternal
Always
Evermore

Safe Haven
Everywhere and Nowhere

Shadow Promised
Strange Days
Weird Nights
Haunted Years

Soul Bound
Prisoner of the Dragons

The Capes
Seductive Powers
Adrenaline Rush
Last Ascension

The Cascade
Haunted Redemption

The Conditioned
Eye Contact
Embraced

Trouble with Mackenzie

Under The Lights

Wings of Artemis
Crashing Into Destiny

Standalone
Bitten Surrender
Mr. Wrong
No Quitting Allowed
Demon Within